CW00767782

SMOKE, MAGIC AND DUST

BOOK 1

T. F. Carroll

authorHOUSE®

AuthorHouse™ UK Ltd.
500 Avebury Boulevard
Central Milton Keynes, MK9 2BE
www.authorhouse.co.uk
Phone: 08001974150

First published by AuthorHouse 8/27/2009

ISBN: 978-1-4490-1687-6 (sc)

This book is printed on acid-free paper.

DISCLAIMER: This is a work of the imagination interwoven with a
lifetime of memories. All characters are fictitious.

DEDICATION

For my family with love and the hope that future generations may live in a world without war.

ACKNOWLEDGEMENT

Thanks to my wife for her constant enthusiasm and encouragement during my writing and to Authorhouse for their advice and support on publication.

CHAPTER ONE

ONE MORNING EARLY IN THE summer of 1925 Tim Ryan shuffled down the prom in Blackpool and into the life of the widow Maria Martinelli. As soon as he woke up that morning Tim knew that something special lay in store for him, he didn't know how, he just knew and he felt excited about it. He'd never had that feeling before, not ever! Usually when he woke up it was to the feeling that the day was going to be even worse than yesterday and more often than not it was. But today things were going to be different. When he crawled out from under a pile of deck chairs on the beach, although he was hungry and stiff with cold, the buzz stayed with him. He heard his joints crack, he groaned, only twenty- seven years old and yet the stiffness in his joints made him feel like an old man of ninety. It was as if somebody had poured a bucket of quick-setting cement over him while he slept. He tried to work off his stiffness by rearranging the deck chairs and he didn't stop until they were neatly piled the way he had found them the night before. Job done, he heaved himself over the sea wall and made a beeline for the gents' washroom on the prom.

By the time he got there he was walking like a young man again, well apart from being breathless and spluttering from that damned cough that wouldn't go away. He spat up some phlegm and it helped him to breathe more easily.

The prom was deserted, not a soul in sight, but out above the sea there was plenty of activity - the sky was teeming with seagulls. Tim didn't really like seagulls. Sometimes when he felt particularly low, he imagined their screams were being directed at him personally, warning everyone that they had a fugitive in their midst. Fugitive? Now don't run away with the idea that Tim was crazy for thinking things like that, it was just that his anxiety sometimes got the better of him when he was reminded of the war. The seagulls' screeching awoke fears in Tim that were lying dormant and when those fears broke through to the surface they frightened him and made his head reel with jumbled images of battle.

Despite all that the birds fascinated him, particularly today. Tim laughed, he actually laughed – today was different - today the noisy gulls hadn't affected him in the least, their raucous calls hadn't brought back memories of those horror years of 1914/18. Gone too was the irrational fear that the screaming gulls were trying to draw attention to him to expose him as a fugitive and a deserter. Today, at last, he was optimistic and his optimism was growing stronger by the hour and for the first time in years Tim Ryan knew what it was like to feel free!

When he entered the washroom the noise of the seagulls faded but he didn't notice he was too busy looking around to see if he had to share with anybody else. Happily for Tim, the place was deserted, he was first of the rough sleepers who regularly used the washroom and using the thumbnail sized piece of carbolic soap he found lying in the hand basin he was able to have a cold top and tail in private. He felt pleased about the privacy; there was no one to see him use his shirt as a makeshift towel. After he had dried himself he rummaged through the torn lining of his jacket pocket and found what he was looking for, a piece of rag wrapped around a Gillette safety razor and blade. The precious three holed blade had been wrapped separately in a piece of greasy lard paper to stop it from rusting After removing the paper, he held the blade between the thumb and finger of his right hand to hone it on the ball of his left hand. When he was satisfied that the blade was sharp enough to use, he tightened it into the razor and very carefully began to shave. He looked at his face in the mirror and spoke to it, "Well, Tim lad, it beats me, here you are in Blackpool, you're broke and don't know where your next meal's coming from and yet you're so happy next thing I know you'll be singing and dancing." It was as though he had been programmed, no sooner were the words out of his mouth and there he was, moving around the floor and doing a Tim Ryan version of the soft shoe shuffle. And beating time with the hand that held the razor he sang at the top of his voice, "The sun has got his hat on, hip-hip-hip hurray, the sun has got his hat on and he's coming out to play.........!"

Tim couldn't remember when he had last enjoyed singing a song, but then he hadn't had much to sing about over the past few years, but today he sang despite the nagging pain of hunger. Again he chorused, "'The sun has got his hat on…," and when he had finished with that one, he followed it with a quick burst of "On the road to Mandalay." His rich baritone voice rang out; it filled the washroom with joyous sound before spilling out through the open window where it was warmly welcomed by the morning sun. A few people taking an early morning walk on the prom heard his voice and stopped to listen. When he finished singing they began to clap their hands, one or two of them cheered enthusiastically. An elderly woman said to her husband, "What a wonderful voice John, that's one of the songs he sang in the north pier show last night, must be that Australian, you know .....?"

"Peter Dawson. Shall I go in Mavis and find out if it is him?"

His wife hesitated, then shaking her head she discouraged him, saying, "Best not dear, you hear some rum tales about the goings on in places like that." She took hold of his arm and led him across the road. A small group remained, waited for a few minutes thinking that the singing might start again and then slowly drifted away.

Unaware of his short-lived popularity Tim picked up a piece of newspaper that was lying on the floor and his eye was immediately drawn to an advertisement, it was for a very smart shaving kit and he looked at it covetously. The fact that he hadn't a bean in his pocket to buy anything didn't worry him, because today he was feeling lucky and if one of those smart shaving kits dropped right out of the sky to land at his feet he wouldn't have been surprised in the least.   Tim sighed, shaving kits and brushes with soft bristles - such luxury.   It reminded him of what it was like to have his cheek brushed by the soft lips of a woman.   A kiss on the cheek from a woman was far better than a shaving brush any day, even if the brush did have the softest of bristles. No contest!   Tim sighed again, when was the last time he had been kissed?   He almost cut himself on the razor blade in his efforts to try and recall the feeling.

The near mishap with the razor put an end to his fantasy.   "Ah, Tim boy," he said out aloud to his face in the mirror, "You've forgotten to brush your teeth."   He put away the razor blade and fished out a screw of newspaper containing a small quantity of salt from the tattered lining of his pocket.   Dampening a finger he sprinkled it with salt, then using the finger like a toothbrush he began to clean his teeth.   He wasn't satisfied; he needed more salt to clean them properly. "Oh, what the hell, in for a penny, in for a pound," he said and poured the last of the salt onto his finger.   He talked as he polished his teeth and the words came out jumpy and jerky, "You never know, maybe today I'll strike it really lucky and find a toothbrush and paste as well."

Tim winced as he tucked the cold damp shirt back into his trousers, he felt uncomfortable but at least he was fresh and clean.   He examined his thin face in the mirror, not a single cut to be seen, not even the slightest graze. He ran a hand over his chin; it was smooth to the touch. "Thank you, Mr. Gillette," he said. "Thank you very much indeed," and he gave a polite little bow of thanks to Mr. Gillette who, he believed, lived over the Atlantic in the United States of America.

Tim peered round the door of the wash-room; he wanted to make sure there were no redcaps or policemen prowling around ready to pounce on him. "Thank God," he murmured when he saw the coast was clear.

He took one last longing look at the shaving kit advertisement before throwing the piece of newspaper into the waste bin and stepping outside. By now there were quite a number of visitors about and the seagulls were getting well fed. Tim didn't need to watch them eating to be reminded that he too was hungry, but Tim the optimist was confident that a meal would soon be forthcoming. And he was right; this was going to be Tim's lucky day, the luckiest day of his life!

That very same morning Maria Martinelli heard that Jake, her handy man, had run away with Elsie, a girl who worked in one of her candyfloss and postcard kiosks. It was Betty Williams, Elsie's best friend and flatmate, who broke the news to her. She stood on Maria's doorstep relating the tale of the elopement and then in the next breath asked if she could have Elsie's job. Maria hesitated, Betty, at only seventeen years of age, had already acquired a doubtful reputation as far as men were concerned.

"Come on, Mrs. Martinelli, we're wasting time and money, give me the key and I'll open up straight away. Talk later, okay?" Betty was smiling, showing her perfectly shaped white teeth.

Maria admired the girl's cheek, decided that she was honest and went inside to fetch the key to the kiosk. Returning, she handed it to her. "Alright Betty, let's have two weeks trial shall we, see how we get on together? By the way, if you hear from Elsie, please let her know that I hope she and Jake will be happy."

"Okay. And thanks Mrs. Martinelli, I won't let you down, you'll see." Betty's blue eyes shone and there was something almost childlike in her manner as she skipped away lightly on the toes of her high heeled shoes. A gust of wind caught her long fair hair and sent it streaming behind her; the sun shone on it and turned it into gold. Maria instinctively ran her fingers through her own dark hair as rumours describing Betty's escapades came flooding into her head - one of the things she was supposed to have done was beyond Maria's belief, "Surely, she couldn't have done **that**," she gasped.

Maria sat at the kitchen table and forgot all about breakfast as she wrote out four identical advertisements hoping that at least one of them would produce a quick replacement for Jake. She wrote one for each of her two shooting galleries, one for a candyfloss kiosk and one for her gift shop in town. She thought about her other business interests but after deliberation decided four adverts would be enough. Her eyes scanned the long list of jobs that the successful applicant would have to perform and lest there should be any misunderstanding she had written them in capital letters. She made no mention of her garden. The omission was quite deliberate; gardening might be the straw that broke the camel's back, a job that could be discussed later, at a time when a new handyman had settled in.

With the advertisements in her hand she left the house by the kitchen door and stepped out into the garden. The garden was larger than most of her neighbours, with a rectangular lawn surrounded by borders of shrubs and flowers. The lawn was divided in the middle by a concrete path that led to a wooden gate; the gate provided a shortcut to the amusement arcades and kiosks on the seafront. One of the gate's hinges was loose which made it difficult to open and Maria had to lift and push hard before she could squeeze through a gap in order to make her way to the candyfloss kiosk. Two scarlet faced youths whom Betty had just served with saucy postcards couldn't get away quickly enough when Maria arrived on the scene. After crossing the road they sat on the sea wall and not for one second did they take their young lustful eyes off Betty.

While Maria was pinning an advertisement to the kiosk wall she told Betty about the difficulty she'd had with the gate. "It's not like Jake to neglect things. I asked him to fix it weeks ago. And the garden too, it's like a jungle."

"Well, he didn't have time, did he?" replied Betty.

"Time? What do you mean he didn't have time? He had all the time in the world."

"Not for work he hadn't, Mrs Martinelli, 'cos most of the time he was shaggin' Elsie. They were always at it." Betty said this without a trace of emotion in her voice; her blue eyes were wide open and staring at something far away in the distance.

To say that Maria was shocked was an understatement. Although she knew about Betty's reputation, she had been totally unprepared for anything like this and as for the language, well? "For goodness sake Betty, do you realize what you're saying?"

"'Course I do. It's true, Mrs. Martinelli. And I'll tell you something else; she couldn't get enough of it. Elsie told me. She told me everything, did Elsie. I suppose after – you know –he was too tired to do any work."

"I hope Elsie will be alright, she can't be more than seventeen or eighteen, Jake must be twice her age."

"Well, you know what they say about old fiddles?" Betty giggled, but when she saw the look on Maria's face she pleaded seriously, "Everybody knew about it, Mrs. Martinelli, everybody knew."

It took a few seconds before Maria could speak. "Everybody knew about it except me it seems." Even though she guessed what the answer would be, she had to ask the question. "And where did all this – activity, take place?"

"In the store room o' course, you know where you let Jake sleep. Elsie said the double bed was lovely. Ooh! I could tell you some stuff. There's lots more, Mrs. Martinelli."

But Maria didn't want to know lots more. The bed Betty mentioned once belonged to Maria and her late husband and she had set it up in the storeroom at the bottom of the garden for Jake because he had nowhere else to sleep. Why was Betty telling her all this about Elsie when she was supposed to be Elsie's best friend? It made Maria feel uncomfortable. Then she saw Betty's face was flushed with excitement. At last Maria understood. "Holy Mother," she whispered to herself, "She's doing all this for kicks." And she thought that perhaps she'd made a mistake employing Betty, maybe those rumours were true after all. There was sharpness in Maria's voice when she said, "All right Betty, that's enough! That's the last I want to hear on the subject. Not a word more, all right?" She noticed the untidy pile of cards on the kiosk counter, "And you can tidy those up for a start."

"Okay, sorry, Mrs. Martinelli," said Betty, her expression composed and innocent now, "But it was those boys, they had the lot down before they bought some."

Maria left Betty and went over to pin an advertisement on the woodwork of the shooting gallery. She didn't have more than four or five yards to go, the two places were almost within touching distance of each another.

Maria had just finished pinning up the notice when she heard a shuffling sound coming down the prom towards her, she was too preoccupied to turn around because she was scrutinising her signature on the advertisement. She had signed, Maria Martinelli (Mrs) and she was wondering if, maybe, she should have written Maria Martinelli (Prop)? She was still considering that when she became aware the shuffling sound had stopped.

"Are you Mrs. Martinelli? I can do all of those jobs on the list Mrs. Martinelli." The voice came from a man with a Yorkshire accent and he was standing right behind her.

Maria turned around to see what he looked like. He was about five feet eight, or nine, with brown hair, thin and a bit scruffy looking. But his face was kind, quite handsome really. She looked down at his feet and laughed outright. "So that's where the shuffling sound came from, it's your shoes; they must be at least three sizes too big." She apologised immediately. "Oh, I am sorry, that was terribly rude of me, I shouldn't have laughed and I'm sorry."

"That's all right Mrs. Martinelli, a kind lady gave them to me for cutting her grass. We knew they were too big, but she said they were better than the ones I was wearing, at least they would keep out the wet." He looked down at the shoes and said ruefully, "Well, they did keep the wet out once. Now they don't." He gave a wry little smile,

"But what can you expect; they've done a lot of miles since then?" He noticed the gate. "That your gate, lady?"

"Yes."

"Mind if I have a look?"

"Go ahead," said Maria.

He shuffled up to the gate. "It's the hinge, two screws missing." He saw them lying on the concrete path and picked them up. "That's lucky," he said, "Finding them easy like that." He wiped the screws on the seat of his trousers. When he was satisfied he had got rid of most of the rust he selected a broken ended blade from his penknife and using it like a screwdriver he screwed the hinge back to its original place on the gate. He swung the gate backwards and forwards, it squeaked a bit but otherwise it opened and closed perfectly. "A drop of oil and it'll be as good as new." He folded back the broken blade and returned the penknife to his pocket.

"Thank you," said Maria. She had already awarded him seven points out of ten and the interview hadn't even started.

"Well, Mr. Whatever your name is, come up with me to the house, we can talk there in private." She emphasised the word private, looking over at Betty as she spoke, Betty was craning her neck trying not to miss a word of what they were saying.

"Tim, my name's Tim Ryan," said the man and followed Maria Martinelli into the garden.

After Maria and Tim had disappeared through the gate, Betty hitched up her skirt, adjusted her suspenders and straightened the seams of her stockings. She did it sensuously, taking her time and all the while giving sly little glances over the road to where the two youths were sitting on the sea wall, watching her. When they couldn't resist the temptation any longer, they abandoned the wall, crossed the tramlines and headed for the kiosk.

Betty smiled her secret smile knowing exactly what they wanted, wasn't she the one who had made them want it?

Meanwhile, Tim shuffled up the path behind Maria. "Grass needs cutting. Got a lawn mower lady?"

"Yes," said Maria, mentally awarding him another point. He was now eight out of ten!

Tim noticed her legs, slim and shapely; he stopped walking, taking time to make a fuller appraisal.

Maria noticed his shuffling had ceased.

She turned around, "What is it, something wrong?"

Tim quickly averted his eyes and pointed to one of the taller shrubs, "Mr Tufty, you've got a Mr. Tufty growing in the border lady and he's a real beauty!"

"What on earth's a Mister Tufty?"

"Mr. Tufty! Why, he's a Mahonia. Take a look at that lovely green coat of his, it never wears out, and by winter he'll have grown a fine head of tufty yellow hair to help to keep the cold out. Sunshine in winter that's Mr. Tufty."

"Oh, that Mahonia. Yes, of course I know about that one," said Maria. It was a lie of course and Maria, being Maria, felt guilty and offered up a silent prayer, "Sorry God for telling a lie, but I was ashamed for not knowing what was growing in my own garden!"

For her penance she awarded Tim another point. The score was now nine out of ten and they hadn't even talked.

"Oh, he's too good to be true," said Maria to herself. Instinct told her that something could be wrong and warned her to take care! Suppose he's in trouble with the police? Suppose he's dangerous? She led him into the kitchen leaving the door open, an escape route – just in case! Maria was about to challenge him about her fears when she noticed the strained look on his face. He looked absolutely worn out. "Heavens, the man's dying of hunger," she whispered to herself. Compassion replaced doubt. As cheerfully as she could, she said, "Look, I haven't had my breakfast yet and I'm starving. Why don't you join me, we could eat and talk at the same time, if that's all right with you Mr. Ryan?" Then she added in a pretending-to-be-stern voice, "Sit down at the table and wait," Tim nodded and sat down at the kitchen table. Within the space of a few minutes the smell of ham and eggs frying was almost driving him crazy.

Maria had put an apron round her waist and she talked as she cooked. "You know, Mr. Ryan, my grandmother used to say that breakfast was the most important meal of the day." Without turning her head she asked him, "One egg, or two?"

"Two please," said Tim.

She stopped spooning the fat over the eggs and turned her head to give him a smile, "That's what I'm having."

Tim smiled back at her; it would be good working for a woman who had a smile like that.

Maria poked a fork at some ham in another frying pan. "Won't be long now," she said. She gave Tim another smile and reached for some plates on a shelf. She was on her toes and having a struggle to reach them so Tim jumped up to help.

"No no, Mr. Ryan, you stay where you are, I can manage."

But she was too late; Tim already had the plates in his hands before she had finished speaking.   He noticed one or two grey hairs growing through Mrs. Martinelli's shiny black hair and the sight of those grey hairs prompted him to make a mental guess at her age.   Tim reckoned she was four, maybe five years older than he but he was wrong, in a few months time Maria would be thirty seven.   She looked years younger and he began to compare what the age gap had done to their looks.   Straight away he knew he was the loser; if he and Maria were standing on the pier with placards round their necks, saying "Guess who's the youngest?" she would get the nod every time.

When Tim first talked to Mrs. Martinelli that morning he thought of her only as someone who might give him a job and provide him with his next meal ticket.   But now he was enjoying being in her company and day dreaming about a relationship much closer than employer and employee.   He pictured himself standing beside her and decided she was just the right height for him.   Oh, and her legs, he didn't think she had caught him admiring them and mentally he thanked the Mahonia for getting him off the hook!   It was Maria's hair he was admiring now, the style was simple, brushed straight back with a tortoise shell comb holding it neatly together.   He imagined it free from the comb, falling to her shoulders and framing her face. For him she had become an Italian princess!

Maria interrupted his dream.   "Forget what I said earlier Mr. Ryan, we'll eat now and talk later.   Is that all right with you?"

"That's fine by me, Mrs. Martinelli," he replied.   He watched as she put their plates on the table and was too fascinated now to turn his gaze away from her and begin to eat.

Maria saw that he wasn't eating and there was concern in her voice, "Aren't you feeling well, Mr. Ryan?"

"Sorry, Mrs. Martinelli, sorry, I was thinking how lucky I am to be sitting here. And as for not feeling hungry, you just watch me." He bent his head down and tucked into his food.

They ate in silence, sneaking glances at one another. Maria always claimed that she could tell what a person was like the first time they met just by looking at them and she'd already made her mind up about Tim Ryan. As far as she was concerned he was a gentle sort of a person, the sort you could trust, competent, too, the repaired gate was proof of that. And as for the garden, well, hadn't he introduced her to Mr. Tufty? The name made her want to laugh, nice touch that, it showed Tim Ryan had a sense of humour. She thought about the Mahonia blossom, "Mr. Tufty's hair," it would become golden in the winter, that's what he had told her and just for a second Maria hoped that Mr. Ryan would still be around when that happened. Then she remembered the earlier doubts she'd had about him. Walking up the path to the house hadn't she thought he was too good to be true and probably in trouble with the police? Those thoughts came back to her again and they were stronger than before. What kind of a man was he? She decided that now was the time to find out but she mustn't be too abrupt in her questioning.

Chapter Two

Tim pushed his empty plate into the middle of the table saying that he couldn't eat any more. Maria pushed away her plate until it touched his. She was conscious of what she had done without knowing why she had done it, but touching his plate with hers had somehow made her feel contented. Tim moved to collect their plates and Maria asked him to leave them saying that Rosy Sharp, her daily help, would be along later to clean up the kitchen.

"Time we had our little chat, Mr. Ryan. Are you ready?"

"Yes, Mrs. Martinelli."

"Tim, may I call you Tim?"

"Yes, Tim's fine, Mrs. Martinelli."

"All right then Tim, let me begin by saying that right from the time you mended the gate and took interest in the garden I felt we could get along together, but..."

Before she could say any more, Tim interrupted, "Thanks. I feel the same. I'd like to stay here and work for you, Mrs. Martinelli."

"I would like that as well Tim, but if there's anything you have to tell me, you know...., it's best if you tell me now. If you're in trouble with the police, you must tell me. If you want to work for me I've got to know the truth. Don't hold anything back. All I ask is for you to be straight with me and I'll be straight with you."

Tim waited for a second and then replied without any more hesitation, "'Course you've a right to know Mrs. Martinelli and I will be straight with you. Yes, I admit I am in trouble; I've been in trouble with the police for the past seven years. Seven years on the run, that's me! Dodging and hiding from the police and the redcaps, summer and winter in all kinds of weather, I'm an expert on hedges and ditches and as for derelict buildings I could write a book about them. Seven whole years, can you imagine?" He looked shamefaced and then continued, "And in case you haven't guessed already, Mrs. Martinelli, the man on the run you're talking to is a deserter!" A nerve in his face twitched and he looked appealingly at Maria as if he wanted her to understand the reason why he had deserted. Maria had never seen a man look so wretched and she wanted to reach out and comfort him. Somehow she managed to resist touching him. She spoke to him kindly, "If it upsets you to talk about it now, I'll wait...."

But Tim said that he wanted to go on, he wanted her to know what had made him become a deserter.

He began his story with a question, "Have you ever seen a man tied to a stake with a blindfold round his head and shot for running away, Mrs. Martinelli? Well I have and I'm frightened that one day they might do the same to me. Sometimes I wake up to find they are putting that blindfold over my eyes...."

"But Tim, the war's been over for years, surely by now they're no longer looking for you? I know that you must have had a very good reason for deserting, so you don't have to tell me about it if you don't want to. You've had enough suffering and I don't need to hear any more. But you will be safe here, Tim." And in a voice shaking with emotion she said, "I shan't betray you, Tim, not ever!"

Tim didn't reply straight away. He was having difficulty breathing and he started to cough and wheeze.

Maria asked if she could get him a drink of water, but he shook his head. They sat quietly for a minute or so until Tim had fully recovered and then he drew a deep breath and continued with his story.

"My Mum and Dad are Staffordshire folk, my Dad used to say, Staffordshire born and Staffordshire bred, strong in t' arm and weak in t''ead."

No laughter from Maria, she wanted him to get on with the story.

"But we were away from Staffordshire, living near Sheffield when we heard that they'd sunk a new pit near Doncaster. We're a mining family and my Dad thought that the prospects at this pit looked good, the owners had built some new houses for the miners and there was enough coal in the pit to provide jobs forever. So, he decided we should go there and it turned out to be the right move. I'll never forget the day we left Sheffield – wintertime, thick snow covering the ground, bitterly cold - we huddled up together with our furniture on an open farm cart. It started snowing again and by the time we reached Doncaster we were nearly frozen. We had a strong horse and an experienced driver or we never would have made it. My sister, Martha, and me were the youngest, so we travelled on the cart with Mum and Dad and the rest of the family joined us later. The new houses were better than anything we'd ever lived in before. They called it a Model Village and when all the building work was finished, King George and Queen Mary came to see it and right to this very day it's still known as Woodlands the Model Village." There was great pride in Tim's voice as he described his family's new home.

"Then in 1914, when the war started, my brothers' Bernard, Jack and Jim left the village to join the army. My eldest brother, Bernard, was the first to volunteer, he'd been a sergeant in the Boer war and he used to tell us stories about Africa - a great storyteller was Bernard. When they all went away, I wasn't quite sixteen, still living at home and working down the pit, I missed them terribly. I wanted the excitement of going off to war but I was too young to join the army. Then somebody told me that if I gave a false age the army would take my word for it. So I went down to the recruiting office and told them that I was eighteen. They believed me, no more questions about age and I was in! "Skilled handler of horses," that's what the officer wrote down about me. "Skilled handler of horses," he said. "I remember laughing when he wrote that. Me, a pit pony boy, a skilled handler of horses, I ask you? Anyway they must have believed him because within a few weeks I was given a team of horses and was hauling big guns to the front. That's when I found out that war isn't exciting; it's the most horrible thing you can ever imagine."

Maria listened attentively, noticing how strained and hoarse his voice had become. His face was beginning to twitch nervously again. "Why don't you stop now, Tim, have a rest?"

Tim shook his head and went on. "Between the time I arrived in France and 1918 I had four teams of horses shot from under me, the last time I was slightly wounded and got fourteen days leave back home. When I walked into the house my mother hardly recognised me and she wept. She wasn't the only one to weep, whenever I remembered the screams of my horses as they lay dying, I burst into tears and when I did, poor Mum couldn't console me. It's too awful to talk about, I try not to remember but the smoke, those stinking clouds of smoke that were always hanging over the battlefield, sometimes I still have bad dreams about that smoke and I wake up choking and gasping for air."

At this point Tim started to cough; perhaps just talking about the smoke was enough to set him off? After taking a few sips from a glass of water Maria offered, he recovered and was able to finish his story. "Instead of rejoining my unit on the 10th of November 1918, I went on the run and I've been on the run ever since. And that's how I ended up here in Blackpool. Thank God my nerves are a lot better now. I'm lucky, some of my mates never recovered." Tim paused, looked up and made a beseeching movement with his hands. "Well, that's it Mrs. Martinelli, no lies and every word that I've said is true."

Maria managed to hide her tears and composed herself again. "The job's yours Tim, if you want it," she said, "I hope you will be happy here and feel safe?"

"Thanks Mrs. Martinelli, You won't regret it, I'll repay your kindness.   And you know something; you've made me feel safe already."

Maria told Tim that the relief she saw on his face was repayment enough and she went on to offer him the storeroom that had been vacated by Jake, saying that unless he had somewhere else in mind, he was welcome to live there.

Tim jumped at the chance of sleeping with a roof over his head and in a warm room at last.

Maria was pleased; it was reassuring to have a handyman living on the premises.

"Right then, I'll talk to Rosie Sharp about it. She'll give the room a good fettle before you go in.   Jake wasn't the tidiest of men." Then she remembered the conversation she'd had earlier that morning with Betty, "Oh, and clean sheets, you'll definitely need clean sheets!"

Maria sounded emphatic about the clean sheets and Tim, not knowing the story about Jake and Elsie, silently searched his memory for the last time he had slept between clean sheets!

Mrs. Martinelli explained that all main meals came to the house from a restaurant in town that she and her brother-in-law owned.   She had a snack lunch at one o'clock and an evening meal at six and Rosie Sharp would take his meals to him in the storeroom.   He would have to make his own arrangements for breakfast although, at first, she would supply him with a loaf of bread, some butter, tea and sugar, enough to start him off.

Tim couldn't believe his ears. Two meals guaranteed every day. "Thanks, Mrs. Martinelli, that's more than enough," he said.

"Taking your food and lodgings into account I think that seven shillings a week wages would be a fair offer. At the end of the summer season we could review that - should your work prove to be satisfactory, that is – and of course, should you decide to stay. Does that sound fair to you, Tim?"

Tim told her that it sounded very fair to him. Most of all, he wanted to tell her that she was the most kind-hearted woman in the world, but at the last minute he lost his nerve and couldn't bring himself to say it.

Maria hadn't quite finished with him. "Look, why don't you take the rest of the day off? Take a walk on the sea front, the fresh air might help to clear your chest, help you to get rid of that nasty cough - and it'll give Rosie time to clean your room. Come back for lunch, take a rest, have your evening meal and be ready to start work in the morning."

Tim thanked her and said he would take her advice about getting some fresh air; he rose to his feet and started for the outside door. He was almost there when she called for him to wait. He turned round to see what she wanted but she had already left the kitchen, so he sat down again at the table and waited. He hadn't been seated for more than a couple of minutes when she returned carrying a pair of brogues. Her eyes were bright as she handed them to him, "They belonged to my late husband. See if they fit you."

"Are you sure, Mrs. Martinelli, I mean, if they belonged to your husband, do you really want to part ..?"

"Of course I'm sure, it's what he would have wanted. Try them on, they're size eights."

Tim tried them on.

"Well?"

"Perfect, just perfect, can I keep them on?"

"Of course, they're yours now."

"Thanks ever so much, Mrs. Martinelli," Tim made for the open door and with every step that he took he managed to turn his walk into a shuffle!

Maria laughed at this latest example of Tim's sense of humour. She called after him. "And you can cut out that pantomime stuff, Mr. Ryan."

Tim pulled a funny face at her through the window and she watched him walk smartly down the concrete path. He opened the wooden gate, looked back to the kitchen window and waved before he disappeared from view.

He didn't wander very far, returning to the store room promptly at one o'clock for his lunch. "Thank you Rosie seems I'm just in time."

"I'm not Rosie," said the woman with the luncheon tray. "I'm more than twice her age and if you must know, I'm twice as nosey as Rosie, that's why I'm here." She set the tray down on the table. "My name's Mrs. Collings-wood, I'm a very good friend of Mrs. Martinelli's and I've come to say hello and have a look at you, see if she's found another Jake." She permitted herself a little smile; still got her own teeth, Tim noticed. Nice dress she was wearing and she had a Marcel wave in her hair. Tim returned her smile. She stared into his eyes as if that was the place she expected to find the answers to everything she wanted to know about him.

Tim didn't say a word and managed to begin eating without taking his gaze away from hers. Seeming satisfied with what she saw, Mrs. Collingswood stopped staring as she slipped the strap of a large bag from her shoulder and dropped it on the floor. "With the compliments of Mrs. Martinelli," she said and opening the bag produced a large bundle of clothes and a pair of working boots, size eights! She put the boots on the floor with a flourish and then dumped the clothes in a heap on the bed. "Eat your lunch while I get this lot sorted out, oh, and by the way, at six o'clock I'll be bringing roast pork in for dinner."

Mrs. Collingswood sorted out three vests, three pairs of underpants, three shirts and three pairs of pyjamas, "Mrs. Martinelli says it's best to have three of everything, one to wear, one in the wash and one to spare." She noticed his empty plate. "Why don't you lie down and have a rest, let your food digest properly? Get your strength up; don't forget work starts for you tomorrow!" Tim nodded sleepily.

"I'll take away the dishes and the bag and I'll see you again this evening." She closed the door quietly behind her. Tim guessed she'd made up her mind that she liked him.

It must have been well past four o'clock when Tim woke up. He decided to take another walk in the fresh air. The promenade was crowded with people, there was a lot of jostling and although it was all good-natured stuff it made him extremely nervous again. More people meant more chances of being recognised, he looked around for somewhere quieter; somewhere he could be on his own, somewhere to rest and feel safe. Across the road he saw an isolated spot where he could lean against the seawall. Hurriedly, he crossed the tram lines to get to it.

The late afternoon sun was low in the sky and there were still quite a number of people on the beach, grown-ups chatting as they rested in deck chairs, children laughing and putting the final touches to forts and sandcastles. Tim sighed with contentment; it all looked so peaceful – idyllic – he wished the scene would stay like this forever. Then he noticed the tide was coming in threatening the sandcastles and forts. A great cry of alarm went up as the grownups stopped lounging and rallied round to help their children. One by one the castles fell, their sand ramparts washed away until there was nothing left on the beach to show for the day's endeavour. But the children's happiness endured and as the bastions fell, the children laughed and cheered.

"It's time for tea," parents called as they packed away buckets and spades. Tim watched the families leave the beach, the children chattering excitedly, planning how they would build bigger and stronger sandcastles, tomorrow.

When he turned away from the seawall and retraced his steps to Mrs. Martinelli's, Tim also began to plan for tomorrow.

Mrs. Collingswood brought in his supper at six o'clock on the dot. "I've come back again to see if I missed any bad bits when I gave you the once over at lunchtime," she teased. She saw the old stained jacket that he had tossed carelessly on the bed, "Oh, I think Mrs. Martinelli would want to see you in a better jacket than that."

"Mrs. Martinelli's very kind," said Tim.

"Kind, that's not the word for it, she's a saint, that woman is, all the things she does for folk you wouldn't believe it."

"Tell you something," said Tim looking up for a moment from his plate, "She speaks very good English for an Italian."

Mrs. Collingswood didn't reply, she spluttered with laughter. At last she managed to get the words out, "Italian! Italian! Mrs. Martinelli's no more Italian than me, she's a Lancashire lass; she was born just a few miles from here, Mrs. Martinelli comes from Preston. Mike Cassidy, her father, was Irish, he came from the west of Ireland, Ballinasloe I think it was. Her dark hair and good looks, she got them from her father."

"Preston? Preston? I could have sworn she was Italian," and thinking that he couldn't be heard, he added quietly, "She's very beautiful."

Mrs. Collingswood heard his whisper, "You're not the only one who thinks that, you know," she said as she brought the tea pot to the table. "Men never stop coming to the door begging Maria to marry them. But she's choosey." Looking Tim straight in the eye she added, sharply, "Mrs. Martinelli sends the lot of them packing."

She poured out a cup of tea, "Milk, sugar, Mr. Ryan?"

Tim took a sip of his tea and then asked if Maria's father was still alive?

Mrs. Collingswood made the sign of the cross, "No, he's dead, God rest his soul. Look, do you mind if I ask you a question, Mr. Ryan?"

"Ask away, but I can't guarantee you'll get an answer."

"It's not that I'm being nosey – well, that's a lie really - I can't help being inquisitive, you'll find that out soon enough. We've been talking about Mike Cassidy, about him being Irish and I'm wondering.....?"

"Wondering about what, Mrs. Collingswood?"

"About you, Mr. Ryan. Ryan's an Irish name if ever there was one. Are you a Catholic, Mr. Ryan?"

"I haven't been to mass for a long time," said Tim. "But I don't want to talk about it if you don't mind Mrs. Collingswood."

"That's fine with me, it's just that I was about to tell you how Maria and her husband met, they were both Catholics you see? Maria took her father to Lourdes because he was ill and Andrew took his father there because he was ill. Maria and Andrew didn't know one another before they met at Lourdes."

"And the miraculous waters cured their fathers I suppose? You read about things like that in the Sunday papers." Tim sounded very sceptical.

For a Catholic – even a lapsed one – to make a remark like that about the holy waters of Lourdes sounded sacrilegious to the devout Mrs. Collingswood, but she managed to reply calmly enough. "No, no, that's not what happened, both of their dad's died soon after their return from Lourdes. However, there was a miracle; Maria and her husband to be were absolutely convinced of it"

Tim returned his cup to the saucer. "How'd they work that one out if both their dads' died?"

Mrs. Collingswood replied with more passion in her voice this time. "Ooh men! When I heard you say that Mrs. Martinelli was beautiful, I thought to myself, now there's a romantic soul for you and I couldn't believe my ears when you talked about the miraculous waters the way you did. Yes, both of their dads' died, that's true, but when

Maria and Andrew met and fell in love at Lourdes, they were convinced that was the way things were supposed to happen - God's will! God works in mysterious ways, or have you forgotten, Mr. Ryan?" Tim stayed silent. Mrs. Collingswood carried on with the story. "'They returned from Lourdes, after a few months they were married and within a year they were blessed with a bonny baby girl. So there was a miracle at Lourdes after all." Mrs. Collingswood challenged Tim, defying him to say that there hadn't been. "Don't you see that, Mr. Ryan?"

"I suppose there was looking at it that way, but it's the stuff newspapers' write about such things that puts me off." Tim wanted to draw the conversation to a close, all this talk about Mrs. Martinelli and her dead father and miracles at Lourdes made it seem as if he'd been prying into their private lives. He was beginning to feel uncomfortable and needed to be alone again.

But Mrs. Collingswood hadn't quite finished. She picked up Tim's jacket from the bed, "We can't let you loose on the street wearing this; we'd have no visitors left in Blackpool. I'm sure Maria said she'd got a jacket in her wardrobe; I'll let you try it on and see if it fits. Oh, and by the way, about your washing, leave that out every Monday and I'll see that it gets done; I don't like my friends going about looking scruffy."

Tim was speechless with gratitude.

Mrs. Collingswood chuckled. "I wish you could see that little boy's look on your face right now. Men are all boys at heart; they'd be lost without a woman to look after them. I ought to know, I've got a little boy at home, they call him Jack and he's my lovely husband."

Tim was touched by Mrs. Collingswood's kindness and didn't quite know how to thank her. In the end he did what came naturally, he stood up, shook her hand and said graciously, "Thanks for your kind offer Mrs. Collingswood, of course I accept and from now on, if there's anything I can do for you, you've only to ask."

"Just one of your nice smiles now and again would be payment enough. I think we are going to get along together just fine and I'll tell Maria what a good choice she's made. Before I go, do you mind if I give you a word of advice Mr. Ryan?"

"I'm listening."

"It's about Betty Williams, the girl who's just started to work in the kiosk. I know about her and she's trouble that one, bad trouble. You keep away from her. Don't say I didn't warn you. Oh, and by the way, leave those dishes; Rosie will deal with them in the morning."

"Thanks for everything, Mrs. Collingswood," said Tim. As the door closed behind her, he noticed that she had taken his old jacket with her.

Tim wasn't used to eating an evening meal, digesting it made him sleepy and he decided it was time for an early night. He rummaged in one of the drawers until he found a clean pair of pyjamas, laid them out on the bed and took down the tin bath that was hanging on the wall. Pouring in two kettles of boiling water and adding as much cold as was needed without making the water too cold, he climbed in and had his first good bath for years!

After the luxury of drying himself on a real towel he put on the clean pyjamas. There was absolutely no doubt about it; he was the luckiest man in the world. Yesterday he had nothing; today he had a job worth seven shillings a week, free board and lodgings, a warm bed to sleep in, and a boss who had a kind heart, and motherly Mrs. Collingswood to give him friendly advice....

Tim still had a few questions to ponder, for instance, what had happened to Mrs. Martinelli's husband, when was she widowed and how had Mr. Martinelli died? And where was Mrs. Martinelli's daughter and how old was she? Tim was sleeping soundly before he could come up with any answers.

Meanwhile, Maria Martinelli lay in her bed trying to recall all the events of the day, starting with the news Betty Williams came to tell her about Jake and Elsie running away together. Poor Elsie, poor Jake, Maria had a feeling that the relationship wouldn't be very long lasting. And then there was Betty, the vivacious young girl with the child-like blue eyes and golden hair who said outrageous things. Although, on the surface, she appeared to be innocently happy, there were times when Maria had caught the girl unawares. These were the times she found something about Betty's expression that she couldn't quite fathom and if truth were to be told it left her feeling uneasy. Then in a lighter mood Maria thought about Tim. She knew she had made the right decision by employing him, she had rescued him, her conscience told her so. The day hadn't worked out too badly and making a mental note of the important things she had to do tomorrow, she said her night prayers and thanked God for helping her to get through another day.

CHAPTER THREE

TIM WOKE UP AT SEVEN the next morning, the ringing from an old alarm clock brought him into the land of the living. He had found the clock last night hidden on a shelf behind some cups and made a mental note to ask Mrs. Collingswood if it was okay for him to keep it.

He treated himself to a strong cup of tea and then went into the shed to get the lawn mower. After his long sleep in a comfortable bed Tim felt fit and strong enough to push the lawn mower all the way to Southport if he had to. A cough to clear his chest and he was ready for work. He locked the door to his room and took his first run at the grass.

An hour later the job was done, the grass cuttings on the compost heap, the lawn mower cleaned and back in its den. Now it was tea and a slice of fresh bread and butter time. He took out the key to his room, but to his surprise he found the door open. Betty Williams, the person Mrs. Collingswood had warned him about, was sitting on the table swinging her legs provocatively.

Tim managed to appear calm. "Good Lord, Betty. You gave me a fright; I thought I'd locked the door."

"No, you couldn't have," Betty said demurely. "From the gate I saw you cutting the grass. The door to your room was open, so I went in. See, I've made you a cup of tea and I brought this nice bacon sandwich so you could have your first breakfast with me." Smiling coyly, she pointed to the steaming cup of tea and the sandwich that lay beside her on the table.

Tim's eyes were focussed on Betty's silk stockings and he reached for the sandwich without taking his eyes off her legs for a second. "Thanks Betty," he gulped, taking a bite at the bread.

Betty didn't say anything. Slowly, deliberately, she crossed her legs, the silk on silk contact made that special sound that always excited him. Betty sensed his pleasure so she did it again, but this time she raised one of her legs higher and whispered, "I never wear anything underneath."

Tim was hypnotised, he stood there, eyes bulging. Betty had lost her innocent look; she waved a hand at the food on the table, "Why bother with that - you can have me." She flung herself backwards on the table, challenging, inviting....

A knock sounded on the door! "Come in," gasped Tim and Betty slid from the table and pulled down her skirt just as the door opened.

"Morning Tim – I'm not stopping," said Maria. "Just popped in to give you .....Good heavens, Betty, what are you doing here?"

Betty was standing by the table adjusting the teacup in its saucer, "I heard Mr. Ryan cutting the grass, I was early for work so I came in and made him a cup of tea and gave him a bacon sandwich. I hope you don't mind Mrs. Martinelli?"

"Mind? Of course I don't mind. No, that was a very kind thought Betty, really lovely." Maria saw the time on Tim's alarm clock. "You should be opening up the kiosk now, Betty."

"Okay, Mrs. Martinelli, I was just about to leave when you came in." Betty turned her back on Maria and faced Tim. "Goodbye, Mr. Ryan, sorry you didn't have time to finish your breakfast." She emphasised the word breakfast and winked at Tim as she said it. She turned to Maria again, "Goodbye, Mrs. Martinelli," and then dazzling them both with the sweetness of her smile she flitted out of the room as lightly as a butterfly.

Tim picked up the remains of the sandwich from the table and then put them down again. His mind was still on Betty's alternative menu when Maria's voice brought him out of dreamland and back into the real world.

"I think that was very thoughtful of Betty to make a cup of tea for you, it just goes to show that there's some good to be found in everybody? Ignore gossip and take people as you find them. Well, that's what I think, don't you?"

"Yes, yes, I agree," Tim answered quickly; he could still hear Betty's voice over and over in his head - "Why bother about that, you can have me ...Why bother, you can have me..." He trembled as he thought about what might have happened if Mrs. Martinelli hadn't turned up when she did?

"Are you alright, Tim?"

"Yes, I'm alright, Mrs. Martinelli. Just need some fresh air. I'll be okay when I get outside." He wondered if she'd noticed the unmade bed and his untidy room. "Sorry about the mess, Mrs. Martinelli."

"That's all right, Mrs. Collingswood has told me about the arrangement she's made with you, so don't worry; somebody will be here shortly to tidy things up." She looked at him anxiously. "Are you sure you're all right?"

"I'm okay, really I am, Mrs. Martinelli," said Tim. He pulled out a chair from the table and asked her to sit down, but she said that she had an appointment in town and couldn't stay.

She gave him a plan showing the locations of her shooting galleries, kiosks and the gift shop and explained she wanted them to be inspected and defects noted, so they could be repaired now, before the season got busy. When she left, Tim reflected on his narrow escape with Betty, forewarned was forearmed, he hoped. Tim concentrated on the plan and studied it carefully. Although it was a rough sketch and not to scale, Maria had made it easy for him to follow, the tower and the piers were clearly marked. "No trouble finding that lot," he said to himself and he folded the paper and tucked it carefully away in his pocket. He would do his inspection later and let Mrs. Martinelli have his report, but first things first, he was determined to make a start on painting the gate before working on anything else.

Betty was doing a roaring trade with her postcards and candy floss when Tim began to sand down the gate. She was only a few yards away but he waited until he had finished doing the priming before he looked again to see if Betty was still hard at work. Now, there was only one person standing at her kiosk - a well-dressed middle-aged man - and judging by his manner he wasn't there to buy postcards. His voice was low and controlled, but his face was flushed and he kept stabbing a finger at Betty. Whoever he was, and whatever he was talking about, he wasn't getting any response from her. Betty's elbows were propped indolently on the counter and the expression on her face was one of utter boredom. She let the man wag his finger at her for a minute or two longer and then after giving a wide yawn she told him in a loud voice that he was a right pain in the arse and the sooner he pissed off the better! The man looked shocked, but he stayed where he was and redoubled his efforts to persuade Betty to do whatever it was he wanted Although Tim strained his ears to the limit, he couldn't make out what the man was asking for, none of his pleading seemed to make an impression on Betty, eventually she turned her back on him and pretended to tidy the post card rack.

Tim knew perfectly well that it was none of his business, but he was intrigued and stood there, paintbrush in hand, watching and listening. It was entertaining, better than going to the pictures and providing that it didn't become violent, Tim was quite content to let the show go on. In his imagination he'd already worked out what the rumpus was about. It was easy, Betty had once been the middle-aged man's bit on the side, but now she must have dumped him and here he was at the kiosk, at first threatening and now pleading with her, in an endeavour to win her back again. But then Betty raised her voice harshly and fearing that things could soon get out of hand, Tim put down his brush and walked slowly over to the kiosk hoping to calm the situation down a bit.

Betty didn't even bother to look up, she knew it was him. "And you can piss off an all," she shouted angrily. "Go away and get on with your painting. Fuck off the two of you, go on, fuck off, and if you don't I'll start screaming." She lifted the lid of the counter and slammed it down hard to show that she really meant it. The stranger, who had kept his face averted while Tim was there, slunk away muttering, "Keep quiet, slut, that's your last warning – if you know what's good for you - keep quiet." Betty stuck two fingers up at him and yelled, "Good riddance and don't come back. Don't try to come back and see me – ever!" She turned to yell the same insults at Tim, but Tim had moved away, he had decided he had more important things to do than listen to barrack room language from Betty.

Tim started on his tour of inspection and reckoned if things went to plan he could get everything done and be back in his room by one o'clock for lunch. He hadn't met Rosie yet, the daily help who was to tidy his room. He laughed wryly; she couldn't be another Betty Williams, could she? Tim felt more perplexed than angry about Betty. What was it with her? Only a few hours ago she was lying on the table in his room and trying her best to seduce him and now she was telling him to clear off. And the angry man he'd seen at the kiosk, what was he warning her to keep quiet about? But why waste time brooding, better to think about his good fortune in meeting Mrs. Martinelli. He was lucky, he told himself, life had got so much better since she had hired him. Why did Betty Williams have to come onto the scene and upset the applecart? He saw images of Betty crossing her legs, heard the sound of silk on silk, and it was difficult to get rid of the feelings she had aroused in him.

Taking all that he now knew about Betty into account, he thought that Mrs. Collingswood was probably right about her – Betty was trouble! From now on Tim made up his mind to be on his guard and keep her at arm's length. It was the only way and safer. That's what he was going to do. Definately!

Looking up at the clear sky, he drew some fresh Blackpool air into his lungs. He hadn't coughed much all morning and that thought cheered him up and helped him forget Betty. It was a lovely day, the weather warm and sunny with a slight breeze blowing off the sea. It was ideal paint-drying weather and he guessed that in an hour's time the undercoat would be dry and then he could give the gate a top coat of green gloss. Meanwhile he would have his lunch and then, after painting the gate, given a fair wind he could complete his inspection of the kiosks and shooting galleries.

He arrived at the store-room at the same time as Mrs. Collingswood. She was in a chatty mood. "Ham salad," she announced. She uncovered the dish with a flourish, "Good healthy food, salad."

Between mouthfuls Tim thanked her, "By the way, the ice cream they sell in the kiosks, where's it made, do you know?"

Mrs. Collingswood told him that it was made by Mrs. Martinelli's brother-in-law, Joseph. With Mrs. Martinelli and his wife Cecilia, Joseph owned one of the best restaurants in town and during summer he and his wife had to work almost night and day running the restaurant and making the supplies of ice-cream for Mrs. Martinelli to sell in her kiosks – during the holiday season they couldn't rake the money in fast enough! Mrs. Collingswood told him all this without a trace of envy in her voice, on the contrary she sounded full of pride for Maria and the family's success.

Tim hadn't quite finished his meal, and he hadn't quite finished asking questions, "What happened to Mrs. Martinelli's daughter, she had a little girl, you told me? And Mr. Martinelli, what happened to him?"

Mrs. Collingswood frowned. "I think you should be asking somebody else those questions not me, Mr. Ryan. All I'll say is this, Mrs. Martinelli's husband, Andrew, died four years ago and when Mrs. Martinelli is ready I've no doubt she'll tell you herself about him and her daughter." She took away Tim's empty plate and placed a dish of steaming sponge pudding in front of him. "I don't know if you deserve this," she scolded, "Hot jam or custard, Mr. Ryan?"

"Jam please, and by the way I'm sorry, you're quite right, I should be asking Mrs. Martinelli those questions, not you. Sorry, I didn't mean to be so nosey."

"Takes one to know one," said Mrs. Collingswood, cheerfully.

Tim remembered he wanted to ask about the clock. "The alarm clock I found last night, now why is it I have this strange feeling that you know something about it?"

"Mea culpa," she said, striking her breast in mock confession. "I hid it there because I wanted you to have a decent night's sleep, you looked worn out. That was yesterday, today, you seem to have made a good recovery." She was beaming; clearly she thought that she was the one mainly responsible for his improvement.

"Thanks, Mrs. Collingswood; it was kind of you to care for me like that."

"It's a pleasure, Mr. Ryan....."

Tim sensed that she had something more to say because she took so much time clearing away his dishes.

"I might have some news for you at tea-time," she said at last.

"Good news, I hope?"

"We'll have to see, won't we?" She didn't say any more, she'd done what she set out to do; she'd whetted his appetite, now she was going to make him wait until the evening before he heard the rest of it.

She stacked the plates on a large tray "See you at six," she promised as he held the door open for her.

Tim returned to complete his work on the gate and as he drew nearer to Betty's kiosk he noticed that trade was steady rather than brisk. After one or two customers had been served there would be a lull and then two or three more customers would drift up - and so it went on.

He prised open the lid from the paint tin with his penknife, gave the paint a stir and set to work. Without giving Betty or the kiosk a second glance, he let her get on with her job while he got on with his. Working steadily, he soon had the paintwork finished and stood back to admire it. Betty's voice called from behind him, "She won't like it."

"Who won't like it?" he asked without turning around.

"Mrs. Martinelli, she won't like it. She only likes white for the gate."

Tim turned towards her, "What's it to you whether she likes it or not? Any way I thought you weren't talking to me, you told me to fuck off, remember?"

"Oh, I'm sorry about that Mr. Ryan. Really I am. But that guy was pestering me; he's always pestering me. He's sick. He was driving me nuts. I didn't mean to be rude to you; I want us to be friends. Please?" Her blue eyes gazed at him, frank and appealing.

Tim didn't take offence easily and he readily forgave her. "Alright Betty, friends it is then, but nothing more than friendship, okay? No more of the sort of stuff you tried on this morning?"

"Okay, okay, I agree, just friends. But can I call you Tim, calling you Mr. Ryan all the time, it doesn't seem like I'm talking to a friend?"

"That's fine Betty, 'though if Mrs. Martinelli or any of the others are around I suggest you call me Mr. Ryan, for the time being at any rate."

"I will. Oh, and thanks Tim." She started to walk back to the kiosk. Before she got there she turned and pointed to the gate again. "Green! Bet you anything she won't like it," she called triumphantly, "White's her colour for the gate. It's always been white."

"Ha! Ha! But suppose she does like it, what then?" Too late Tim realized that he shouldn't have replied, he had given Betty an excuse to come skipping back. She stood up on her toes and whispered in his ear, "Bet you............"

Tim couldn't believe what he was hearing, after all that had happened earlier in the day he was not prepared for what she had just proposed. "Christ Betty, where'd you learn all that stuff? Only two minutes ago you promised to behave yourself and here you are, you're at it again."

Betty tripped away laughing, "I was only teasing Tim, only teasing."

But Tim knew that she wasn't teasing, she was testing him to see how he would react to what she had promised if she lost the bet.

He managed to squeeze through the gate without causing damage to the wet paint and cleaned the brushes in the shed so that they were ready for the next job. As he put the green paint away on the shelf he noticed the tin of white and it was then that Betty's words came back to him, "She won't like it you know, white's her colour ......" Tim decided to leave things as they were until he heard from Mrs. Martinelli. If she liked it, fine, if not – well, he'd repaint the gate white - no problem!

It was almost six o'clock by the time Tim had completed his tour of the kiosks. He unlocked the door to his room and as he washed his hands it dawned on him that he had made a big mistake agreeing to be on first name terms with Betty. What an idiot he was, instead of keeping her at arm's length, he had invited her to take not one but two steps closer to him, even though he knew by now, she couldn't be trusted an inch.

When Mrs. Collingswood came in with his tea, she didn't waste any time in telling him the news she had promised earlier. Mrs. Martinelli had agreed to let her have one of the ice-cream kiosks at a give-away price and had consulted with Mr. Beswick her bank manager this very morning, in order to get the sale moving. Running the kiosk meant that by mid August, Mrs. Collingswood's husband, Jack, who was retired and bored, would have something to do to keep him occupied. She went on to say that Mrs. Martinelli was going to rearrange all of her own business commitments, so that from now on she could take things a bit easier and spend more time enjoying the garden. Humming a little tune and sounding as bright as a lark, Mrs. Collingswood balanced a tray of empty dishes on her arm and left Tim to work out the significance of what she had told him about Maria.

Tim woke up the next morning to find that it had rained overnight. A glance at the garden was enough for him to see that the rain hadn't made the ground too soggy but had softened it so it was just right for weeding. The weeds came up easily from the damp soil and soon he had quite a large pile ready to be carted away.

As he pulled out the wheelbarrow from shed, he was surprised to see that Mrs. Martinelli had come out to join him. She was wearing stout shoes and carrying a pair of gardening gloves and asked if she could help him. Clearly it hadn't entered her head that he might say "no" and just for a moment Tim, out of sheer devilment, was tempted to refuse. But instead, he assumed an authoritative air and reminded her that he was the head gardener and that she had better do strictly as she was told if she wanted to keep her position as his assistant. Maria went along with his jest and said that she was aware of her humble position and would do her best to please him – sir! They worked steadily together for about two hours, pausing occasionally for a chat about this plant or the other and then, during one of those pauses, she invited Tim back to the house for a cup of tea.

They left their muddy shoes in the porch and Tim sat down at the table while Maria went to fetch food from the pantry. Not since he was at home with his own family had Tim felt so relaxed and contented in a woman's company. After pouring out their tea, Maria sat facing him and apologised when her feet accidentally brushed against his under the table. A weak "that's okay" was the best Tim could muster because the light contact with Maria's feet seemed to have affected his breathing and made speech difficult. He wondered if Mrs. Martinelli had been similarly affected. Apparently not, because she was laughing and talking, telling him to stop calling her Mrs. Martinelli, to call her by her first name, Maria.

The words rang out like music to his ears. No breathing difficulties now. He heard himself saying repeatedly, "Yes, Maria, Maria."

Now they chatted together like friends who had known each other for years. Mostly they talked about their families. Some things she spoke of, such as her husband's death four years ago, he already knew from Mrs. Collingswood. But then she told him that her husband had been an invalid for a long time. He had been very badly wounded in the war and had never really recovered. Maria bowed her head overcome by sad memories. Tim, who had been totally unprepared for any of this, instinctively reached out and took her hand. They sat quietly for a while, Tim holding her hand, until at last she raised her head and said in a voice barely louder than a whisper, "Can I ask you a personal question, Tim?"

"Sure," said Tim. "Anything."

"Are you married Tim?" she asked, then hurriedly added, "You don't have to answer if you don't want to."

"That's alright. No, I'm not married." He smiled ruefully, "The last job I had involved a lot of travelling, no time to fall in love and settle down in one place, I had to keep on the move..."

Maria laughed because Tim's description of his life on the run was meant to be funny, but she could sense the sadness in it. "Oh, I don't know Tim; you could always give up the travelling job and settle down in Blackpool. There are plenty of pretty girls here to choose from. What about Betty Williams?"

A look of alarm crossed Tim's face; thank God Maria didn't wait for an answer.

Maria continued, "She's pretty and bright as a button, I can vouch for that. Would it surprise you to know that since she took over at the kiosk it's doing a hundred per cent more business? She's a hard worker is Betty and she'll get a good bonus from me at the end of the season, she deserves it. I'm sure that with the right sort of man she could settle down."

Tim was silent, he longed to say, "It's you Maria, it's you that I want."

Maria sensed something was embarrassing him. Had Tim grown quiet because she'd gone too far by talking about marriage and settling down in Blackpool? She quickly changed the subject to her daughter Bernadette, who was eighteen, married to a ship's engineer and living in Glasgow. Her face was glowing when she told him, "Their first baby is due just before Christmas."

"Lucky them, lucky you," said Tim.

"You've still got time, Tim, time for your luck to change. It'll happen one day, you'll see."

Tim thanked her for the tea. He said it was time he was getting back to work and plucking up courage added tentatively, "Maria, when you've time, when you have spare time, can we work together in the garden.....?"

"Of course we will. I was getting worried. I thought you'd never ask."

"Thought I'd never ask? Come as often as you can Maria, I'd like that more than anything."

"That's settled then," said Maria firmly. She opened the door for Tim and watched as he laced up his working boots. He had taken a few steps down the concrete path when she called after him. "By the way Tim, the gate looks good. It's time we had a change from white."

Tim spun round, gleefully gave her the thumbs up sign and went to see if the gate needed a second coat of green gloss.

He hadn't been there for more than a few seconds when Betty appeared standing beside him. Tim glanced in the direction of the kiosk, two or three people were giggling at the postcards. He could hear a little girl demanding candyfloss and her harassed mother waved to attract Betty's attention.

Tim pointed to the queue, "Shouldn't you be serving, Betty?"

"I will, I will. But tell me first, she wants white doesn't she? She always has white."

"Not this time Betty. Mrs. Martinelli likes the green. Time for a change, she said."

Betty's face expressed total incredulity and then anger. "She likes you, Tim," she spat out. "Don't say I didn't warn you. You must be stupid not to have noticed, all that helping in the garden and all those cups of tea in the house after. Bloody hell Tim, she's nearly old enough to be your mother." She ran back to the kiosk and slammed down the lid of the counter so hard the flimsy walls shook. The little girl, still waiting for her candy floss, put her hands over her ears and screamed!

CHAPTER FOUR

TIM DIDN'T SEE MUCH OF Betty for a while, he suspected she was deliberately keeping out of his way and that suited him fine, but as the days of the season sped by he found himself seeing more of Maria. At least twice a week she found time to work with him in the garden and after about two hours or so they would go back to the house for tea and a chat. During one of these chats Maria told him she was selling the two shooting galleries and when the sale was completed she would be able to spend more leisure time in the garden.

She took out a box of clay pipes from a drawer and presented it to him. "It's a souvenir," she said, "When the galleries go, that's all that will be left of them." The gallery prize appeared expensive but wasn't, the box was made of red cardboard designed to look like real leather, Maria's name, address and telephone number were printed on it in gold. A gift from Maria was special; Tim vowed to himself that he would always keep it.

Maria asked Tim to tell her again about his mother and father. "Alright, but I haven't seen them for five years so things could have changed a lot since then," Tim said.

"Five years - so you did keep in touch then, earlier I mean?"

"For the first two years I did. I kept dodging in and out to see how they were. Then the redcaps' got wind of it. They were sniffing around and it frightened me off. I stayed away and never dared go back again."

Maria nodded as though she understood. "Let's pretend things are just the same as they were five years ago, shall we?"

"Right, well, my mother's name is, Mary." He raised his eyes to hers, "Maria, Mary, both names are the same aren't they?" Maria nodded.

"But most of the villagers' call her Granny Twiceover, Mum always repeats what she's said if she thinks it's important. Judging by the number of times she repeats things, I guess she thinks that most of what she says is important." Tim had the most loving expression in his voice. Maria, whose eyes had never left his face, guessed that he was missing his mother terribly.

He took a sip from his tea and continued talking. "How old do you think my Dad was when he started to work down the pit, Maria?"

Maria shook her head.

"Eight! He was only eight years old. Can you believe it, only eight years old and working down a coal-mine?"

"Surely at that age he should have been at school?"

"In those days if you gave the head teacher a letter from your parents saying you had a job, you could leave school and start work at almost any age. People were poor then, even poorer than they are now and a few coppers earned by a child made a big difference to a family."

"But what did they expect him to do; surely he was too small and weak to hew coal?" The thought of a child in a coal mine appalled Maria.

"Oh, they found him a job alright," said Tim. "And it was an important job too. They sat him down in the dark and put a piece of rope in his hand, told him to pull and release, pull and release. An easy job, they said."

"What was it for?"

"Well, it was vital really, because what it did was to open and close a wooden door into the shaft that acted as a ventilator. Every time he opened and closed the door it drew fresh air into the shaft for the miners. So you see, although Dad was only eight years old he had a very responsible job, without him the miners could have suffocated." Maria saw Tim gazing into the distance, staring into a past that only he, with his knowledge of the pit, could see.

"But Tim, he must have been frightened half out of his wits sitting there all alone in the dark?"

"Yes, he told me he cried at first, but he got used to it and the thought of earning money for the family helped him to stick at it. At least life was easier for Dad when he grew up and married. He enjoyed our childhood – it made up for the one he didn't have. And later, after the war, I heard they had some good times at home, especially when my eldest brother, Bernard, and his mate's, Long Andy and Short Andy went to see them. Mum said there was never a dull moment when they were around!"

"Long Andy, Short Andy?"

Tim laughed. "They're gamekeepers and after the war they went to see a local land-owner, Major Wilberforce, hoping to find a job. He asked for their names and both replied at once, "Andy Smith." Major Wilberforce found they were both crack shots and experienced gamekeepers and he set the two of them on. He called the six foot-sixer, "Long Andy" and the five foot-sixer, "Short Andy." I shouldn't be surprised if everybody in the West Riding of Yorkshire knows who they are by now....."

"Is there any more to come?" prompted Maria.

"Plenty! There's my brother Jim. Jim's the scholar in the family; he works down the pit and is a trade union representative. Dad thinks Jim will finish up being prime minister one day! Then there's Martha my sister and my two other married sisters, Polly and Annie..." Tim didn't get the chance to explain more because Mrs. Collingswood came into the kitchen, Mr. Beswick, the bank manager, was on the phone and wanted to speak to Mrs. Martinelli.

Maria went to answer Mr. Beswick's call, "Wait, Tim," she said. "This'll only take a few minutes, and then we can pick up where we left off."

When the door closed behind Maria, Mrs. Collingswood reported to Tim that Betty Williams had complained her counter flap wasn't working properly, a friend of Betty's had brought the message. She said the counter flap should be fixed urgently, because it might cause an accident.

Tim got up straight away, "Where are you going?" asked Mrs. Collingswood.

"Get the job done. Best get it done now. Don't want anyone to be injured if I can prevent it."

"Surely you're not going until Mrs. Martinelli has finished talking to Mr. Beswick? She's expecting you to stay. Couldn't you stop a minute longer?"

"Sorry, Mrs. Collingswood, I'd never forgive myself if someone got hurt. Mrs. Martinelli will understand. Tell her what's happened. The family history can wait."

Mrs. Collingswood raised her eyebrows, it seemed to her that Tim was giving precedence to Betty Williams and she didn't like it. Tim ignored her disapproval; he hurried away from the kitchen, collected his toolbox from the shed and set off to make the repair.

At least twenty yards from the kiosk he could clearly hear the sound of the counter lid being smashed down, and the same red faced man he had seen before was in fast retreat followed by a torrent of abuse from Betty. Tim was pretty certain it was the hinge that needed fixing; it couldn't possibly stand up to the sort of treatment Betty was dishing out. Silently he set to work tightening up the hinge screws, then, job done; he rummaged about in his toolbox, produced a metal rule and presented it to Betty.

"What's that for?" she said crossly

"If you've got to bash the counter with something, use this and not the flap – otherwise you'll have me back here every day to mend the dammed thing."

"Ooh, that's a promise is it?" Betty fluttered her eyelashes, and gazed longingly at him. It was a first rate performance.

"Okay, okay, funny, funny," Tim laughed. "But seriously, you've got to stop bashing that counter lid up and down, otherwise the day will come when you're going to hurt somebody and that won't be a laughing matter. It's got to stop, Betty. Do you hear what I'm saying?"

Betty heard, but she didn't like what he was saying, "Know something, Tim? You've got no sense of humour. You had a sense of humour when you first came here, but now you seem to have lost it. It's that Mrs. Martinelli, you've let her turn you into a right boring old fart just the same as she is."

After Tim left, Betty picked up the pile of post-cards intending to sort them, then, one by one, she allowed them to fall from her fingers into an untidy heap. She watched as the last card fluttered down and smiled to herself - she'd hatched a plan – it couldn't fail and she wondered why on earth she hadn't thought of it before. All she needed was the right opportunity to put it into action and hey presto when that was done, she could just sit back and wait for the fireworks that would blow Tim right out of Mrs. Martinelli's arms and into hers! Love can change into hate overnight, Betty Williams smiled at the thought; she knew now exactly what she had to do to make Mrs. Martinelli hate Tim.

Betty daydreamed about a future with Tim. The pile of money hidden on top of her wardrobe - a small fortune – was enough to set them up in business together. She indulged herself imagining what they would do with the money, their lives bound up together. Now all the other men in her life would merely be subscribers to her special future with Tim.

She was startled by a man's voice, "Excuse me miss. Excuse me ...." and glanced up to see a stout, well-dressed man, aged about fifty, she guessed. He wore a gold watch chain slung across his ample midriff, obviously wealthy and not at all bad looking.

"Yes sir, can I help you?" Betty was bubbling over, still glowing with the excitement she felt as she imagined her life with Tim.

Marcus Kellner nodded politely. "Well, I hope so. A friend of mine who knows you," he leaned over and whispered a name into Betty's ear –

"Oh him, yes, we see one another quite a lot, he's lovely."

"He said I could ask you if you would - if you would ...."

"You want to talk about having sex with me, is that it?"

He flinched at the bluntness of Betty's question and looked around to make sure that he wasn't overheard before replying, "Yes, if that's alright."

Betty seductively unbuttoned the top two buttons of her blouse and leaned forward on the counter. "Before we talk business," she said slowly, "you've got to buy some cards."

Without taking his eyes off her, the man reached for the card rack.

"No, not those," corrected Betty. "Take them from that pile on the counter." She picked up the cards, "Look, why don't you buy the lot, save me the trouble of putting them away?"

She noted that he was sweating nervously; Betty undid another button to keep him nicely on the boil! He paid her for the postcards, fumbling as he tried to put them away in his pocket. Betty's blue eyes darkened and she whispered, "Tell me what you would like me to do for you and then, when I've finished here, perhaps we can go somewhere nice and cosy.....?"

CHAPTER FIVE

TIM TURNED THE KITCHEN COLD-WATER tap on and off testing the new washer he had fitted, it worked perfectly. The door to the kitchen was open and as he dried his hands he could hear the murmur of Maria and Anne Collingswood's voices in the sitting room.

Anne loved to spend time with Tim and Maria. She enjoyed their company to be sure, but it was the role of observer she liked best. Several months had past now since the "day of the shuffle," as Maria sometimes called it, and it made Anne immensely happy to see them growing closer to each other every day.

Tim joined the women to await the arrival of Anne's nephew, Michael. He was late and Anne was growing impatient. "I'll die with thirst if I have to wait for Michael much longer, that boy must be the worst time-keeper in the world."

Almost as she spoke there was a loud bang on the front door. "Bring him in before he batters the door down," said Maria, "then we can all have a cup of tea."

Michael entered the room like an actor walking onto a stage, tall, handsome and just twenty-three years old he was a newspaper reporter full of confidence and at an age when a young man feels that nobody can teach him anything.

"Hello everybody," he said and before Maria could speak, he introduced himself to Tim. "My name's Michael, how do you do?"

"Pleased to meet you, Michael, I'm Tim Ryan, the Jack of all trades around here. Your Aunt Anne has told me about your work on the local newspaper."

"So, she's told you about the local paper, but has she told you I'm leaving to join The Manchester Sentinel after Christmas?"

"No, she didn't tell me. Does she know about it?"

Michael couldn't say more because Anne was embracing him and Maria congratulating him for being appointed to such a prestigious newspaper. He made no attempt to subdue the women's praise; it appeared he thought he deserved every bit of it.

When Anne released him, Michael took Maria in his arms and hugged her warmly assuring her he would do his very best in the new job and thanking her for all her years of encouragement. For the first time in his life, Tim knew what it felt like to be jealous.

Maria sensed Tim's change of mood. Struggling free from Michael's bear-hug, she said, "Once upon a time I nearly became Michael's mother-in-law, you know."

Tim managed a smile for Maria's sake and Anne declared she knew very well why Maria never became Michael's mother-in-law. "It was because Bernadette hardly ever saw him," she scolded. "He was always dashing about going somewhere or other for the newspaper. And never a telephone call or a written word or anything to Bernadette the whole time he was away. So, one day when he got back from his travels and asked, "Where is she?" we had to tell him he was too late, that Bernadette was married and living in Glasgow. And who can blame her?"

Tim noticed how Anne gazed affectionately at Michael during the whole of the time she was scolding him.

"Just goes to show you, doesn't it," said Michael centre stage, addressing his audience. "If you love somebody, you've jolly well got to move quickly or somebody else will get first prize." He had adopted a wounded look and tried to sound sad, but he was putting on an act and everybody knew it. Although he wasn't taken seriously, Anne did think that both Maria and Tim looked just a wee bit uncomfortable. Good, she thought, perhaps Michael's little speech might ginger them up a bit.

Michael was just about to take a bite of cake when Anne said, "Anything exciting happened since we last saw you, Michael?"

Michael was waiting for his cue. He always kept a store of exciting news items to entertain and had developed the knack of matching the right story to his audience. He put the piece of cake back on his plate and began. "I've just got back from Paris, reporting on the Exhibition. It was absolutely marvellous. And Josephine Baker's show, she is a must, you really have to see her dance......" Just as he was about to get into the swing of his story, Maria interrupted.

"Paris? What a coincidence, Michael, that's where Anne and I intend to go at the end of the season! If my memory serves me right, that should be the first week in October?" She was looking across at Michael so didn't see the hurt on Tim's face. Anne saw and realized this was the first Tim had heard about Paris. Oh, the poor man, she thought, we should have talked to him about our trip a long time ago and not let him hear about it like this. She decided to play the diplomat, "Yes, Michael, we are **thinking** of going to Paris with some other business people at the end of the season, but Maria says she can't agree for sure until she clears it first with Tim. You wanted to ask Tim if he'd be willing to hold the fort while we are away, is that right, Maria?"

Maria was grateful to Anne for throwing her a lifeline and could have bitten off her tongue announcing the Paris trip before Tim knew anything about it. "Will you Tim?" she asked. "If we do decide to go to Paris, will you stay behind and hold the fort for me, otherwise I can't?"

Quickly, Tim interrupted, and said he'd do that happily for her; the way it had been put to him now made all the difference between feeling slighted and feeling needed.

Michael was concerned when he heard Tim's agreement come so readily. "I hope you're aware of what you are letting yourself in for, Tim Ryan? It's a big responsibility, guarding the Martinelli Empire. I'd volunteer to help you out, but I'm afraid I'm too busy, what with the Exhibition report and then The Manchester Sentinel..."

"That's okay Michael, I'll manage," said Tim firmly.

"But if you get really stuck, Tim, you've only to ask and I'll help, promise. You've a lot of money to look after." He grinned at Maria, "I don't suppose you've told him that you're one of the richest women in Blackpool...."

Maria smiled, "I knew you couldn't keep a secret!" she said.

During the evening Tim and Michael relaxed in each other's company and when Maria explained that she was selling the shooting galleries so she could have more time to herself, Michael was all in favour. "Well, you know what they say about all work and no play, Maria…?" Without waiting for an answer he asked if she'd had a good year. Maria told him, yes, so far. 1925 was beginning to look like it would be a fantastic year, but with so much unemployment about she just couldn't understand why, "Perhaps the Manchester Sentinel reporter can tell me?"

"How long do you want me to talk, Maria? An hour? Half an hour?"

Tim said, "How about two minutes?"

Michael laughed and promised he'd be quick. "Maria's quite right of course," he said, "There is a lot of unemployment around in South Lancashire, oh, and in lots of other places too. But in June I did some research into the new electrical and motorcar industries that are springing up in the midlands, Coventry and around that area. Looks like you missed reading the article? Anyway, there aren't many people out of work in those places and with money in their pockets many of them are coming to Blackpool to spend it. So, in a nutshell, Maria, that's why I think Blackpool is having such a good year."

Maria was pleased with this explanation and Tim, who thought Michael had covered the situation well, clapped to show his appreciation. "Just under two minutes Michael, congratulations," he teased.

"Any more questions from the floor?"

"What about next year? What's 1926 going to bring?" Anne said, she sounded anxious.

Tim wondered why she should be worried.

"1926 - Bit of a tricky one that," said Michael seriously. "Take our pre war trade, I don't want to sound pessimistic, but I don't think we'll ever get it back to what it was then. Overseas competition's very fierce, especially when it comes to coal. And talking of coal, I can see nothing but trouble for the coal industry."

"What sort of trouble?" asked Tim. Michael was on familiar ground now and it was Tim's turn to be anxious, all his family and the villagers' he had grown up with depended on mining for a living.

"Work it out, Tim, there's competition from overseas, and that means cheap imported coal. Well, the coal-owners aren't just going to sit back and let Johnnie Foreigner take their trade, are they?"

"Suppose not. But what do you think they might do about it?"

"Without taking a cut in their own profits they'll try to force the miners' to work longer hours for less money in order to remain competitive. They'll….."

"That's not fair, the owners ought to sacrifice something too," said Maria and Anne.

"Not fair? Do you think the mine-owners' bother about **fair**?" Michael's face was red and his voice rose. Maria and Anne were stunned into silence; Michael had never talked so passionately. This was a new Michael speaking who wasn't all outside show and detached charm, a genuine caring Michael. Tim listened to him with respect.

When Michael fell silent, Tim said, "They won't stand for it, you know, the miners. They'll fight every inch of the way and if the other unions join in with them, there'll be a national strike and they won't lose this time, not with all that clout!"

Michael shook his head sadly. "It's not going to be like that, Tim. Take my word for it. The government and the coal-owners are in this together and they're ready for it, it's exactly what they want. They've already laid their plans and are set to take on the miners' and anybody else who supports them. The miners' will be starved back to work, the trade unions will be smashed, the government will be relieved and the coal-owners satisfied - job well done chaps and hand-shakes all round!"

"Well, let's pray that it doesn't come to that."

Maria and Anne glanced quickly at one another; did they hear right, did Tim actually say "pray"?

They all sat silently, each one deep in thought until Michael jumped up and checked the time, "Sorry folks, I have to dash, another engagement, sorry."

Tim couldn't resist asking cheekily. "Who is she, Michael, anyone we know?"

Just for a second Michael hesitated, but he recovered instantly and quipped, "Haven't you heard the saying Tim, he travels the fastest who travels alone?" He wished them all goodnight and turned to leave. Anne was determined not to let him off the hook so easily, "And that's how you lost Bernadette isn't it Michael, you're travelling so fast you can't see what's happening to those who are closest to you. Carry on like this and you're going to be a very lonely person, do you really want to go through life alone.....?" Michael paid no attention to her. He left the room calling, "Goodbye, goodbye," and Anne winced as she heard the front door close with a bang!

Tim said it was time he was off too, there was still enough light left for him to finish doing a job in the garden. Anne gave Tim a minute to get clear then she too did a disappearing act but she was back within seconds.

"What was all that about?" asked Maria.

"I just went to take a peek through the kitchen window to see if Tim is working in the garden."

"That's what he said he was going to do."

"I know, I know," said Anne impatiently, "but I wanted to make absolutely sure he'd left the house so he couldn't possibly hear us talking about him."

"So, we're going to talk about Tim are we? I thought you'd want to talk about Michael. Didn't you notice the look on his face when Tim asked if he was going to meet a girl friend?"

"'Course I noticed. All that business about he travels fastest who travels alone, it was a cover up, anybody could see that. But Michael wouldn't actually lie to us, Maria, he just evades the question. He's got a girl friend all right - I wonder who she is and why he doesn't want us to know her name?"

"Are you worried about him, Anne?"

"Well, don't you think it's about time he found a nice girl and settled down, because I do Maria? What worries me is the thought of him letting some painted hussy sink her claws into him, he's daft enough. Oh, why did he let Bernadette go, Maria?"

Maria moved her chair closer to Anne. "Listen to me," she said, gently. "Michael and Bernadette were both very young and it just wasn't to be that's all. Bernadette's happily married and Michael's moving to his new job in Manchester and he's ambitious - don't worry about him, Anne. He's plenty of time to think about settling down once he's established in his career and he'll do what his conscience tells him to do. Life may not always run smoothly for him but he's honest and won't easily be put off course, not even by a painted hussy with long claws! Trust him, Anne, I do. I know you're proud of him already, but mark my words, Anne, one day you'll be very, very proud of Michael."

There was no doubting the sincerity of Maria's message, since Michael's mother had died Anne had raised him like a son and enriched by her love Michael lacked for nothing.

"Thanks Maria, you don't know how much it means to me to hear you say that."

"Good. Now Anne, here's an offer you can't refuse. How about drinking a toast to celebrate Michael's new job? He's not here, but that's no reason why we shouldn't drink to him, is it?"

"What shall I get you Maria?"

"Dry sherry, please, Anne Oh! And since it's a big occasion, let's make it large ones shall we?"

Anne poured the drinks and Maria stood up and raised her glass, "Here's to Michael, his new job and a brilliant future. God Bless him!"

They clinked glasses, "I'll drink to that," said Anne.

Their thoughts gradually turned from Michael to Tim. Maria was missing him, wondering how he was getting on alone in the garden and Anne was wondering, while she had Maria to herself, would this be the opportune moment to air her opinion on Tim and Maria's relationship.

"Look Maria, why don't you stop all this dilly dallying with Tim?" she said at last. "The strain's not good for either of you. You're both Catholics so why don't you get it over and done with, a nuptial mass at the church round the corner, I'll be matron of honour and we can all live happily ever after. Now what could be better than that?"

Maria sighed, "I wish it was as simple as that, Anne. If we get married the authorities will know who Tim is and where he is and he'd be arrested, then I would lose him and God only knows what they would do to him. I don't know what the answer is. Sometimes the problem seems too great to have any solution?"

"Maria, switch on brain. We've got to get some answers."

Maria took a large sip from her glass, "Ooh, that's better," she giggled.

"What's so funny?"

"Nothing," said Maria, innocently.

Anne knew Maria too well to be put off. "Will you take the innocent Legion of Mary look off your face and tell me what it is you find so amusing, Maria Martinelli?"

"The other day, I was looking in the wardrobe and saw some trousers, so I thought I would take them to him and …"

"And did you?"

"Yes,"

"What happened?"

"I knocked on his door and went in. He was standing in that tin metal bath having a stand up wash."

"Naked?"

"As a baby," said Maria.

"Was he ...?

"Complete? Oh, yes....!"

"What did you do?"

"Said I was sorry, dumped the trousers and ran!"

"Idiot!" laughed, Anne, "What a waste of good warm water!"

Maria became serious again. "There's another thing I've got to consider, Anne, to start with I'm almost ten years older than Tim. I don't want to be accused of cradle snatching, do I?"

"Go on with you, there are plenty of men married to older women. Take me for example; I'm five years older than Jack..."

"I know, but Tim might want to have children, Anne. Remember I'm nearly thirty-eight..."

"What's the problem with that? My mother was forty three when I was born. If you are so much in love with one another, there's only one way to be together, Maria."

"Don't think I don't want to, Anne, but the thought of living in sin.... However much I want us to live together, I can't give up my faith."

"Things change through time," said Anne. "It'll turn out right in the end...."

"Then we'll wait," Maria said, determinedly, "Even if we have to wait for a miracle to happen."

"Well, as long as you don't expect Tim to take you to Lourdes for it!" said Anne. "Let's go and see if he'll finish in the garden and come in to drink a toast with us to Michael."

CHAPTER SIX

DURING EARLY SEPTEMBER, BLACKPOOL BASKED in the warmth of an Indian summer. One glorious day Maria asked Tim if he would leave his work to walk with her to the shops and help carry the shopping. Tim was delighted to have the chance to accompany Maria through the town, "Give me ten minutes to wash and I'll be ready."

Tim held the garden gate open for her. "Why have you pulled your cap so far down on your face?" Maria asked.

"In case there are any red-caps or police about," Tim replied nervously, "Well, you never know," he pulled the peak of his cap down a bit further.

"I won't let them hurt you," murmured Maria. She thought Tim was being unnecessarily nervous and slipping an arm through his she gave him a reassuring squeeze.

Their first few yards led them past the candy floss kiosk where Betty was busy dealing with an unruly queue of children. "Me next, me next." they clamoured and a sea of arms waved frantically under her nose. Betty was in top form, she had the kids laughing and jumping up and down with excitement and even when they'd got their candyfloss they still hung around the counter.

"I think they like her as much as the candyfloss," said Maria, admiring Betty's performance. "And yet, if you listened to some of those gossips in town, they'd have that poor girl hung, drawn and quartered by now. Just look at her Tim, I know I've said it before, but I'll say it again, one-day I think she'll make somebody a fine wife and you can see for yourself how much she loves children." As they drew level with the kiosk Maria called to her, "You're doing a wonderful job with those kids Betty."

"Thanks, Mrs. Martinelli. I love them!"

This interruption nudged Maria's memory, "Oh, I've forgotten the letter for Bernadette and I do want to post it today. I'll just run back for it, won't be a minute, Tim."

Betty seized the opportunity to be alone with Tim. She abandoned the kiosk and the children. Sidling up to him she whispered, "She's wearing you out, Tim. Too much nooky - remember what it did to Jake?"

"Why do you always have to bring sex into it, Betty? Sex isn't the only thing in life you know." Tim spoke quietly, but his tone was angry.

Betty didn't care, "Take my word for it, Tim, sex is what most people think about most of the time, I should know, I'm an expert." And turning her back on him she went into the kiosk and clapped her hands. "Now children," she called brightly, "Who's next?"

"Me Betty. Me Betty, I'm next," they all clamoured, happy to have Betty back with them again.

Maria reappeared and slipped her arm through Tim's again. They fell into step with each other, enjoying the novelty of walking out in public together. An army of workmen were busy uncoiling what seemed to be mile after mile of cable along the promenade and in the small group of people watching, Maria spied Anne.

"What's all this about?" Tim asked her.

"Today's a big day for your diary," Anne explained, "This is the first time we've seen this since the war started in 1914. Take a good look, Tim and then you can have three guesses to tell me what they are doing."

Tim shook his head. "Not if you gave me a hundred guesses, Anne. I've no idea."

"No need to guess. I'll tell you," laughed Maria. "They're preparing for the Blackpool Illuminations. After more than ten years we're going to have them again and they're due to run for a month, from September 26th to October 26th. What do you think about that?" She paused, waiting for Tim's reaction.

"All those illuminations – I'm flattered, but you shouldn't have gone to all that trouble for little old me."

"Why you cheeky devil....."

"Those dates, Maria," Tim said, thoughtfully. "They fit around your holiday dates. You're not going to Paris until the first week in October, so you'll be here when the lights are switched on and then be back before everything ends on the 26th."

Maria nodded, but for some reason she didn't want to talk about the holiday, so the subject was dropped. Anne said it was time she was getting home and left Maria and Tim to continue with their walk to the town.

When they reached the gift shop, Maria introduced Tim to the girls' who worked there and while she discussed business with them Tim looked around the building to see if anything required repair. Their next stop was at Joseph and Cecilia's and after a chat and a coffee with them in the restaurant they walked out into the sunshine to do some window shopping.

Tim noticed engagement rings sparkling in the window of a jeweller's shop and made up his mind to buy one for Maria; she might refuse his proposal but the only way to find out was to ask and if Anne could let him know Maria's ring size he would buy the ring tomorrow morning. He quickened his step to a skip and Maria almost had to run to keep up with him. Tim held her arm more tightly, happy with his secret.

There was a heavy shower during the night and in the morning the sky was overcast. Tim went to do a bit of tidying up in the garden, for a moment the clouds parted and the sun shone on tiny beads of moisture which glistened on the leaves of shrubs and flowers making them sparkle like the ring he wanted to buy for Maria.

He recognised Anne's voice calling, "Morning Tim, garden looks lovely in the sun."

"I came out, waiting for you to turn up, Anne, there's something I want to ask you."

"Snap," said Anne. "There's something I want to ask you too. After the heavy rain last night, Jack says there's a leak in the roof of the kiosk. I know it's our responsibility now, but a bit of advice from you wouldn't come amiss."

Tim told her not to worry and that he would have the roof fixed before the day was out, meantime, could Anne help him, could she tell him the size of Maria's ring finger?

Without a second thought Anne gave him the answer straight away and she was halfway up the path leading to the house when she realized why he had asked. "Congratulations!" she said in a stage whisper

"Thanks Anne, please not a word to Maria. If she notices I'm not here, tell her I'll be back in an hour."

"Trust me; I can keep a secret," promised Anne.

An hour later he stepped into the kitchen just as Maria and Anne were finishing a cup of tea. As soon as Anne saw him she stood up, "Oh, Tim, seeing you reminds me, I'd forgotten that I was supposed to phone Michael ten minutes ago." She made for the door leading to the hall and as she passed Tim, she mimed, "Did you get it?" Tim winked and nodded.

Anne made a great show of closing the door behind her. Maria thought that was rather odd, Anne had never been one for privacy. But she had no time to dwell on it because within seconds, Tim was holding her and kissing her. "What's all this about?" she gasped when she got her breath back. Tim kissed her again more gently and then sank to his knees. Maria noticed that his hands were trembling as he produced a little box from his jacket pocket. He opened the box and took out a sapphire ring "That's what it's all about Maria."

Maria slipped the ring on her finger and pulled Tim to his feet. At last she found her voice again, "It's beautiful, and yes I do love you, Tim, I do want us to be engaged."

She flung her arms round his neck and kissed him and then called out "It's all right Anne, you can come in now."

Anne wasn't in the least embarrassed about listening behind the door. She hugged them both. "Congratulations, dear Maria and Tim, I'm so very happy for you."

"It was Anne who told me the size of the ring," said Tim.

"I guessed as much, thank you Anne," Maria held out her hand for Anne to see the ring more closely. She turned her hand first this way and then that, to admire the blue stones as they caught the light.

"Oh, it's gorgeous, it really is," said Anne. She paused and asked very seriously, "Are you two keeping this a secret for now?"

"Yes but I'll always wear my engagement ring," said Maria. "I'll put it on a silver chain and round my neck. No one will know about it except Tim and me and you, Anne. That's alright with you, Tim, isn't it?" Tim, smiling fondly at Maria, said everything was fine with him.

Tim needed an excuse now to leave Anne and Maria alone and remembered the kiosk roof. "Did Anne tell you about the leak in the kiosk after last night's rain?" he asked.

"Yes, do you think you can fix it, Tim?"

"I'll go and do it now," replied Tim. He kissed Maria's cheek and then waved to Anne, the women watched through the kitchen window as he went down the path to collect his tool box from the shed.

Anne and Maria sat down at the table. "Is that the end of the celebration to mark your engagement? Aren't we going to do anything else? Is that it then?" Anne sounded terribly disappointed.

"No, it isn't the end of the celebration and yes we are going to do something else."

"What is it then, Maria? It should be something special!"

"Depends what you mean by special. How long is it since Jack and you went to a dance, Anne?"

"Ooh, ages," said Anne. "And yet we love dancing. Well, you know we do, Maria, it's just that we've got out of the habit somehow...."

"Well I thought that you and Jack might like to join Tim and me for an evening out. We could start by having a meal at the restaurant and then finish off with a dance at The Tower ballroom. Arthur Davies and his orchestra are playing, people were talking about it in the gift shop, they said he's very good. Maybe we should ask Michael too, you know, celebrate his Manchester Sentinel appointment?"

The very mention of Michael's name and a celebration in honour of his promotion excited Anne. "I'll phone him straight away Maria and ask him, but before I do, tell me how did you do it?"

"What do you mean, how did I do what?"

"How on earth did you persuade Tim to go dancing? And to The Tower ballroom of all places, with all those people around ....?"

"I haven't, not yet." said Maria. "I've only just thought of it – He'll be fine, I'll disguise him to look like Rudolph Valentino and he'll have no excuse! No-one will recognise him looking like that. Tim'll do it for me, I know. We're engaged and he loves me....and ..."

"What about you, Maria, are you going in disguise too?"

"Oh, I've thought about getting done up as Bebe Daniels," joked Maria, "So they won't know me from Eve and they won't know Tim from Adam."

"Brilliant! I'll phone Michael straight away and see if he can come with us."

As Anne was leaving the room she remembered something and stopped. "Rudolph Valentino and Bebe Daniels, they're in that new film, "Monsieur Beaucaire," aren't they?"

"Yes," said Maria, "That's how I got the idea." Anne smiled, raised her eyebrows and disappeared into the hall.

She came back from the phone with a face as long as a fiddle. "It's no good, Michael can't make it. He's got a prior engagement and says it can't be broken."

"Never mind, Anne, with Michael there it would have been perfect, but we'll ask him out with us another time."

Anne was frowning now.

"What's the matter, Anne, is something wrong?"

"Michael's fobbed me off Maria. He says he's got a prior engagement, a prior engagement my foot! He's seeing a girl, that's what it is. I'm not daft, I could tell. But she can't be up to much if he can't tell us her name, can she? And you wonder why I'm worried?"

"You've really got to stop worrying about Michael," Maria said firmly. "You've got to let go, Anne. Let him lead his own life, if he makes a mistake and needs your help, well, you will always be there for him, won't you? Why can't you content yourself with that?"

"I'm an interfering old woman Maria, giving you the third degree about Tim and now sticking my oar in over Michael. But you are right about him; he's a man now and must be left to make his own decisions and his own mistakes. I apologise my dear, forgive me?"

"I'll forgive you Anne, but only if you do the washing up. Do that and we'll forget all about you being an interfering old woman? Come on, the water should be nice and hot, Tim did something to the boiler and it's made a big difference," Maria reached for a tea towel.

"I'll tell you something Maria, I don't think Tim will let you do it."

"Never let me do what?"

"He's a Yorkshire man isn't he?"

"You know perfectly well that Tim's a Yorkshire man What's all this Yorkshire business about, anyway?" Maria closed the cupboard door as she put away the last of the dishes.

"Disguise or no disguise," said Anne, "Do you think a Yorkshire man will let you get near his face with make-up because I don't."

"I didn't know you were so knowledgeable about Yorkshire men, Anne."

"Hmm. Well, Jack's not been the only man in my life, you know. People come to Blackpool, even from Yorkshire - I'll tell you about it one day. But for now Maria, what do you advise me to wear tonight; if only Jack and I were younger we could go as Jack and Jill!"

Tim returned while they were still discussing dance dresses. "Don't tell me," Anne said to him, "The roof can't be repaired?"

"Don't be such a pessimist Anne. Job's done, it only took five minutes."

"Oh, thanks Tim, thanks Maria, it's ever so good of you. But you've been gone a long time Tim, I thought it must be a big job?"

"No," said Tim, "Somebody forgot to order the ice-cream, didn't they? I've been helping Jack, that's what made me late."

"Oh my God, that was supposed to be my job," said Anne. "I'd better be off, but we'll see you tonight." A quick hug for them both and she was gone.

"Are Jack and Anne coming here tonight? Jack didn't mention it," said Tim.

"He didn't know about our night out."

"What night out?"

"Tonight we're all going out to celebrate our engagement, Anne and Jack and you and me. We'll have dinner at the restaurant and go on to the dancing at the Tower and, before you say no, don't worry about people recognising you because we are both going in disguise." And when Maria told him the details of what she had planned, Tim said he rather fancied being made up to look like Rudolph Valentino, "Wasn't he the man who was irresistible to women?"

"Don't even think about it!" said Maria.

Chapter Seven

THE TWO COUPLES SAT AT a small table close to the edge of the Tower ballroom dance floor sipping their drinks and talking while the orchestra took a short break. Jack suggested a toast to Maria's brother-in-law and his wife for providing them with such a magnificent dinner in honour of Tim and Maria's engagement. They raised their glasses, "To Joseph and Cecilia" and Jack said he'd heard the restaurant was getting a reputation as the best in town, bit on the expensive side, but worth every penny.

"Thank you, they'll be really pleased when I tell them that," said Maria.

Out of the blue Jack surprised them by asking Tim if he'd heard anything about the two runaways, Jake and Elsie. None of them responded, even the Tower Ballroom seemed hushed. Jack stirred uncomfortably in his seat and looked embarrassed; he couldn't understand why his simple question wasn't answered.

All eyes focussed on Tim. "I don't know what you're staring at me for," he said, "Jake and Elsie were before my time in Blackpool. When Jake disappeared with Elsie I got his job and that's all I know about them.

Maria came to his aid, "Tim's right, they had left before he arrived. But I knew them very well, I thought they would have had the decency to drop me a line by now, but they haven't.

And I can't understand why she hasn't heard from Elsie, she was supposed to be Betty's best friend. Right up to yesterday, Betty was saying that she hadn't received as much as a card from her. She sounded really hurt. It's as if they've forgotten everybody and just disappeared off the face of the earth."

Anne turned to her husband, "Why did you ask Tim about Jake and Elsie in the first place? It's not as if you knew them. I can't ever remember you speaking to either one of them." Sometimes when the mood took her, Anne could make her questioning sound like Judgement Day. Poor Jack became flustered and his face reddened. In fact Tim thought that his face looked a bit too flushed and was concerned. "Are you feeling okay, Jack?"

"Fine," said Jack, "Well, apart from a bit of indigestion."

Anne insisted, "Come on then, why did you want to know about Jake and Elsie?"

"It was because of Michael. We were talking and I can't remember how we got on to it, but at some point he asked if you and I had heard anything about them. You know what Michael's like, he's always asking questions.

Well, that's his job isn't it? Anyway, I told him that as far as we knew they hadn't been in contact with anybody, but I'd try to find out for him......."

Anne's face was now as red as Jack's. "Michael! So you've been meeting Michael, have you? Why didn't you tell me?"

Tim and Maria glanced around to see if they were being overheard by folk at other tables but there was too much buzzing excitement and laughter in the air for that to happen. Maria fingered the engagement ring hidden on the chain around her neck; it was a comforting distraction from the argument between Anne and Jack.

"It wasn't arranged, Anne, we just bumped into one another at the kiosk, it was the same morning Tim helped with the ice cream. You forgot to order it, Anne. I don't know what I'd have done if Tim hadn't been there to help me. I'd been so busy; I just forgot to tell you about Michael." Jack's voice sounded weary now, and he slumped in his chair.

Anne realized she had made a terrible mistake losing her temper. Poor Jack, he hadn't done anything in secret, he hadn't done anything wrong at all but Anne still harboured resentment for an old hurt and now, if she so much as suspected that Jack had done something behind her back, it relit the fuse again. But she was wrong this time and felt guilty. She reached out and took Jack's hand in hers and held on to it tightly, "Sorry my dear, it's my fault. I'm to blame for everything, forgetting to order the ice cream – everything. The devil must have got into me! I shouldn't have talked to you like that. It's not fair to you, my love. Forgive me?"

Jack squeezed her hand. "There's nothing to forgive. You're the best wife a man could have. I wouldn't change you for the world."

"I don't deserve you, Jack Collingswood," she said.

"No, you don't deserve him." Tim and Maria teased.

The orchestra had returned from their break and started to play a tango. "Dance with me Anne, I love a tango," said Jack, happy now that Anne was happy. And like a couple of young lovers they tripped onto the dance floor.

Maria took a long look at Tim. He didn't resemble Tim Ryan the deserter, with his hair combed back, well pomaded and sleek, he looked more like Valentino than Valentino himself.He wasn't relaxed and Maria recognised the signals, he was working out the odds, whether to stay or make a bolt for it.She put her arm around his shoulders and whispered reassurances until she felt he was confident again. Then she issued him with a challenge, "Okay, Mr. Ryan, so you look like Rudolph Valentino, can you dance a tango like Valentino? Come on Tim; let's see what Mr. Arthur Davies and his orchestra can do for us." And before he knew it, Tim was on the dance floor with Maria's body pressed close to his, moving to the sensuous rhythm of the music and swept up in a wave of near intoxication. No panic now, all that he was aware of was Maria's closeness and warmth. Ta dum dum tum tum, the tango beat pulsed through his body and following Maria's footsteps he discovered that he had a natural sense of rhythm and soon he could do the basic steps of the dance. When the music demanded more, Tim wanted to show Maria that he could add some drama and, keeping a deadpan expression, he gave his head a couple of those quick jerky movements he had seen some of the other more experienced dancers doing.   Deadpan face, jerk jerk with the head – great! Maria laughed, so Tim did it again. Deadpan face, turn away with the head -- and that's when he saw, Michael! Oh, it was Michael all right. He wasn't alone, there was a glamorous girl with him, blonde hair piled up on top and wearing a dress that seemed to reveal more of her than it covered. One more jerk of his head and Tim recognised the girl. Then Maria saw her too, "That's Betty, doesn't she look absolutely gorgeous!"

"They've seen us but they don't want us to see them," said Tim. "Look Maria, they're heading for the exit." Then Maria lost sight of Michael and Betty because Tim's latest tango movement had her lying across his knee with her hair almost touching the floor and at that moment the music stopped.

Maria stood up, smoothed down her dress and said approvingly, "Nice timing Tim. Valentino couldn't have done better." She could see Anne and Jack threading their way back through the dancers to the table. "Do you think they saw Michael?"

"No way, he left so quickly."

"Well, Anne and Jack look happy enough," she said.

"And they wouldn't be looking like that if they'd seen Michael with Betty Williams. So, if you don't want to spoil their evening, don't say anything about it, Maria."

A perspiring Jack and Anne flopped down beside them at the table but after a few minutes rest, they all began tapping their toes to the music and were off dancing again.

Not once during the evening had Tim coughed. Dancing seemed to be doing him a power of good and even when they returned to their table feeling tired, the band had only to strike up again and he would lead Maria back onto the dance floor. They were having the time of their lives and as they danced, Maria whispered into Tim's ear how much she loved him and that this was the best party, ever! She was right; it **was** the best party ever. Tim put his arm around her waist as he led her back to the table.

Anne was looking anxiously at her husband, "How do you feel now Jack?"

"Bit tired. I've still got indigestion."

Tim was alarmed to notice that Jack's flushed cheeks were now putty coloured. He lowered his voice to speak to Maria, "I think Jack's ill," he said urgently. "He needs a doctor. We'll have to do something about it. Do you want me to...?"

"No, no," said Maria, "I think it'll be better coming from me." She turned to Anne, "Jack's so pale and still in pain, maybe he needs a doctor? Perhaps we should get him to the hospital, Anne."

Jack overheard her, "No. No hospital for me. We'll go home. Let's walk, get some fresh air. Anne'll look after me...."

"Better if we get a taxi, Jack," said Tim.

"No. No taxi. We'll walk." He was having difficulty with his breathing and once more, Tim asked if he could call a taxi. Jack ignored him, "Let's go home," he gasped and began to stagger towards the exit. Tim caught up with him, took his arm and steadied him. "Thanks Tim, take it – slowly."

"Slowly it is then Jack." They set off down the promenade, Jack leaning heavily on Tim.

Anne and Maria followed, Anne was weeping and Maria did her best to console her. They reached the house and as Anne rummaged in her handbag for the key she asked Maria would she stay the night with them? Maria took the key from Anne's trembling hand, opened the door and promised to stay.

Once Tim had helped Jack upstairs and seen him safely tucked up in bed, he asked if there was anything more he could do? The women shook their heads; Jack appeared to have fallen asleep. Anne sat on a chair beside the bed and held his hand, "I won't let go until he wakes up," she murmured.

Tim wished her goodnight and Maria took him to the door. "Thanks love; I don't know what we would have done without you. You don't mind me staying the night with, Anne, do you?"

"'Course not, she needs you, Maria. And if you want any extra help in the morning, well, I'll be there for you." He held her closely, "Maria, maybe this isn't the best time for me to say this - but our engagement party, it was really great, wasn't it?"

Maria kissed him, "Oh, yes the very best party ever. And when Jack gets better we'll have another one and we'll dance the tango again."

"You really think he will get better, Maria?"

"To be honest love, I don't know. I'm sure of one thing though, he stands a far better chance of recovery if we can get him into hospital, so that's what I'll try to do. There's one more thing you can do, Tim. On your way home will you call at the presbytery next to the church, explain to Father MacDonald what's happened, he'll come and maybe Jack will listen to him and agree to go to hospital. It'll comfort Anne if I tell her what you are doing."

"Of course I will. I'll go straight away. You think it's as serious as that, then?"

"I don't know. But ask Father to come as soon as he can." She raised herself on her toes and kissed him again, "Goodnight love, and thanks for a wonderful time."

It must have been almost eleven o'clock when Tim arrived at the presbytery. He pounded heavily on the door, thinking the priest might already be in bed and asleep. Almost instantly a light went on in the entrance hall and Father Macdonald opened the door. "Good evening young man, I think you'd better come in before you knock my door down," He led Tim into the hallway. "Coming at this time of night, your visit must be urgent?" Tim nodded and with a statue of the Sacred Heart standing beside him like a companion, he began to tell the priest what had happened. The hall light shone down on Father Macdonald's grey head and lined face, Tim guessed his age at nearer to sixty than fifty. He reassured Tim he knew where Jack and Anne lived and would find his own way there. Then, scrutinising Tim like a doctor, he advised, "As for you, young man, I suggest you go home now, you look worn out, go home and get some rest."

"Thanks Father, I think I'm ready to take your advice."

Father MacDonald led him to the door to show him out. "You'll be Mr. Ryan, Mrs. Martinelli's gardener?" Tim was surprised, he wondered how the priest knew his name and apologised for not introducing himself earlier. "Sorry, yes, that's me, Tim Ryan."

"I thought you must be the gentleman," said Father MacDonald, smiling, "There's not much that goes on in my parish that I don't get to hear about." He seemed about to say something more, but changed his mind, "No time to talk, my friend Jack needs me. Now goodnight to you Mr. Ryan, get yourself straight home and to bed."Tim started on his way home and without Anne and Jack and Maria for company, he felt very lonely.

Tim was glad to get into bed but couldn't sleep. He thought about Jack and for the first time in years tried to pray, he made the sign of the cross and pleaded for God not to let Jack die. But he found praying was too difficult for him to sustain for more than a couple of minutes. All kinds of thoughts came flooding into his mind to distract him. Wide awake now, he reached out to switch the light on so he could see the clock; he rubbed his eyes in disbelief when he found that it was only a quarter past midnight. He got out of bed, dressed, put on his raincoat and went out for a walk. Maybe, after the exercise, he would be able to get some sleep.

He opened the gate at the bottom of the garden, not going anywhere in particular, and walked towards the prom. The notion that Jack might die made him think of his own mortality. Images of his past whizzed around in his head, it was as if he was being forced to watch a film of his life, except that the film was all jumbled up and out of sequence   Most of the images were unpleasant and mostly they were about death.   Death in the pit, well there was nothing unusual about that, mining was a dangerous job, and death in the war ..... the film whirred on.   It was the war that affected him most and even now, after seven years, those blurred battlefield scenes terrified him. Sometimes he had nightmares about the corpses shrouded in smoke as they lay rotting on the battlefield. He could feel the smoke in his throat and it made him cough for the first time that day.

He thought about Jack again. It seemed like only yesterday that Maria had sold Anne and her husband the ice-cream kiosk and Jack was delighted telling everybody how lucky he was to be his own boss at last with something to occupy himself in his retirement. And everything was going along just fine until tonight. What sort of luck was that - to have something given to you one day and to have it taken away from you the next? Tim shrugged his shoulders, he had learned that luck didn't have any logic and didn't give a damn about peoples' feelings; it could give or take just as it pleased.

Chapter Eight

THE MOON WAS BRIGHT ENOUGH for Tim to recognise that he was approaching the little park known locally as the "Cuckoo's Nest." It was a green, shrubby sort of place, with a few seats scattered around nicely sheltered by trees. In summer time, when the days were hot, old people sat in the shade and gazed out to sea. Sometimes they would sit there quietly for hours, but when darkness fell, and long after they were fast asleep in their beds, the "Cuckoo's Nest" rustled with activity, the night birds were coming home to roost.

Michael knew all about the place and when he told Anne some of the minor goings on there during the night, she would clasp her hands to her ears and say she didn't want to hear any more and what was the human race coming to? Later, she had repeated some of these stories to

Tim and Maria who concluded that the park had been very aptly named.

Tim stood still, he was almost sure that he heard a woman screaming. The screams were faint and stopped abruptly; in the silence Tim told himself he must have imagined them. A few seconds later the screaming started again, this time loudly and definitely coming from the "Cuckoo's Nest." Tim didn't want to become involved, but he couldn't ignore a cry for help, instinct pulled the trigger and he shot off to rescue the victim. Assuming they were a woman's screams, he yelled, "Hold on lady, help's coming, I'll knock hell out of him if he's hurt you." He winced at the sound of his voice, coarse and threatening, threatening enough, he hoped, to scare off the assailant. Several times the tangled undergrowth snared him and brought him crashing to his knees. He picked himself up again and ran faster convinced that he was on a life-saving mission. Eventually he broke through a clump of rhododendron shrubs and saw a woman lying on her back on one of the benches, threshing the air with her legs to try and ward off her attacker. In the shadows cast by the bushes, the moonlight wasn't bright enough for him to distinguish the man's features. He could see that the man was small and thin. Clenching his fists Tim closed in and the man ran. Tim started after him but out of breath and easily outpaced, he gave up the chase. Seconds later he heard the sound of a car door closing, an engine springing into life and the roar from a car's exhaust. A cloud covered the moon and the night became almost pitch black. For a moment the "Cuckoo's Nest" was silent as a grave, then the woman started sobbing. She was slumped forward on the bench and Tim put a protective arm around her, telling her she was safe now and not to be frightened. He tried to think of something funny to say to divert her. He joked that the man who had attacked her had run away so fast his trousers had caught fire. She raised her head and said, sharply, "Seems you haven't lost your sense of humour after all, Tim Ryan." The woman in distress was none other than Betty Williams!

Tim didn't know what to do or say. Of all the women in the world, Betty was the last one he had expected to rescue! He sat with his mouth open until at last he scolded, "I'd no idea it was you, Betty. I think your second name should be trouble!"

"Bastard," said Betty cheerily.

Tim chuckled, relieved that his rescue mission hadn't come to an end in blows. "No, I really didn't think it was you, Betty, weren't you out with Michael, didn't I see you with him at The Tower?"

Betty evaded the question, "Thanks Tim," she whispered. "I don't know how I'll ever be able to repay you for this." She touched his face with her fingers and shivered. "Hold me Tim, please hold me, I'm so cold."

She felt cold as ice to his touch and little wonder, she had no coat, all she wore was that same skimpy dress she had on at the ball-room earlier in the evening. He noticed that she was clutching a small, beaded purse, it was open and its contents had spilled onto the ground. "When I hit him with it everything fell out," said Betty. Tim helped her find lipsticks and a powder compact and she put them back in the purse. He took off his raincoat to wrap around her; "Come on Betty," he said, "It's time we got you home."

Betty buttoned Tim's raincoat up to her neck and giggled when she saw that the coat reached down as far as her ankles. "Hides all my best bits," she said as she rolled back the sleeves. She said she was warmer now and didn't want a taxi; she wanted Tim to walk her home, it would help steady her nerves. Tim knew not to argue.

They seemed to have for walked miles before Betty announced they'd arrived at her flat. It was on the ground floor of an old Victorian building close to the railway station and she pleaded with Tim to go inside with her in case there was someone lying in wait. "You stay by the door, Betty, I'll go in first and look around," he said.

Betty lifted up a stone beside the step to uncover her hidden key and handed it to him. Tim opened the door and found that the hall light was on. He looked around and beckoned for Betty to follow him, then closed the main door and gave her back the key. They stood in the middle of the hall while Betty described the layout of the house; the large central staircase led to more flats upstairs, to the left of the hallway was her flat and to the right was Elsie's old flat which was still empty, tenants paid six month's rent in advance and Elsie's rent still had a couple of months to run. Betty took the key for her flat from under the hall carpet and asked Tim to go ahead again. Tim checked each room and then gave her a short lecture about keys and security. Betty replied testily that she knew all that, thank you, and Tim wisely dropped the subject, he didn't have the strength left in him to withstand one of Betty's tantrums.

He took a long look around the large bed sitting room, the wallpaper and paintwork were in good condition, the room well furnished and carpeted. Betty told him proudly she also had a nice kitchen and bathroom. Tim reckoned she must have been paying a lot more in rental for the flat than she was earning at the kiosk. Perhaps she had another source of income? He told himself to mind his own business, where she got the extra money from had nothing to do with him.

He asked to use the bathroom and when he came back into the sitting room he found Betty had lit the gas fire and changed into a dressing gown. She was perched cross-legged on the bed and announced she was feeling much better now, thawing out quite nicely! Tim saw the time on the mantelpiece clock, it had just turned three. "Good God Betty, I'd no idea it was so late, it'll soon be time for work." Hurriedly, he picked up his raincoat, but that was not what Betty wanted; she slid off the bed and placed herself between Tim and the door. Gripping the lapels of his jacket she pleaded with him, "Don't go Tim, please, don't go - not just yet. Please." Was this just one of Betty's little tricks, pretending to be scared, or was she genuinely afraid? Tim gave her the benefit of the doubt and, dropping his raincoat back on the chair, agreed to stay for a little while longer.

"Oh, thanks, Tim, I'm so hungry – are you?"

"Starving."

"You sit there and I'll make us some sandwiches." She went into the kitchen to prepare the food and then brought out a tray which she set down between them.

"Remember that bacon sandwich I made for you the first day you started to work for Mrs. Martinelli? 'Course you do, I can tell." Wrapped in her long woollen dressing gown Betty looked the picture of innocence and Tim was relieved that she wasn't trying to flirt with him again. She was talking to him more like an old friend and confidante, reminding him of some little secret they had both shared in the past.

"Betty, what were you doing at The Tower ballroom with Michael?" he asked. "Michael said he couldn't join us there because he had another appointment, it must have been with you. Did you know that Michael's Mrs. Collingswood's nephew, she brought him up when his own mother died?"

"That old cow, Collingswood, she hates me and yes, I did know he was her nephew and Michael and me, we were just talking, it wasn't a proper date."

"Okay, okay, sorry. I must say though, you did look nice and cosy together."

"I wouldn't want him for a boyfriend, ever. Are you blind, Tim Ryan? I want you, not Michael Topliss. And tonight you saved my life - I'm yours forever now Tim - I'll never stop loving you." She put down the tray that separated them and moved closer to him.

Tim didn't know how to deal with Betty's confession of love without sounding harsh and dismissive and hurting her feelings. He stood up and reached for his raincoat again and as he put it on, words came to him at last. He tried to make them light and pleasant, "We agreed to be friends Betty, remember? You know I love Mrs. Martinelli, but you and me; we can always be friends, can't we?"

She was desperate now, she would tell Tim everything if only it would keep him with her for a while longer. "Don't you want to know about that man who attacked me?"

"Of course I want to know about him," said Tim. "But you were so quiet on the way home, I thought maybe you didn't want to talk, well, you know ... you were still frightened."

"When you're with me, Tim, I'm not afraid of anybody or anything. Sit down and listen and I'll tell you everything."

Reluctantly, he sat down beside her.

Betty pressed closer to him as she spoke, "The man owed money to Elsie, fifty pounds. When she ran away with Jake the last thing she said to me was, "Make sure you get that money for me, Betty. If things don't work out with Jake, at least I'll have some cash to come back to. You know what Jake's like, he spends all he can lay his hands on." That's what Elsie said."

"So you're telling me you met this man after you had left the Tower ballroom - after you had left Michael?"

"That's right, Michael and me didn't say goodnight straight away, we went for a drink first and then afterwards I met the man. It was still early. He said he had the fifty pounds with him but, since it was a nice evening, we could go for a drive and make a night of it. He looked a decent enough sort - things were fine at first and we went to a pub, had a few drinks then drove on. When we got to The Cuckoo's Nest he stopped the car and said he had to relieve himself, he seemed to have been gone a long time so I went to look for him and that's when he attacked me – I never did get the money." She snuggled closer to Tim. "You came just in time and rescued me."

"What about your friend, Elsie?" asked Tim, eager now to hear the whole story, "How did the two of you become friends?"

Betty told him that Elsie was a customer of hers when she used to work in a ladies dress shop, the one next door to Mrs. Martinelli's gift shop. During Elsie's shopping sprees they became friendly and then one day, when Elsie was trying on a new dress, she told Betty that the girl who rented the flat opposite hers was leaving Blackpool to go to work in London. She asked if Betty would like the flat - the offer came just in time because her stepdad was trying to mess about with her and her Mum had told her to get out. That was almost two years ago when she was fifteen, she told the agents that she was almost twenty and they believed her, they were only interested in the money, they wanted six months' rent in advance! Elsie and she had always got on together like a house on fire and Elsie loaned her the rent and told her to pay it back when she could manage it. She stayed on at the dress shop and Elsie worked in the kiosk for Mrs. Martinelli. Sometimes at night when they didn't go out she'd sit with Elsie in her room and Elsie would tell her about her men friends' and they'd have a great laugh. But after a while, the only man Elsie wanted to talk about was Jake, Mrs. Martinelli's gardener. And although Jake was old enough to be Elsie's father, she was nuts about him. Then one night Elsie told her they were running away together and she asked Elsie if they were alright for money. Elsie reminded her to get the fifty pounds back that was owed to her - but apart from that she said they had no money worries. So Elsie packed her bag and off she went. She didn't say where they were going, promised she'd write with their new address, but never did. And that was the last she had seen or heard of them.

Betty was yawning now, tired at last after all her talking and Tim said firmly that she should get some rest and that he must go. It was almost four in the morning and he only finally managed to get away by agreeing to come one evening after work to fit a security bolt to the door of her flat and some safety catches on the windows. He couldn't be sure when, exactly, it all depended on Jack and he told her briefly how Jack had been taken ill at The Tower ballroom. Betty said she liked Jack, she was sorry to hear he was poorly, but she couldn't resist adding that she didn't know how he had put up with that bitch of a wife of his and Tim knew it was useless to try and persuade her that she'd made a mistake about Anne. As the door closed behind him, he heard Betty turn the key in the lock.

Tim walked home trying to make sense of everything that had happened since he first heard Betty screaming for help at the Cuckoo's Nest. The sifting process threw up more riddles than answers and he almost wished that he was back in Betty's flat to ask the questions that still bothered him. Maybe he would get the opportunity when he went to fit the bolt and security catches? He reached the cold, windswept promenade and, remembering old times with a shudder, he smiled to himself at the joyful thought of having his own safe, warm shelter to go home to and a comfortable bed to sleep in.

The sound of Maria's voice awakened him. He rolled out of bed and switched on the light. "Coming Maria," he called sleepily. Pulling on one of Andrew's old dressing gowns, he unlocked the door and Maria fell into his arms. He stood with her just inside the door; gently rocking her as he held her. "It's Jack," she managed to say between sobs.

"I guessed. I guessed." he whispered.

"It happened at half past four this morning in the hospital. He had a massive heart attack. Anne and Michael and I were with him when he died." Maria tried to dry her tears; her face was pale and drawn. "I didn't have time to let you know, it was so quick."

"I'm glad Michael was there."

"He was passing Anne's about mid-night and saw the lights were on. Father Mac had rung for an ambulance and Michael came with us to the hospital."

"Poor Anne, is Michael with her now?"

"Yes. He brought me home to get some sleep and went straight back to her. I'll go back in a couple of hours so they can get some rest. Michael feels terribly guilty for not spending time with us all last night."

"Did he say anymore about that? Did he say why he was with Betty at the Tower?"

"Not a word. And don't ask him just now, please, Tim."

"I wouldn't dream of bothering him now, Maria, not while he's grieving and trying to comfort Anne."

Maria dried her tears and Tim led her to the table and sat her down. "You look tired out, my love. Try to eat some breakfast and then I'll take you up to the house. I'll call at Anne's during this afternoon; see how you are and if I can do anything to help. D'you want me to walk you round to Anne's after you've had a sleep?"

"No, that's okay, Tim, I'll go by myself when I'm ready and I can't eat now, it's too early. I'll just have a cup of tea with you - and Tim…"

"Yes Maria,"

"I love you, Tim."

Tim walked her up to the house and tucked her into bed. For a while he lay on the eiderdown beside her, then, when she fell asleep, he tip-toed out of the room, down the stairs and closed the kitchen door behind him. It was a bright dawn but, he was glad to get into his bed again to catch up on his sleep. He overslept and was woken at two o'clock in the afternoon by a loud knocking on the door. Barefoot and in his dressing gown he opened it to find Betty Williams standing there. She said she had come to find out when he was going to the flat to fit the bolt and window catches. All the time she was talking to him she was straining to see inside the room and she spotted the unmade bed.

"You got somebody in there with you?"

"No I haven't," said Tim. Afterwards he could have kicked himself for not telling her to mind her own business.

Betty asked why he wasn't dressed, was he okay? Tim told her sharply, he had overslept because she had kept him up late last night. Betty smiled but didn't make any comment. She expressed sympathy when he told her of Jack's death and then immediately asked him again when he was coming to fix the safety catches.

Tim thought quickly. "Between seven and eight, yes, I'll see if I can do it then, get it done before it's dark. By the way who's looking after the kiosk?" he asked, hoping to get rid of her

"Nobody, I closed it for five minutes so I could talk to you. See you later then. By the way I'd get a shave if I were you, you look awful."

Tim shaved and dressed and went out into the garden to cut some roses for Anne. There weren't too many left to choose from, but he managed to find enough for a bouquet and set off with it to her house. Maria had been there for a few hours when he arrived. "Left you sleeping like a baby," she said, "I peeped in on you!"

Anne wept when he gave her the roses and said how thoughtful he was. She went off to find a vase while Maria clung to Tim as if she didn't to want to let him go. Tim knew she was remembering her own bereavement. "Don't worry love," he said, "I won't leave you, I promise to live until I'm a hundred."

"You always manage to comfort me," she said.

"I was thinking exactly the same about you," said Tim.

Anne wanted Tim to stay for a meal. "Maria's prepared a lovely salad Tim, why don't we eat together?" Tim thought, dear Anne, she was trying so desperately hard to carry on with her every day routine. While they ate she told him that Michael had seen the undertakers about the funeral and Father Mac had made all the arrangements for Jack's requiem mass.

Tim didn't want to tell them what had happened last night after he had left the presbytery but he did need to explain why he must leave them later to go to the iron-mongers, so he told them that he had seen Betty today and she'd said how scary it was living next to Elsie's empty flat and asked if he could fix some security bolts to her windows and doors. Maria said she could understand Betty feeling frightened and Tim should help her straight away. Anne was grudging when it came to doing something for Betty Williams, "Girls like her bring trouble down on themselves," she said sourly. Nevertheless she agreed that Tim was right to help her.

After his meal, Tim left to collect his toolbox and call in on Mr. Nightingale. As far as the bolt was concerned, the ironmonger recommended one which he said was strong enough to give a charging elephant a sore head and insisted on talking Tim through the procedure of doing the fitting. Tim thanked him and listened patiently to his advice. Mr. Nightingale was satisfied, he liked customers to appreciate his knowledge and he hummed a merry tune as he locked up the shop. He'd had a good day, Mr. Ryan was the tenth who had said thanks, making it ten out of ten and that meant trade was picking up again.

Tim knocked on Betty's door and to his surprise she opened it straight away. He thought that was downright careless of her, she should have checked to see who it was before opening the door and he told her so.

"I knew it was you," she snapped defiantly. She was not in the best of moods. Tim knew that one word too many and she would tell him what he could do with his advice, so he dropped his critical father tone and replied cheerfully, "Oh, it's like that today is it, Miss Williams? We'd best make a start then, hadn't we?"

She locked the main door behind him and then unlocked the door to her flat with the key she still kept under the carpet! Tim made no comment, what was the point. She stood behind him watching, not saying a word, leaving him to wonder what it was that had upset her? While he was fixing the door bolt he chatted away about things in general and pretended not to notice how unresponsive she was. Gradually he managed to draw her into conversation until her mood changed and now she was doing most of the talking.

When she paused, Tim asked her, "So what made you so bad tempered this evening, Betty?"

"What made me? I'll tell you what made me. It was that pal of yours, Michael Topliss. Ooh! That man, I could kill him, he's just full of lies. He's so deceitful, I just can't stand him."

Tim protested, "Oh, come off it, Betty. I know Michael and he's not a liar."

"He bloody well is a liar and sly with it. He told me that he was going to write a funny article about the sort of people who bought saucy seaside postcards and he thought that I was just the sort of person to help him, knowing all I did about customers at the kiosk. That's what we were supposed to be talking about last night …"

Tim interrupted again. "Well, that's not a lie is it Betty, you must have sold hundreds of those postcards ………?"

"The lie is, he never intended to write the article in the first place, he only asked one or two daft things about the postcards then he went on and on grilling me about Elsie and Jake. When did I last see them? Why did they leave? Why did they leave so quickly? Did they take any documents or large bulky envelopes with them? I said to him, the way you're talking about them, anybody would think they were bloody spies!"

Tim had to smile. "What did Michael say to that?"

"Nothing, he didn't get the chance. I told him to piss off."

"So, when Michael left, that's when you went to meet the man who attacked you at the Cuckoo's Nest?"

"Yes."

"D' you know his name?"

"'Course I do. Elsie had to give me his name so I could contact him and get the money. As far as I'm concerned though, he can stuff his fifty quid. And if Elsie wants it that badly, she can bloody well go and get it from him herself."

"I don't blame you, Betty, he's a dangerous man. But who is he?"

"It's Mr. Beswick," said Betty, adding with a sneer, "He's Mrs. Martinelli's bank manager!"

"Christ! Mrs. Martinelli's bank manager, have you reported what happened to the police?"

"The police, no way and I don't want you to tell them either. So promise. I don't want nothing to do with the police, okay?"

"Okay, okay, I promise," said Tim. He didn't want to get involved with the police anymore than Betty did. Tim had run out of questions now and picking up his toolbox he took it out into the hallway towards the front door. Betty barred the way; she faced him with her back pressed against the door. "Don't leave me Tim. Stay, spend the night with me please, please?"

"Betty, we've been through all this before and more than once. You said you'd behave, remember?"

"I know, I know and I'm sorry but I can't help it, Tim. Listen, just listen to me, just two minutes and don't interrupt, okay?"

Tim sighed. "Okay Betty, I'm listening and I won't interrupt."

"Right then, I know you're not sleeping with Mrs. Martinelli, I know that for a fact. That's the first thing..."

Tim tried to cut in to ask how she was so sure of that, but she shouted him down, "You promised not to interrupt, you promised..."

Tim nodded his head. "Sorry, go ahead," he said quietly, hoping the people in the upstairs flat had not heard her shouting.

"I've been thinking about this for a long time, Tim, let me share you with Mrs. Martinelli – even a little share of you will do for me. That proves I love you, doesn't it? And I'd always be here waiting for you, always, you can be sure of that. And Tim, you don't have to tell Mrs. Martinelli about it, she'll never know. It would be our secret, forever. What d' you say, Tim?"

"Sorry Betty, I can't enter into a pact like that. Cast your mind back just a few minutes and remember how you were accusing Michael of telling lies and being devious." Tim spoke patiently now, as though talking to a child, "Remember how angry and upset that made you?   Well, all that stuff about Michael, it's nothing compared to what you are proposing we should do to Mrs. Martinelli?   I love her Betty; I couldn't ever deceive her like that. Look, we've both had a couple of bad days, what happened to you at Cuckoo's Nest and then poor Jack dying, that's emotion enough for us surely, without adding more to it? As for me, all I want now is some peace and quiet, so come on Betty, open the door so I can go home. Please."

Betty reluctantly moved away from the door and Tim opened it. Without saying goodbye he stepped out into the street. He felt relief to have escaped into the fresh air and relief, too, that Betty had answered all he had asked about Michael. But now he had questions for Michael. What was his interest in Elsie and Jake? Tim smiled when he recalled how Betty had accused Michael of talking about them as if they were spies. And what was Maria's bank manager doing, owing fifty pounds to Elsie? What was that about?

There was something unpleasant about it all and, although Betty's behaviour was bad enough to raise the hackles of anybody, Tim shuddered to think what her fate might have been if he hadn't rescued her from Mr. Beswick. As soon as Jack's funeral was over he would talk to Beswick and make sure that he left Betty alone in the future. And what was Michael's interest in all this? Michael had used Betty unfairly to discover more about Jake and Elsie and sympathised with her on that score. He would tell Michael how he felt about that as well.

When Tim left the house, Betty closed the front door behind him and leaned against it for a long time before she went back into her flat. As far as she was concerned Tim was still with her, she imagined his thin handsome face and his blue eyes gazing into hers, inviting her ... She sighed and said aloud, "I love you Tim Ryan more than you'll ever know. I'll never let you go. I'm going to make your precious Maria hate you and send you away and tell you never, ever, to come back to her. But don't be sad, 'cos I'll be here waiting and we'll run away together, just like Elsie and Jake...."

Chapter Nine

Jack's coffin was brought to the church in the evening and placed on trestles facing the altar to await his requiem mass. A few close friends and family kept vigil. Anne noticed the flickering light of the sanctuary lamp as she looked up at the tabernacle and made the sign of the cross. "Don't be afraid, Jack, our Blessed Lord will watch over you tonight and keep you company until we come tomorrow." Michael held a protective arm around her and led her home.

In the morning, despite the fact that it was a weekday, the church was almost full. Tim could see Anne sitting close to the communion rail and the coffin. She was leaning on Michael who sat beside her, Maria's daughter and her husband sat at his other side and Maria and Michael's father were in the pew behind. Even on this solemn occasion, Tim, from his position in the shadows at the back of the church, couldn't help noticing the eye contact between Anne and Bernadette. He didn't know when Bernadette's baby was due, but guessed that this new life would be a consolation for Anne as well as for Maria. Tim imagined Maria with the baby and felt very happy for her. Then he remembered Betty's wild ideas about sharing him; what if Betty got up to her old tricks again and tried to undermine his relationship with Maria? When Father MacDonald emerged from the sacristy and reached the altar, Tim was glad to forget Betty. He concentrated his thoughts on Jack and the requiem mass.

Father MacDonald's grey hair shone like silver against the sombre black of his chasuble. He turned to face the congregation, "In nóminee Patris, et Filii, et Spiritus Sancti. Amen." The congregation joined him in making the sign of the cross. As Tim stood in one of the few empty pews at the back of the church, it both surprised and pleased him that he still knew the Latin responses to the prayers; the smell of incense reminded him vividly of attending mass with his family as a child. He drifted into a reverie until, looking up, he saw the priest walk round the coffin and incense it three times on either side as the mass ended. Soon the procession to the cemetery would begin. Without waiting for the final blessing, Tim slipped out of the church unnoticed and made his way to the cemetery, alone.

In mourning for Jack, Maria had closed the gift shop and kiosks and given all her employees the morning off to attend the funeral. Betty decided to skip the requiem mass, all that mumbo jumbo stuff bored her. It was nearing the end of the season and once the illuminations were over the kiosk would be closed until next spring, so Betty thought that she'd do a bit of paper work, check the total sales to get some idea of what bonus might be due to her. She figured that she could do all that and still be able to get to the cemetery in time to see Jack buried. There was a nip in the air and a cool wind blowing in from the sea when she set off for the kiosk. Instead of her usual working clothes, she was wearing a stylish black woollen coat and had wound an expensive black silk scarf in a neat band round her head, carefully tied in a bow at the back. As she walked along the promenade the breeze teased the tails of the silk bow and sent them fluttering. She looked glamorous as she passed by, holidaymakers stopped to gaze admiringly at this girl with the golden hair and elegant clothes. "Wonder who she is?" they asked. Someone in the crowd thought she was an actress, the leading lady in the new show on the North Pier. "She must be the star." An old man raised his hat in Betty's direction, "Well, she's a star alright, and a real bright one at that...."

Betty opened the kiosk and got on with her paper work without much interruption. She became so engrossed she didn't hear footsteps approach. A man's voice made her jump. She recognised it straight away. "Christ, Mr. Beswick, you nearly gave me a heart attack. You're a sneaky one aren't you? Are all bank managers tarred with the same brush?"

"Don't be so rude," said Mr. Beswick, "I haven't come to cause trouble, Miss Williams, I've brought Elsie's fifty pounds." And he slapped a wad of notes down on the counter. Betty moved to take the money; Beswick closed his hand over it. "Not so fast young lady. Haven't you forgotten something? First, I get the envelope, then you get the money, that's the deal isn't it?"

Beswick sounded in control but that didn't fool Betty, she knew that he was worried. "What envelope? I haven't got any bloody envelope. How many more times do I have to tell you?"

"But there is, a large buff envelope, like this," the bank manager insisted and with his forefinger he outlined the size of the envelope. "Elsie showed it to me, it had my name on it." His manner was no longer confident and his face twitched anxiously.

"Well, I've searched everywhere for it," said Betty. "It's not in her flat; I've been over it with a fine tooth comb. Elsie must have taken it away with her. Anyway, what's in it that makes it so important?"

"Don't you know?" asked Beswick. He looked surprised.

"No, and I don't bloody care, either," said Betty, emphatically.

"I believe you – I really believe you don't know what's in it," he said with relief. "You are quite right, Miss Williams; Elsie must have taken the envelope with her. She's probably keeping it safe for me until she returns. Yes, that's what must have happened. You don't know when Elsie intends to pay us a return visit do you?"

"No. I haven't heard a dicky-bird from her since she left."

"What shall I do about the money?" Beswick asked.

"Why don't you stick it up your arse," said Betty.

Beswick ignored her insult and pocketed the notes. "It seems that I've been wasting both my time and yours,

Miss Williams, so I'll bid you goodbye. Don't worry; I don't propose to call on you again."

"Oh please, you're breaking my heart," mocked Betty. Mr. Beswick turned quickly and walked away. Quite unperturbed by his interruption, Betty completed her accounts and in fifteen minutes was ready to lock up the kiosk.

At the cemetery it began to rain. She saw Tim sheltering under a tree a short distance away from the open grave and went to join him. "Am I glad to see you Tim," she said. "I hate funerals. Can I stay with you until it's --- over?"

"Fine by me," said Tim. "You're not the only one who hates funerals..." He stopped talking abruptly when he caught sight of a small thin man in a dark suit making his way towards the graveside. There was something familiar about the way the man moved. Then it dawned on him. "That's him! That's him Betty! That's Beswick, that's the man who attacked you." And before Betty could stop him, Tim left the cover of the tree and ran to intercept him.

"Excuse me Mr. Beswick, my name's Tim Ryan, I'd like to have a word with you."

Beswick looked startled at first but then he recognised Tim. "You're Mr. Ryan, aren't you? Mrs. Martinelli has told me about you, I've seen you working in her garden. What is it, what do you want to talk to me about?"

"Well, it's not about Mrs. Martinelli's garden, the Cuckoo's Nest, that's what I want to talk to you about. You were there, I saw you."

Beswick gasped. "So it was you. It was you who ran after me?"

"That's right. Now, can you explain to me what you were doing, or do you want to talk to the police...?"

"For God's sake Mr. Ryan, there's no need to call in the police. What happened at The Cuckoo's nest, it wasn't as you think, I assure you. I'll tell you everything you want to know, but not here - this isn't the time or place. Please, Mr. Ryan, the hearse is coming through the gates. I'll speak to you tomorrow, I give you my word."

"Where?" Tim demanded.

"Tower aquarium, lunchtime tomorrow, twelve thirty."

Tim nodded agreement and Beswick moved away to join the mourners at the graveside. The rain was falling steadily now. Tim returned to the shelter of the tree and found Betty waiting for him. Affecting grief, she took his hand and held it tightly as the short graveside service began.

Father MacDonald was liberal with the holy water, he shook the sprinkler vigorously, sending droplets flying into the air to mingle with the rain and fall as tiny pools on the coffin lid. As the rain continued, the pools joined together making larger pools which overflowed into the grave. Mr. Beswick watched the rivulets of water coursing down the sides of the coffin and reflected on his own miserable life. With all his heart, he wished it were he and not Jack Collingswood that they were lowering into the watery pit.

Tim and Betty saw Anne, Maria, Michael and Francis each crumble a small clod of damp soil between their fingers to drop down onto the coffin. Betty flinched and Tim felt her hand tighten on his as they heard the dull sound of earth thudding against the wood.

Father MacDonald said a final prayer and Tim was relieved to release his hand from Betty's to follow the priest in making the sign of the cross. Betty hurried off and the mourners started to drift away. Tim went over to talk to Maria and Anne; Anne asked him to come with them to Joseph and Cecilia's for a meal but he excused himself, thinking the occasion should be for Jack's closest family and life-long friends.

By the time he reached home he felt miserable and isolated. Changing out of his damp clothes, he flung himself down on his bed and thought how empty his life was without Maria beside him. Hours later, Maria kissed him awake. "I've been waiting all day to do that...." she said. She sat on the bed holding his hands in hers. "Honestly, Tim, I don't know how I could have got through it all if I hadn't known that you would be here waiting for me." She stroked his forehead and it was then that she noticed how unhappy he was. "Oh, my God Tim," she said, "You look really awful. What's the matter? It's the funeral isn't it, is that what's brought it on?"

"No, not the funeral," he said. The cause of Tim's unhappiness wasn't the funeral, he had been very fond of Jack and would miss him but that didn't compare to the way he missed Maria whenever he was away from her. He wanted and needed her so much that the strain of not being able to live together as man and wife was sometimes unbearable.

"What's the matter, Tim?" Maria asked again. Tim felt too nervous to tell her the truth, instead he said he regretted not spending time with Bernadette and Robert – would they ever be able to accept him as a granddad for their baby?

"Bernadette and Robert couldn't stay, Tim – Michael and I saw them off at the station and they'll be well on their way to Glasgow now. Shall we wait until the baby's born, Tim, before we worry about that?"

"You're right – now's not the time," said Tim.

Maria asked tentatively, "Tim, if that minor miracle we're waiting for doesn't happen by Christmas and we still can't get married, shall we live together – as man and wife?"

"I want that more than anything, but it's not right for you, Maria. What about your reputation, what about your faith? You shouldn't have to lose all that for me...."

"It's for both of us," she said firmly. "Especially me - I want to be with you all the time, Tim, my mind's made up......"

"I wish with all my heart we could get married Maria, but I daren't, I'm scared they'd find my name in the register and come and get me and I don't want to leave you. I don't want to go to prison and..."

She spoke to him softly, almost crooning to him like she would to a child. "Don't be frightened Tim, we can live together and nobody need ever know anything about you."

"I love you, Maria Martinelli," he said and Maria was content with that, they were the only words she wanted to hear.

Maria decided it was time to cheer themselves up. "I know this has been a sad day for all of us, but just for a little while let's celebrate Jack's life, just the two of us. Jack liked to dance, so come on Tim, let's dance; it will be like a special celebration of the last evening we spent with him." She slipped off the bed and held out her arms for Tim to join her.   For a minute they stood in each other's arms, then Tim took a step away from her, "Okay, Maria, Jack liked to tango, so let's do the tango." He hummed out the beat – "Ta dum dum tum tum" and together they danced round the room, "Ta dum dum tum tum," – deadpan face, jerk, jerk with the head, "Ta dum dum tum tum," jerk, jerk, with the head and now Tim was smiling...

Maria laughed happily; Tim was back to his normal self again.

They danced until they were breathless and then collapsed onto the bed, lying face to face.

"Penny for them, Maria," Tim said.

"You might well ask," said Maria. She turned to lie on her back. "Believe it or not my thoughts were on the war. What a strange thing imagination is. There I was being danced round the room by this crazy man who thinks he's Rudolph Valentino, then when I'm lying on the bed peacefully, all nice and relaxed, my mind turns everything upside down and decides to think about the war - I had horrible thoughts about you being arrested if we got married...."

"My mind plays tricks like that," said Tim. "Slightest thing can set it off and before I know it I'm in the middle of the war again, best if we don't talk about it."

"No, I won't, except to remind you that the last war was the war to end all wars. That's what they said. Marvellous, no more wars, ever! There now, that's my last word on it."

She took a closer look at Tim's pale face, "Have you had anything to eat at all?"

"Slice of bread and a cup of tea at breakfast...."

"You must be starving; we'll go up to the house, Anne and Michael are there so we'll all have our meal together."

Tim didn't need to be asked twice. They opened the door and peeked outside; it was raining again. "Follow me Maria," he said, "Do what I do and you won't get wet," and he hopped, skipped and danced first to the left and then to the right all the way up the path leading to the house. Maria followed him, copying every step he made. When they arrived at the door she stopped to brush the rain off her jacket. "I did what you said but look, I'm wet. See?"

"Then you couldn't have done it properly," said Tim severely,

"Tell me then. Tell me what we were supposed to be doing?"

Tim raised his eyebrows, "What a question to ask Maria. We were dodging the raindrops. Now, don't tell me your granddad never taught you how to do that?"

Maria pretended to be angry. "Dodging the raindrops! You're plain crazy Tim Ryan." Then she whispered, "Perhaps we shouldn't say anything to Anne and Michael about our plans, not on the day of Jack's funeral?"

Tim agreed and solemn faced they went into the house.

Michael and Anne were waiting for them and Maria immediately took Anne into the kitchen to help prepare a meal. Tim was glad to be left alone with Michael so that he could ask him what he was doing with Betty Williams at the Tower ballroom on the night that Jack had been taken ill?

Michael looked surprised. "You saw us then? What about Anne, did she see us?"

"No. Just Maria and me and we didn't tell Anne or Jack."

"Thanks," said Michael, looking relieved. "You know Tim, Anne doesn't like Betty much."

"Understatement of the year." replied Tim.

Michael decided to confide in Tim, "That evening I spent with Betty at The Tower is not what it seems. I wanted some information and I thought she could give it to me. It was important, that's why I turned down Anne's invite to your engagement party."

"And you lied to get her to see you. Betty told me."

Michael shrugged his shoulders. "I know, but Betty's pretty smart, she soon rumbled me and she made sure she didn't give much away."

"What was it you were after, exactly?" said Tim.

"I've already said it's not what you thought, she's not my type."

"Oh, come off it Michael, you know what I mean. What information had Betty to give?"

"It was about some letters," said Michael, "It all started with the letters."

"What letters?"

"Letters to the newspaper," said Michael. "Editors get lots of letters, Tim. Most of them are serious, but we also get some from cranks and anonymous letter writers as well. Usually we sling the anonymous letters in the bin, but not this time because a few of them seemed to be forming some kind of a pattern and my editor thought it might be worth our while if we investigated, so he put me onto it. I can just see his face now, the sly old devil, he said it would be my last fling before joining The Manchester Sentinel and if there was anything in it, well, who knows? "You could go out in a blaze of glory my boy," he said.

Michael paused and Tim took the opportunity to ask him what he meant by "some kind of a pattern"?

"A blackmailing pattern, husbands and wives caught while playing out of bounds and being forced to pay a price to keep a blackmailer quiet. Got the picture?"

"You don't think Betty was involved in blackmail, do you?"

"No, she hadn't a clue what I was talking about. The only thing was – I thought it strange that she didn't know where Elsie and Jake had gone and stranger still, after all this time, that she hadn't heard a word from Elsie. Elsie was supposed to be her best friend."

"Are you saying that Elsie and Jake were involved in blackmail?"

"Yes, I spoke to a detective pal of mine and he said that the police had heard one or two whispers about Elsie and Jake, nothing positive, just enough for them to be suspicious and put the word out. Elsie and Jake will be detained for police questioning when they come back to Blackpool, or whichever town they finally turn up in."

Tim decided to tell Michael about the incident at the Cuckoo's Nest and the arrangements he had made to see Beswick the bank manager, the following day.

"Beswick! Not banker Beswick, Maria's Beswick?"

"The very same gentleman," said Tim.

"Oh, my God," breathed Michael.

Tim wondered if, maybe, the Cuckoo's Nest incident was somehow tied in with the blackmail business and Michael asked if he would let him know the outcome of his meeting with Beswick. They were just about to arrange a time to see each other again when Maria came into the room to say their meal was ready.

"Have you boys had time for a nice long chat? Have I missed anything interesting?"

"I was just about to ask Tim what he thinks about the ghost," said Michael, nonchalantly.

"Well, he doesn't know, I haven't told him yet, so you can tell Tim all about the ghost while we are eating. We're having our meal in the kitchen, it's cosier," said Maria as she led them through to the table.

Anne was pale and the dark circles under her eyes seemed to have grown darker. Tim was grateful Michael did most of the talking and as he listened to him, his respect for Michael grew. There was nothing in the least bit forced about Michael's conversation and on a day that had been marred by so much sorrow; he managed to talk in a way which was soothing, healing, and amusing. Anne looked adoringly at him and everybody took comfort from him. Maria and Tim knew that with Michael around, Anne wouldn't lose heart.

Michael diverted them with the subject of the ghost, "Maria is convinced this house is haunted, it's true, isn't it Maria?"

"If I tell you about it, promise not to laugh," said Maria. She waited until they had all given their assurance, "Okay, well, sometimes when I'm working around the house I come across something, maybe a cushion, or the small coffee table, and I think to myself that's not where they were last night before I went to bed." She shrugged, "I put them back where they were before and then the same thing happens again. And cupboards and drawers, sometimes they seem as if they've been rummaged through...." Maria shivered slightly as she stopped talking and waited for their reaction. Nobody said a word. "They must think I'm nuts!" she said to herself.

Anne was the first to break the silence, "If you're looking for a ghost to blame, you're wasting your time, Maria Martinelli. When you're dead you are either up there with Him, like my Jack is, or down below trying to find a shady spot to cool off."

"Hear, hear," said Michael, who didn't believe in ghosts, either. "Has anything been stolen? Anything missing, Maria?"

"No, nothing as far as I can tell."

"W-e-ll," said Michael slowly. "As long as you're okay, Maria, and nothing is missing, I don't think there's anything to worry about."

"I'm not worried, Michael, it's probably just my imagination."

"If you are worried, even the least bit, Maria, let me know and I'll keep popping in to see that you are alright. In fact, I'll do that anyway," said Tim.

"Thanks Tim, I'd really appreciate that," said Maria gratefully.

Anne looked at the clock. "Nearly half past ten, think I'll try to get some sleep. It's been a long day." She bit her bottom lip to stop herself crying. "Thanks for letting me sleep here, Maria, I couldn't face the house tonight without Jack." Maria made a move to get up. "No, it's alright, Maria, you stay with the others, I'd like to be on my own for a while. Come and see me before you go to bed?"

"Of course I will, Anne."

"Goodnight," they all chorused.

"It's about time I was going," Michael said when Anne went upstairs. "I'll pop in tomorrow though and see if everything's okay. D'you think Anne will be alright, Maria?"

"Don't worry, Michael; I'll take good care of her for you."

Maria and Tim talked for a while after Michael had gone, happy to be alone again. But it had been a long day and a very emotional one and Maria confessed to Tim that she felt absolutely shattered. "Once Anne's settled down, I'll turn in," she said.

Tim put his hand up, "Please, Mrs. Martinelli, can I go to bed now?" Maria went with him to the door, reluctant to part from him she watched as he walked down the path to his room.

Although Tim felt exhausted he couldn't sleep. He tried counting sheep and, almost imperceptibly, drifted into a dream about sheep. The sheep' heads became human heads, they turned towards him so that he could see their faces and the eyes in the faces were open wide, staring at him, rows and rows of heads with open staring eyes, waiting for Tim to count them. And every face, in every head, was the image of Mr. Beswick!

CHAPTER TEN

TIM WOKE NEXT MORNING FEELING refreshed despite the bad dream and after breakfast he went out into the garden to do some digging and a lot of thinking. As he dug in the spade and turned over the soil, he was trying to work out how he could get away from Anne and Maria at lunch-time to see Beswick without making them curious. He knew that it would be difficult because Anne was bound to ask where he was going, Anne was naturally nosey! He couldn't possibly tell them that he was meeting Beswick at the Tower Aquarium, otherwise the whole Cuckoo's Nest business might come out, Anne could question people like a detective. It started to rain but he ignored it, he bent his back over the spade, his brain always seemed to function better when he was doing manual work!

Maria looked through the window and seeing he was getting wet through, went out with an umbrella to rescue him. On their way up the path she suggested that in future they should have all their meals together, she didn't care a fig what people said. And Christmas couldn't come soon enough, they wouldn't just be sharing a meal together, they would be sharing their whole lives.

In the house, Maria insisted Tim take off his wet jacket and stay while it dried out. He asked about Anne,

"She'll be down soon," Maria said, "I woke up once or twice and heard her crying, but she seems much better this morning."

"Good, and what about Paris, is that still on?"

"Not sure about that, I'm still working on it," said Maria. "Leave it for now, talk to Anne about anything but Paris, okay?"

As they sat in the living room they could hear Anne in the kitchen. She came into the room and saw them cuddled up together, "Excuse me, aren't you two old enough to know that you can't live on love alone? Come into the kitchen, I've made some toast and tea."

They had settled down around the kitchen table when Anne said, "They tell me that Betty Williams has been spreading it all round Blackpool that you've made a good job of her windows."

Tim almost choked on his toast; he took a long drink from his tea to clear his throat before he explained, "I've made her windows secure, Anne, if that's what you mean?" He couldn't understand how Anne had heard that Betty Williams' was gossiping about him fixing her windows. Who was the source of Anne's information? He knew it couldn't have been Betty directly; she and Anne were at daggers drawn, so it had to be somebody else. Whoever it was, Tim was sure of one thing, although Michael might be the top-notch reporter, when it came to updating local Blackpool gossip his Aunt Anne scooped him every-time!

Anne picked on the word, secure. "Secure, that's it," she said, "Security's what I want. Without Jack in the house, I'll have to make sure everything's safe and......"

"That's okay; I'll fix them for you, Anne." Unwittingly, Anne had provided the solution to his problem, now he knew that the meeting with Beswick at the Tower Aquarium could go ahead in secret and he surprised and delighted Anne by saying he would have the job on her windows completed by teatime.

Tim planned that first he would meet Beswick at twelve thirty and next he would collect the fittings from Mr. Nightingale the ironmonger and then go to Anne's. Mentally checking his timing again, he told Anne she could put the kettle on about five and over a nice cup of tea he would tell her exactly what he had done to make her windows secure.

"Thanks, Tim, that's a great relief, I'll just get you my front door key." Anne sounded more confident now. "I'll go back home after tea, tomorrow, Maria," she said. And despite everything Maria said to try and persuade her to stay for a while longer, Anne wouldn't change her mind, she was going home tomorrow and that was that! Tim looked at the clock, ten minutes to twelve, time to get ready! Maria went out into the garden with him and he asked her why Anne seemed to dislike Betty Williams so much.

"Honestly I don't know," said Maria. "And she won't talk to me about it, so I've stopped asking. It's a shame really, because usually Anne doesn't have a bad word to say about anybody. The other day, you should have seen the strange look she gave me when I told her I thought Betty had a lot of good in her."

"Well, nobody's all bad," said Tim. Maria had expected him to agree whole heartedly with her about Betty and his response puzzled her. He left her with little time to dwell on the subject; a quick kiss goodbye and he was on his way to the store room.

Maria called after him, "Don't forget Tim, its back here for tea when you've finished?"

Tim waved in acknowledgement and as soon as he opened the door to his room a wall of damp chilly air met him and reminded him he must get a new can of paraffin from Mr. Nightingale.

He changed out of his gardening clothes and, catching sight of his reflection in the mirror, decided he looked very smart in his brown tie and white shirt and Andrew's expensive sports jacket. Then he remembered they were the combination of colours his mother liked – brown and white. He stared at himself in the mirror, and just for a moment he heard his mother speaking, her voice was warm and approving, "That shirt and tie, Tim, that's what I like, brown and white, I said that's nice Tim, brown and white together." Tim whispered "Love you, Mum, love you "Granny twice-over," I'll come and see you one day soon - promise."

With a cap pulled low over his brow he was ready. He locked the door, reassured that there was little in his appearance now to identify him as Ryan the deserter, if there were any redcaps about they wouldn't recognise him.

He reached the promenade and hurried on towards the Tower.

It was the first time Tim had been in the Tower since the engagement party and a flash back of Jack being taken ill came to him just as he reached the admission kiosk. It brought a lump to his throat and his voice echoed in his ears, sounding as if he was speaking in a tunnel. "Hello miss, the aquarium, how much is it to go in?"

The girl behind the glass slapped down the book she was reading so hard on the counter it reminded him of the way Betty used the counter flap to show her annoyance, but that's as far as the comparison went, the girl in the kiosk wasn't in the least attractive. She didn't bother to answer; she pointed to the notice board close to Tim's elbow and gave him a look which said, "Use your eyes." Tim glanced at the notice board, "General Admission, one shilling including tax. Children, half price. Fish fed eleven thirty."

He paid his shilling; she gave him a ticket and went back to her book.

"Thanks," said Tim. There was something about the sad, sullen look on the girl's face that reminded him of someone. At the moment, for the life of him, he couldn't think who that was and he had no time to speculate. It was twelve thirty and Mr. Beswick would be waiting for him.

The aquarium was undoubtedly one of the most unexpected delights of Tim Ryan's life; there was an aura of tranquillity about the place which he sensed as soon as he walked through the door.   The subtle lighting and the fish gliding noiselessly through the great luminous tanks of water made it beautiful as well as peaceful. The thought came to Tim that maybe that's why Beswick had chosen this place for their meeting; perhaps he hoped the tranquil atmosphere would lessen his inquisitor's hostility?

Beswick entered the aquarium after Tim, spotted him and hurried to join him.   Anxiously, without any formal greeting, he muttered, "You didn't tell the police did you?"

"Not yet," said Tim. "Depends on what you tell me. I want everything, and the truth - or else!"

The threat in Tim's voice frightened Beswick, he shrank back and held up his hands like a shield, "We don't have to fight Mr. Ryan, that's not why I'm here; I've come to tell you the truth."

"I'm listening," said Tim, in a less threatening tone.

Beswick breathed a sigh of relief and lowered his arms, "Thanks." He gave another furtive look around.

"What's up?" said Tim.

"Just checking, making sure nobody can hear me," said the bank manager.

"Come on, Beswick" said Tim, impatiently.   "There's nobody here, you've seen that for yourself. They'd finished feeding the fish when I arrived and now everybody's gone for lunch. You can talk your head off if you like, there's nobody to hear you."

Tim was right.   They saw the door close on the last of the visitors and Beswick and Tim had the aquarium to themselves.   The place was now as quiet as a confessional.

Beswick coughed nervously, "You aren't married, are you, Mr. Ryan?"

"Hell, what sort of a question is that? I can't believe it," said Tim. "Look, I'm not asking you for a bank loan you know and it's me who's asking the questions so why don't you start explaining?"

"I know, I know and I will I just wanted to try and establish a starting point that's all."

"Tell it from the beginning," said Tim, coldly.

"Right, that's what I'll do, I'll tell it from the very beginning. It all started a long time ago. My wife, Edna, and I worked as clerks in the same bank in Liverpool, that was, oh way back in 1908 and we were both 24 years old. During the Christmas party that year, Edna and I slipped outside and in the heat of the moment we …. Well, a few weeks later Edna told me she was pregnant, so we got married. The following year our baby was born, Lily we called her. She's sixteen years old now - you would have met her this morning when you paid to come in - the girl in the kiosk?"

That was it; Tim could have kicked himself for not getting it right sooner. There was no doubt about it, she reminded him of Beswick – she was Beswick's double!

It was obvious that Beswick was expecting Tim to make some comment about Lilly and, because Tim hadn't the heart to hurt him, he lied and said as brightly as he could, "Nice girl, very helpful."

Beswick shook his head, "Hates the job," he said vehemently. "When she left school she said she wanted to be a writer. That's wonderful, I thought, so I bought her a typewriter and waited for her to say, "Dad, what do you think about this?" But she never did, she locked herself in her room and day after day I listened for the click of the typewriter keys, I never heard them, she showed me nothing, not a single page of anything. Then one day she forgot to lock her door, so I had a good look around, the typewriter still had its cover on, there wasn't a single scrap of typing to be seen - nothing! I insisted she find a job. They needed someone to manage the kiosk at the Tower and I persuaded Lily to apply. She got the job but it won't last, she's not interested in people, hates it here. They'll let her go at the end of the season and you can't blame them."

This outpouring from Beswick about his family embarrassed Tim. "Look," he said, "I'm sorry if things aren't going right for you at home, but I can't see what that's got to do with what happened at the Cuckoo's nest."

"Please be patient Mr. Ryan, let me tell you about it in my own way."

"Alright, but I'm sorry I can't stay long."

"I'll be as brief as I can. I've told you about Lily, but I have to tell you about Edna because the day Lily was born, that's when our intimate life ended. You'll notice I didn't say anything about love? Edna never loved me but we carried on living together as a family under the same roof, all a sham." He paused and tilted his head so that his face, now part hidden in shadows, looked grotesque. His mouth opened and closed without sound, more like the fish in the tank than a man. But it was an illusion, a trick of the light, and when he moved his head again his face was composed, except that his sadness seemed deeper than ever. "I adored Lily when she was a baby, when I held her in my arms I was tremendously happy. Then, as the months and years passed by she changed, became morose just like her mother, eventually locked me out of her heart, just like her mother had done."

He paused again, overcome with emotion, and Tim led him to sit down on a bench beside the exit door. "Sorry Mr. Ryan, I don't usually allow myself to get carried away like that. The last time I cried was when we went to war with Germany - it's true, when war was declared I wept with relief because at last I could see a way out of all my misery. I've never told anybody that before. And I'll tell you something else, when I volunteered for the army I thought I'd soon be dead, the thought that I might actually die a hero made me feel good. Edna thought I would be killed too, "And don't come back," that's what the look in her eyes said. I was only at the front for the last six months of the war, before that I was on admin duties. When they got really short of cannon fodder, they sent for people like me. In the trenches it took me less than an hour to realize I didn't want to die after all. Death became the enemy, not the Germans. I didn't want to kill Germans and if truth were told, they probably didn't want to kill me either. In fact, I didn't want to kill anybody. Then they discovered that I was a crack shot. It was no surprise to me; even on admin duties I'd been trained for the day when I would have to use a rifle."

Tim looked at the thick lenses of Beswick's spectacles and couldn't believe that he knew one end of a rifle from the other - and as for being a crack shot – well?

"You don't believe me, do you? Well, I was a crack shot, the best. So good, you know what they made me do?"

Tim decided to humour him. "Okay, you were a crack shot, so tell me."

Beswick's face began to twitch "They'd keep one or two like me behind, in case some of the boys who went over the top got frightened and ran back."

"What – you actually shot your own mates?"

"Yes, that's what they made us do, "Cowardice in the face of the enemy," that's what they called it." He saw the shocked look on Tim's face. "But I never killed anybody, Mr. Ryan, I was a crack shot, remember? It was up to me. I aimed to wound one or two and that's all. Then they took me off the job and the war ended."

"But the soldiers you wounded, they gave them time to recover, then they shot and killed them just the same, didn't they?"

Beswick looked ashamed and hung his head. "Yes, I think so. Perhaps I should have aimed to kill in the first place? But I couldn't, I couldn't kill anybody and I've lived all my life since then realising I was more of a coward than them."

Tim couldn't prove if Beswick's account was true or false but he gave him the benefit of the doubt, "No, you weren't a coward Mr. Beswick, well, not in my book anyway."

Encouraged by the warmth of Tim's voice he continued with his story. "After the war, back in my old job, I was promoted, made manager of the Blackpool branch, moved the family here, bought a new house. But life continued just as it was before – without any joy.

Then one day my luck changed. I was walking down the prom by the kiosk where they sell post cards and candyfloss when I saw a little child drop her candyfloss on the ground. She began to cry, so I bought her another - and that's how I met Elsie, the girl working in the kiosk. Elsie seemed to be really touched by what I did for that child, we started to chat and within five minutes I felt I'd fallen in love with her. It's true! When I found out she was a prostitute it didn't bother me at all and the next day I was in her flat and making love to her. I called at Elsie's often after that, I really cared for her – really loved her. Then one day when we were making love, a man sneaked into the room and before I could stop him he took photographs of us. I tried to wrestle the camera from him but he was a big brute of a man, threw me to the floor and threatened me. He raised his foot ready to kick me - Elsie saw that too and she screamed - told him not to hurt me. She pushed him away. The tender way she looked at me, Mr. Ryan, if I never see love in anybody's eyes for me again, at least I saw it that day. The man ordered us both to get dressed. It was obvious he was Elsie's pimp and she seemed to be afraid of him. He told me it would cost me fifty pounds to buy the negative. Elsie tried to persuade him against that, "Jake," she pleaded, "You ought to be satisfied with the money he's already paid me." He told her to shut up, said Elsie would give me the negative when I gave her the fifty pounds and threw me out of the flat. I didn't have the opportunity to get the negative and pay them the money because Elsie and Jake suddenly disappeared and it was Miss Williams who said that she wanted the fifty pounds I owed to Elsie. She told me Jake and Elsie had run away together and Elsie had asked her to collect the money. We arranged to meet – she chose the venue. That night at the Cuckoo's Nest I had the money with me but she denied all knowledge of the envelope with the negative. I wouldn't hand over the cash without the negative. That's when she became hysterical and lashed out at me, kicking me, I didn't retaliate and when you came along I ran away. Next day, I went to visit her at the kiosk hoping she'd calmed down enough for me to reason with her. She was calm enough at first but, when I demanded the envelope in exchange for the fifty pounds, she said again that she didn't know what I was talking about, said they must have taken it with them. It was clear to me then, that she had no idea what was in the envelope or anything about it. She lost her temper and told me what I could do with the money, said that Elsie could collect it from me herself when she came back. So I pocketed the money and left. Oh, there's just one thing more, she seemed to think that the relationship between Elsie and Jake wouldn't last. She could be right, I checked around, seems Jake was a gambler and a drinker." Beswick shrugged his shoulders, "That's it Mr. Ryan, that's everything and it's the truth." He looked imploringly at Tim, "You won't go to the police will you?"

"No, Mr. Beswick, I believe you. I won't say a word to the police and I'll make sure that Betty Williams won't say anything to them, either."

"Oh, thank God. Thank God for that."

"Look, I'm sorry you've had such a rotten time of it Mr. Beswick, believe me, I really am. If I were you, I'd go home now and try to forget about what happened in Elsie's flat and at the Cuckoo's nest. And I shouldn't worry about Jake, he won't be coming back, I've heard that the police in Blackpool don't have much regard for him."

"Thanks, Mr. Ryan. You've no idea how worried I've been. Thanks for taking the weight from my shoulders."

He shook hands with Tim and they left the aquarium together just as the afternoon visitors started to come in. At the ticket kiosk, Beswick stopped to speak to his daughter, "See you this evening then, Lily?" Lily ignored him completely and picked up her book. If she had struck his face, her father couldn't have looked more hurt and Tim remembered what Beswick had said to him earlier, "Gradually she became more and more like her mother and then she too shut me out of her heart." Tim felt protective towards him, "Come Mr. Beswick, we've finished our business here, let's leave shall we?" And taking the bank manager's arm he led him away from the kiosk and out into the fresh air. Over the top of her book Lily watched them walk away.

The sun was shining as they stood on the promenade. Mr. Beswick said that was a good omen, a sure sign that at least some of his troubles were over. Tim waited until he was lost in the crowd. "I hope you are right, Mr. Beswick," he said to himself, "I hope your troubles really are over...," Tim had his doubts, once you were in Lady Luck's bad book you had the devil of a job to get out of it.

Mr. Nightingale sold Tim the window fasteners and a gallon of paraffin. Tim apologised for forgetting to bring a container but Mr. Nightingale told him not to worry, "Just bring an empty one back next time you're passing", he said cheerfully. He was keen to know how Tim had got on with the last lot of fasteners and when Tim said the job had gone well and that he was grateful to him for his advice on the fitting, Mr Nightingale turned pink with pleasure. He accompanied Tim to the door. "Goodbye Mr.

Ryan, don't forget, if you need any help you know where to come.........."

The work at Anne's went well; Tim was way ahead of schedule. He was putting the finishing touches to the downstairs bay window when Michael pressed his nose against the glass and grimaced at him.

"Well," said Michael, after plonking himself in an easy chair and making himself comfortable, "Did Beswick turn up?"

"He sure did," said Tim.

"So, what did he say?

Tim sat opposite Michael and repeated Beswick's story almost word for word, about his wife, his daughter Lily, about the war – every sad episode.

Phew!" said Michael when he'd finished. "What a life. Poor bastard, thought he'd found love and it all ended up in blackmail!"

"Looks like it."

"And Betty's got nothing to do with it?"

"I don't think so. Beswick doesn't think so either. When he offered her the fifty pounds in exchange for envelope, she said that she didn't have a clue what he was talking about. They had a bit of an argument about it and then she told him what he could do with his money."

"I bet she did. What about the envelope?"

"It wasn't in Elsie's room, at least that's what Betty said. She told him Elsie must have taken it with her and he'd have to get it from her if she came back to Blackpool but as far as Betty was concerned, she didn't want to have any more to do with it."

"So, when she said that, Beswick went away, did he?"

"Yes, there is something else, Michael, about Betty though it's got nothing to do with what we've just been discussing."

"What's that?"

Tim told Michael about the middle aged men he'd seen hanging round the kiosk, particularly the one Betty had slammed the counter lid down on, the one she had told to "piss off.""

"What did he look like?"

Tim described him and Michael smiled, "Sounds like Billy Braithwaite to me."

"Billy Braithwaite?"

"Big-shot Blackpool bookie, sounds like Betty was getting him off her books."

"What do you mean, getting him off her books?"

"Do I have to spell it out for you Tim? Betty's on the game and very selective she is too. Billy must have done something to upset her."

Tim said, "I did wonder about that. I saw her flat when I went to fit the window catches, very expensive place - what she earns from the kiosk couldn't even cover the rent."

"Well, her second income will pay the rent," said Michael, "And with plenty to spare."

"I'd better go now, Michael, and report to Anne, "I promised to be back for tea."

"That's alright, I'll come with you," said Michael, "Maria's invited me as well."

Michael waited while Tim collected his tools and his can of paraffin, then they set off together and took the promenade route to the house. The tide had come in; they could hear the waves crashing against the sea wall, sending great clouds of spray high above the railings. The gulls loved it, playing some kind of dare game, swooping in and out of the spray, screaming with excitement. Tim made no comment; seagulls were at the bottom of his favourite bird list. He opened the green gate to the garden and Michael followed him up the path to the kitchen door. Before they had reached halfway, Tim stopped, "I don't think we should say anything to Maria or Anne about Beswick and Betty, do you?"

"Mum's the word," said Michael.

Chapter Eleven

At the end of the month, Blackpool illuminations were lit for the first time since the war. Tim, Maria and Anne were among the hundreds of people thronging the promenade waiting for the lights to be turned on. "First time since 1914," blared the loudspeakers, "On this night of September 26th 1925, you will witness a truly fabulous spectacle."

"As if we didn't know," said Anne when they had been reminded for the umpteenth time.

Then at last a switch was flicked on and Blackpool sparkled and shone under a thousand electric stars. There was a moment's silence whilst the awe stricken crowd took in the magnificence of the brilliant tableaux, and then the cheering started. "Oh, see the children's faces," Maria exclaimed, "Just look at them, they can't believe what's happening!"

"It's fairyland," cried the children.   Then Maria said quietly, "I never expected it to be as good as this. It really is out of this world."

Maria's remark must have stirred Anne's imagination, "Maybe it's like this in heaven for Jack," she said dreamily.

Was Anne being serious about that? Tim looked and saw that she was and later in the evening she announced happily that she had made her mind up about the trip to Paris – she wanted to accompany Maria after all.

When the time came for their holiday, Tim didn't go with Maria and Anne to the railway station; he thought it safer to say his goodbyes to them at the house. Maria told him to take care and promised to phone him from Paris before returning to Blackpool. They kissed and said goodbye again and then Michael drove them to the station.

After they'd gone, Tim sat in Maria's chair daydreaming and already feeling lonely. They had arranged that he should stay in the house while she was away, but here he missed her even more than he did when he was alone in his own room. He roused himself from his reverie, realising he should have started collecting cash from the various outlets at least half an hour ago to be sure of getting it to the bank in time. Bank! The very word brought images of Mr. Beswick and his unhappy family and he wondered how Beswick was getting on.   Was life still so miserable for him?

Tim emptied the money from the till in Betty's kiosk and although it was the tail end of the season he was surprised at the large amount of cash people were spending.

Betty was obviously doing very well but, when the illuminations were switched off in October, the cash tills would be emptied for the last time and the kiosk closed and shuttered. Tim asked Betty if she'd made up her mind about working in the gift shop in town when the season ended. "I will, if Mrs. Martinelli lets me come back and work in the kiosk again next year. She wants to train me to manage the shop, but I like it here, the people I meet here are far more interesting." I bet they are, thought Tim, remembering her encounter with Billy Braithwaite the bookie! But Tim couldn't understand why working in the kiosk meant more to Betty than the gift shop or that very smart dress shop she had left in order to take Elsie's place. Maybe she didn't mind the pay being less, but the kiosk could be a damned uncomfortable place to work when the weather was bad. Still, if she'd made her mind up, Tim knew it would be a waste of time trying to persuade her to change it. "Oh, she'll probably agree to that, Betty, best if it comes from you though, you could tell her when she gets back from Paris."

Betty's eyebrows shot up. "Oh, so they've gone then?"

"This morning."

"You'll be on your own then?"

"Afraid so."

"Diddums," said Betty, "So my little boy will be lonely." Then she dropped the baby talk. "Tell you what, come to my flat tomorrow, it's my eighteenth birthday today, but I can't celebrate it until tomorrow. A few of my mates will be there to see I don't gobble you up and there'll be plenty to eat and drink. Say you'll come, Tim. Celebrate my birthday. Please?" And she took his nose between her thumb and finger and tweaked it hard, "There now, that's for nothing, so you know what to expect if you refuse!"

The nose-pinching made Tim chuckle. It would be churlish not to accept the invitation, and with her friends there he should be safe from Betty's romantic notions.

"What time?" he asked.

"About eight, okay?"

"Eight's fine. So now can we get on with what I came for, collect the cash and check the float?"

Tim had spent more time at Betty's kiosk than he intended, so he had to rush around collecting cash from the other tills until he finally arrived at the bank just two minutes before closing time. He asked the teller if Mr. Beswick was in his office and was told he was busy, "But if the matter's urgent, Mr. Ryan, I'm sure Mr. Beswick will see you."

"No, no, it's nothing that won't keep," said Tim and he left the bank and returned to Maria's without seeing him.

It must have been about seven in the evening when the phone rang. It was Cecilia, Maria's sister in law, ringing from the restaurant to remind Tim that he was supposed to be eating with them whilst Maria was away and she wanted to know what time he'd be with them for dinner. "Can I leave it 'til about nine," said Tim, "First day on my own you know and I've been pretty busy."

"That's fine," Cecilia said, "See you about nine, talk then."

Tim had a long soak in Maria's bath and after that he took his time getting ready. He put on a clean shirt and was adjusting his tie when his coughing started. It wasn't a bad attack, but it was the first time he coughed like that in weeks and he put it down to all the rushing about he'd done when he was collecting cash and then that mad dash to the bank. He poked his head outside the door to check the weather, it was cold so he put on his raincoat and buttoned it right up to the neck.

He was on the other side of the road from the restaurant when he saw Betty. She came out of the restaurant door, swaying slightly; she refused the helping arm of her escort and trailed a white fur stole carelessly on the pavement behind her. The man was stout and middle aged, no one Tim recognised. They got into a waiting taxi and as Betty turned to wave goodbye to Cecilia and Joseph, Tim noticed her necklace; it sparkled in the light from street lamps. The taxi sped away and Tim crossed the road and went into the restaurant. Joseph greeted him and led him to a corner table, "It'll be just the two of us dining together tonight, Tim. You'll have to excuse Cecilia, we're busy and she drew the short straw."

They sat down and Tim asked Joseph if he knew the name of the man who had just left with the young blonde girl.

"Why, not jealous are you Tim?" Joseph was laughing.

"I thought she looked like a girl who works for Maria, but I don't know the man she was with," said Tim.

"He's no stranger, Tim. His secretary calls regularly to book him a table. Marcus Kellner, that's his name. Property man from London, been here for weeks. Rumour has it he's got a big deal going through in Blackpool. They say he's loaded. Did you say you know the girl?"

"If it's the same girl, she works in one of Maria's kiosks."

Joseph shook his head in disbelief. "Well, whoever she is, that Marcus Kellner's really nuts about her and you don't need specs to see why. They've been coming here once or twice a week you know, and he spends a fortune on her. Did you see those ear rings and that necklace? Diamonds, I would guess! He gave her the earrings tonight, said it was her birthday present."

So that was why Betty had told Tim she couldn't celebrate her birthday until the following night; it was because she was celebrating the evening with Marcus Kellner. What neither Joseph nor Tim knew was that Marcus Kellner had only become acquainted with Betty a few weeks ago; he was the man who had arrived at Betty's kiosk to ask if he could talk about having sex with her. The same man she had flirted with – "Just to keep him nicely on the boil!"

Tim had to make an excuse to Cecilia and Joseph about dining with them the next evening. The least complicated thing he could do was to tell them he wanted to stay in and have a quiet evening – stay indoors and get rid of his cough. After finishing his meal he made the same excuse to leave early and that suited Joseph; the waiters and Cecilia were still working flat out and now he was free to help.

Tim went straight to bed and coughed himself to sleep, but not before wondering why Betty hadn't told him about the date with Marcus Kellner. Then he thought, why should she, after all it wasn't any of his business?

The next morning he decided to try and sweat out of his system whatever it was that ailed him, so he set to digging round the ragged edges of the lawn and widening all the borders. He sweated a lot but it didn't seem to help his cough much and when he finally arrived at Betty's flat at quarter past eight that evening, he was still feeling pretty rough.

Betty took his coat and led him into the room. Tim presented her with the bunch of flowers he had been hiding behind his back, "A bit late, but Happy Birthday, Betty."

"Thanks Tim, they're beautiful; they are the best birthday present a girl could wish for." Her voice sounded as if she really meant what she said - or did she? Tim noticed she was wearing her necklace and the diamond earrings which were her birthday gift from Marcus Kellner!

Betty went to put the flowers in water and Tim was left waiting alone, the other guests were obviously late in arriving. He had a good look around the room again and was surprised to see a bundle of knitting lying on the settee. Betty reappeared and stood the vase of flowers in the middle of the dining table which was set for two - she told him that the other guests couldn't come because of a mix up with the birthday date. But not to worry, she had cooked a meal especially for him and she was ready to serve it now.

She gave him a plate of roast beef with Yorkshire pudding and all the trimmings, Tim's mother who was a brilliant cook couldn't have done better and when Tim told Betty, she blushed with pleasure. She made coffee and added a measure of whisky, "Might soothe your cough a bit," she said. Tim asked her about the bundle of knitting on the settee.Betty explained that she was knitting a pair of bed socks for her grandma who was eighty years old and lived a few streets away. She loved her grandma, she said, in fact it was her grandma who had taught her how to knit.

The whisky and the coffee seemed to be soothing Tim's throat so when Betty refilled their cups and added even larger measures of whisky, he found himself nodding his head with approval.   While they were enjoying the drink she told him she had spent a lot of her childhood with her grandma; if Tim had enjoyed his meal all the credit for that should go to her grandma who had taught her how to cook. Tim raised his cup, "To grandma, and to you Betty, a toast to two great cooks!"

Tim felt inquisitive, now. Was he becoming as nosey as Anne, or was it the whisky that was making him bold? "Didn't you learn anything at home from your own parents?" he asked.

"Yeah, how to keep out of their bloody way," said Betty. Her eyes had narrowed and she fidgeted with her hands.

"Keep out of their way; keep out of their way from what?"

"My Dad – look, I don't want to talk about him. He was a right bastard. In the end he ran off. End of story."

"But things got better after that, after he went away, I mean?"

"No, and don't keep on about it. I thought I'd told you before about all that. I left home and I haven't been back since and I don't intend to. I see grandma all the time though. I make sure she's all right. Now let's change the record, okay?"

Tim thought about Betty's family, especially about her grandma, and found he was more in agreement with Maria who always maintained that there was some good in Betty.

When he started to cough again Betty suggested he should stay on in the flat and let her look after him until he was better. "Maria won't know," she said, "She's in Paris having a good time. When the cat's away..." She sat on the arm of his chair and crossed her legs. He struggled to control his breathing, trying to suppress a cough. The phone rang in the kitchen. Betty excused herself, left the room and closed the door behind her. When she returned she told him her grandma had fallen – the phone call was from a neighbour. "Grandma's not badly hurt, a bit bruised that's all, but shaken up - wants me to go round and tuck her up and say goodnight to her. I'll have to go. But you wait; I shouldn't be more than an hour. You could go to bed here, have a sleep while you're waiting?"

"No, no, you look after your grandma Betty; she may need you to stay the night. I'll go home and try to get rid of this cough. You go to her Betty, its best you look after her, better all round." Tim was glad of an excuse to leave. He should have known better than to accept her birthday party invitation and not for the first time he blamed himself for being so gullible, blamed himself for coming here at all.

"You're right, Tim," Betty said. "I'll probably stay the night with her. Wait, I'll get your coat."

Tim stood up and steadied himself; the whisky had made him light headed.

She was back within seconds and helped him on with his coat. "Look after yourself, Tim. You know I love you more than anybody else in the world, don't you? Come to the kiosk and see me tomorrow, I'll know more about Grandma then. And you take something for that cough, okay?" She raised herself up on her toes and kissed his cheek before she closed the door firmly behind him.

With her ear pressed against the front door, Betty waited until Tim's footsteps had died away then she scurried back into her flat, got dressed up in one of her most glamorous outfits and packed a little overnight bag. Thirty minutes later the doorbell rang. She greeted Marcus Kellner and together they got into his car and drove away.

CHAPTER TWELVE

KELLNER DIDN'T TELL HER WHERE they were going but Betty, who knew Blackpool like the back of her hand, looked out of the window and said, "Why are we going to the marina, Marcus?"

"A spot of business on the Isle of Man, Betty, say "hello" to some interesting people and there's one man who lives there I particularly want you to meet. We need the boat to sail there, unless, of course, you prefer to swim."

"Boat please;" said Betty, "I can't swim."

"What! Can't swim and lived by the sea all your life, unbelievable! You must be joking," said Kellner.

"So, who's this person you particularly want me to meet then, Marcus?" said Betty, more to divert attention than out of any curiosity about Kellner's friend. She had reluctantly given Tim some idea of life with her family, but she certainly wasn't going to tell Kellner why her childhood memories didn't include jolly beach picnics and swimming lessons.

"It's a surprise, darling," said Kellner as they boarded the boat and Betty couldn't persuade him to tell her any more about the trip. She went down below, poured herself a drink, selected a sailing manual from the shelf and flicked through the pages.

Marcus Keller was now a contented man, his business plans were highly successful but as far as he was concerned the jewel in the crown was Betty. "How'd you like to take the wheel?" he called down to her. Betty finished her drink quickly and climbed on deck to join him.

"Keep it on this heading," said Kellner, pointing to the compass. "Throttle setting's okay; we're doing about fifteen knots. At this rate, we'll arrive with time to spare."

"What will she do flat out?" asked Betty, as she took over the wheel.

It wasn't the first time Kellner had been asked that question and he knew the answer off pat. Wanting to impress Betty, he pretended he had to calculate the answer. "Twin engines, eight horses apiece, if push comes to shove I reckon she'll do a good twenty knots, depending on weather and sea conditions of course. There aren't many cabin cruisers like this one in Blackpool, Betty. Petrol consumption's a bit high, but for that turn of speed I reckon it's well worth it." He looked at Betty, eager for her to ask more questions, but she shrugged her shoulders and said, "Thanks, Marcus, nice to get the answer from an expert."

Betty hadn't been fooled by all the technical stuff he seemed to be working out so carefully, everything he'd said she'd already learned from the manual in the cabin. Poor old Marcus, from experience Betty knew that some men liked to show off their knowledge. Betty let him take charge of the wheel again. Her eyes brimming over with mock admiration she said, "Clever old you Marcus, you can sail me round the world anytime!"

If Kellner had dared let go of the wheel, he would have grabbed her in his arms and danced her round the deck. "Thanks for the vote of confidence Betty. And yeah, hey! What a great idea you've just come up with, I mean sail around the world. Brilliant! D'you know, one day we might just do that."

Betty had no intention of sailing away from Tim - she changed the subject again. "Are the weather and sea conditions okay now, Marcus?"

Kellner had checked out the sailing conditions before they came on board, "Everything's fine, Betty. If you want to give her a two minute blast go ahead, take the wheel, open her up, a burn will do the engines more good than harm."

Betty took the wheel again and pushed the throttles wide open, the boat leapt and bounced on the swell. They were speeding at twenty-two knots for a while before Kellner decided it was too dangerous and asked Betty to reduce speed. She eased back the throttles and held the wheel steady until Marcus took the wheel from her; it had been a wonderful thrill to unleash all that power. Kellner gave her the thumbs up and Betty went below to repair the damage the sea and wind had done to her hair and make-up. She could hear Marcus yelling out one of Peter Dawson's songs, one of Tim's favourites, "On the Road to Mandalay." She listened while she poured another drink and murmured, "Hmm. Not bad Marcus, but you can't sing it like my Tim."

Oh yes, Marcus Kellner was a very happy man and his wild singing gave way to laughter when he recalled the first day he had met and talked to Betty at the kiosk. "Before we do business, first you have to buy some postcards," that's what she'd said to him. It had cost him the price of ten postcards before she'd talk business, but he considered that was the best deal he'd ever made in his life. Without any thought of danger now, he flung the throttles wide open so that the whole world might hear and celebrate with him. The engines responded with a magnificent roar and the prow rose above the swell, sending the spray flying higher and wider than ever. Kellner burst into song again through the sheer exhilaration of it all, "On the road to Mandalay where the flying fishes play....." His mind filled with romantic dreams of Betty and a nomadic sea-faring life together. He completely forgot about his wife and family in London, it was as if they had never existed.

The Isle of Man business had been concluded entirely to Kellner's satisfaction and it was almost six o'clock the following morning when he eased the cabin cruiser slowly back into Blackpool marina. A few minutes later he was lying next to Betty on the luxurious bed in the cabin. He wanted to make love to her, but couldn't, and he groaned, "Christ! What's wrong with me Betty........?"

"You're tired, Marcus, that's all," Betty said, and without waiting for an answer she began whispering into his ear while she caressed him; whisperings he had never heard or dreamed of before, wild ideas which breathed new life into him until he roared out and pulled her beneath him. A few minutes later he rolled onto his back and gasped out apologies. "I hardly knew what I was doing. You just make me feel so young."

Betty made little throaty, growling noises for him, "My pleasure Marcus." Her growling reassured and amused him; laughing, he seized Betty in his arms and holding her tightly rocked her about the bed until they were both quite dizzy. Exhausted, he stopped. "Betty Williams, one day you'll be the death of me," he wheezed. Then, getting his breath back, he laughed gleefully and this time Betty Williams laughed with him.

Betty didn't go to bed when Marcus dropped her off at the flat, she felt she could go without sleep forever, there was too much excitement in her life to bother about sleep. It was half past seven in the morning now, and almost time to go to work. After a quick bath and gulping down some breakfast, she changed into a skimpy red dress and lingered to look at herself in a full-length mirror. She ran her hands down the smooth curves of the dress and tried to imagine what it would be like if Tim's hands were caressing her. She sighed, if only they were!

Satisfied with her image, she said out aloud, "If this doesn't turn you on Tim Ryan, nothing will!" She slipped on a warm coat and started out for the kiosk. As she walked, she began to think about all that had happened on the Isle of Man last night and for a while Tim was forgotten.

Kellner's meeting had taken place in a large house on the outskirts of Douglas. Betty thought that it was going to be one of those boring business gatherings where she would be put on display as one of Marcus Kellner's trophies but, although the night started out like that, in the end it turned out to be surprisingly different.

There were about a dozen people in the room, three of them women. The women were polite when they were introduced to her, once they had heard her speak however they kept well away from her. That didn't trouble Betty, she knew they were whispering about her, "Who cares?" she said to herself, "I prefer talking to men any day." And there was no shortage of interest in Betty from the men; they were mostly middle aged - except for one. She didn't know him; he must have come into the room after the introductions were made and now he was standing on his own in a corner, looking across at her. Betty stared back invitingly, he seemed different from the others, younger for a start and she guessed his age to be about thirty. He was untidily dressed but definitely not scruffy. He had an air of something about him that she couldn't quite put her finger on. She was absorbed in trying to work out what it was when her thoughts were interrupted by Marcus, who excused himself, saying that he had to talk to a business colleague. He waved to someone to come over and keep her company during his absence. Several men in the room were absolutely sure that the wave was intended for them. Like moths to a candle they came, old moths to be sure and they fluttered around Betty each trying to gain her attention with their own brand of small talk. To her satisfaction, the group grew until she was the single centre of attraction.

But through gaps in the crowd Betty could see that the man in the corner was staring at her as intently as ever. Now she noticed his hair, he had the thickest mop of black hair she had ever seen in her life. Her eyes swept the circle of heads surrounding her; there was not a full head of hair amongst them. She giggled as she imagined that he had enough hair to cover all their bald bits and still have plenty to spare. When she looked over again for him, he had disappeared. Betty was disappointed, he was the only man there who didn't look boring and now he had gone!

There was an announcement for the meeting to begin, please would everyone proceed to the library. Betty's admirers drifted away and then Marcus was beside her, "I've got to go into the meeting now Betty, I'd like to leave you with my friend, Martin Kershaw."

Betty turned; the man standing next to Marcus Kellner was the young man with the mop of black hair. Betty gladly shook hands with him.

"Martin's the mystery man I spoke to you about," said Kellner. "He's an artist and I'd like him to paint your portrait, well, if that's okay with you, Betty? Look, why don't you two discuss it while I'm at the meeting? Let me know what you think?" Marcus kissed Betty lightly on the cheek and strode away, closing the library door behind him.

"He's a nice guy," Martin Kershaw said.

"How come you know him?" asked Betty.

"Through commercial work, artist's impression stuff, he gives me most of the property work he's involved in."

"Is that what you do for a living?"

"It provides me with a living, if that's what you mean. But no, my real work is painting portraits and figure painting – that's what I think I do best."

"I saw you staring at me," said Betty. "Would you like to paint a picture of my figure?" Martin Kershaw hesitated, overcome by her directness. "Well, to be absolutely honest yes, well, that's what I'd really like to do, but then, I'd be the last to ask in case you were - uhm – shy. And then there's Marcus to consider, he definitely wouldn't want that. What he wants is a portrait of your face."

"What Marcus doesn't see, Marcus doesn't know about, does he?" Betty challenged

Kershaw shook his head. Without his friend's approval the idea was strictly a non-starter. But Betty had no qualms about secrets or deception; they made her life more exciting. Anyway, posing naked for Martin might prove quite interesting, something to keep her mind occupied until the time came for Tim to say that he would run away with her. Kershaw might also fit into her future plans; instinct told her he could be useful.

"Now listen, Martin," she said firmly, "This is important. Sometimes in life you've got to grasp opportunities when you can. D'you hear what I'm saying?"

Martin hesitated again, "You're saying I should paint you in the nude, whatever Marcus wants?"

"That's it Martin. Marcus won't be upset because he'll never know. Look, all we have to do is tell him that I've agreed to have my portrait painted. We keep the nude thing a secret between you and me and you can paint the sort of thing he wants as well."

Martin agreed. At that moment he would have agreed to anything that Betty had proposed and she basked in his admiration.

It was Martin's adoring gaze Betty remembered as she arrived at the kiosk. She felt good when she opened up the shutters and through the slats she could see Tim coming to ask how her grandma was. In a flash, she took off her coat and dumped it on a pile of cardboard boxes in the corner. Tim ducked under the counter flap and stood beside her. He thought that she looked tired, "Looks like you didn't get much sleep last night, Betty, having to take care of your grandma. Is she feeling better this morning, is she okay?"

Betty stifled a yawn, "I was kept awake most of the night, but yeah, she's okay now. What she really needs is for me to spend a bit more time with her though, to make sure she's really better." She looked up and fluttered her eyelashes. "Look, Tim, do you think I can get the weekend off, I've got plenty of days due to me?"

Tim was sympathetic, "That's no problem Betty, Maria left me a list of people I can call on, I'll arrange for someone to take over for a day or so. You take off from mid-day Friday and I won't expect to see you again until Monday morning. Would that help?"

"Thanks Tim, you're an angel." Betty stretched across for something on the counter so she could move closer to him, but she felt a tugging at the hem of her dress. Looking down she saw a child's face peering under the counter flap. She recognised her at once; it was her favourite little girl customer - Fred.

Somehow Betty managed to return the child's smile. "So it's you," she said, hiding her annoyance at the interruption. "You crawled under the counter again, didn't you? What is it Fred, what d'you want?" The little girl laughed, she loved it when Betty called her Fred. She'd got the name by accident; a slip of the tongue made by Betty ages ago when she called her Fred instead of Freda and now the name singled her out and made her special. "Betty, you promised to give me an extra big candyfloss, if I came early."

"All right, a promise is a promise, see I haven't forgotten?" And with a dazzling smile Betty whisked a cloud of pink floss and presented the child with the largest candyfloss she had ever seen. But Betty was bitterly disappointed; her special moment with Tim was lost.

Freda spoke to Tim as he stood in the shadows inside the kiosk, "See mister, see what Betty's given me?" and she held the candyfloss up triumphantly, "I love Betty, d'you love Betty?"

"Betty's a lovely, kind person," Tim said weakly. The little girl crawled out and away under the counter flap taking care not to scrape her candyfloss on the pavement.

Betty turned to face Tim, "You know that I love you Tim Ryan, ever since I first set eyes on you, if it takes forever for you to decide that it's me that you want and not Mrs. Martinelli, then I'll wait Tim, I'll wait."

The child's interruption had brought Tim down to earth and put him on his guard. "Sorry Betty, got to go now," he said and before she could reply he ducked under the counter flap and walked away from the kiosk towards the house with his mind racing. He feared he wasn't as strong as he thought, well, when Betty was around, anyway, and he resolved not to give her the chance to flirt with him again – not ever!

Betty pulled the shutters wide open so she could watch Tim all the way to the garden gate. She knew that he didn't love her, he'd never given her any encouragement and when the little girl had said, "I love Betty, do you?" Betty had listened very carefully to his reply and it didn't surprise her that the word love didn't even get a mention. So what, things could change. Maybe he didn't love her, but she'd make him want her. Tears stung her eyes and she muttered angrily, "Don't worry Tim Ryan, when Mrs. Martinelli tells you to clear off – and she will - I'll go away with you and we'll make love all day, every day and you'll forget all about your precious Maria and you'll want me instead. Just see if you don't."

When the weekend came, Betty and Kellner set sail for the Isle of Man again. Once more Kellner allowed her to skipper the boat and she pleased him by turning onto the correct heading without having to be instructed. Betty was a quick learner. They settled down on course and were doing a steady fifteen knots when Betty asked if it was okay to open the throttles and give the engines a two-minute burn. Kellner gave her the thumbs up and the cabin cruiser leapt over the waves. Betty was in a hurry to meet her young artist again, she wanted him to make a start on the painting.

Kellner's week-end business diary was full of appointments, the deals he hoped to set up would all bring in plenty of cash. But there was something else that pleased him even more than the chance of lucrative business; it was that Betty would be with him for the whole week-end. He reflected on how his life had changed since he met her and he knew he couldn't live without her. He watched admiringly as she made a minor adjustment to their heading and he remembered his promise to sail around the world with her. It was a promise he was determined to keep and in a few months, after concluding his business in the Isle of Man and Blackpool, he would start divorce proceedings and ask Betty to marry him. Marcus made a quick mental calculation – Christmas - by Christmas at the latest; all deals should be done and dusted. At Christmas he would ask Betty to marry him.

Martin Kershaw met them on the quay at Douglas. Kellner suggested that after a drink at the hotel, he should take Betty to his studio so he could make a start on the portrait. "The sooner it's done, the sooner I can have her back for myself," he smiled. He arranged for a car to take them to Martin's cottage and told Betty that he would send the driver back in the evening to pick her up in good time for dinner. "See you later, darling," said Marcus as he waved them off.

Martin led Betty into his studio, sat her down on a chair and without saying a word began to paint her portrait. He worked silently for about an hour until Betty became bored. She was tired of sitting. Languidly she stood up and started to take off her dress.

"What are you doing?" Martin sounded alarmed.

"What d'you think?" said Betty. "Look, is that the couch over there, is that where you want me to lie down and pose for you?" She glanced at the canvas on his easel. "Hmm, that's nice, but this should be better," she said, stepping out of her underwear.

"Okay," Kershaw agreed and when she was naked except for her jewellery he led her to the couch and showed her how to pose for him. "Take off the necklace, but please wear the earrings," he said, "I'll call the painting, "Girl Wearing Diamond Earrings."

"Call it what you like," said Betty, she lay comfortably on the couch and watched with interest as he began to paint.

Martin worked on, his face set, uncommunicative. Betty couldn't cope with this silence. She blurted out, "Oh, for fuck's sake, Martin, say something."

The coarseness of her language shook Martin; he had never heard a woman swear like that before. He laid down his brushes and came over to the couch. "Don't you know why I'm so quiet, Betty? Don't you know what's troubling me?" His thick hair fell forward as he knelt beside her and when he tried to smooth it back his hands were trembling.

"No, I don't know," Betty's tone was contemptuous.

"I adore you, Betty. Can't you tell?" And he began to stutter. "I want to m-marry you Betty – if you'll have me. I want to marry you."

Martin's proposal of marriage was a shock for which Betty was totally unprepared. Propositions of a sexual nature - yes, she was always ready to deal with those, in fact she'd had so many she'd lost count. But this time it was different; this was for her, Betty Williams, someone actually wanted to marry her and it had nothing to do with the selling and buying of sex. She suddenly felt contrite. "I'm sorry I shouted like that, Martin. Sorry I was such a cow. But this is a bit sudden, isn't it? I mean we hardly know one another......" And that was all Betty could think of to say.

But now that Martin had blurted out his proposal, he regained his confidence and had plenty to say for both of them. "When I was standing in the corner of the room and you were surrounded by all those men, I looked at you and I knew. I knew the very first time I saw you, that you were the girl I wanted to marry. Say "yes" Betty, then we can come out in the open and tell Marcus. You're fabulous, beautiful, wonderful! I love you, Betty, and I want the world to know about it and celebrate with us."

Betty almost panicked. Martin knew about Marcus, but he didn't have any idea about Tim or the other men in her life. He didn't know about the money she was saving, money she'd hidden, money ready for the day she ran away with Tim. She had no love at all for Martin, yet she couldn't afford to lose him. He was the first man who had asked her to marry him, her first chance of any real security. Eventually she managed to say, light heartedly, "Thanks Martin, I'm really, really flattered, but you've sprung it on me a bit quick, haven't you? I need more time. Give me time to think about it, will you? Tell you what. Christmas, I'll let you have my answer by Christmas. What we've talked about just now, let's keep it our secret until then. I've got two weeks holiday coming up, I arranged it a long time ago with my boss. Just think Martin, we'll have two weeks to get to know each other better, much better, you know what I mean?"

Martin Kershaw didn't need words to tell him what Betty meant, her look explained everything. He took out a key from his pocket and gave it to her. "It's the key to the cottage, Betty. It's yours now. You keep it, come and go whenever you please. I'll always be here for you; you can rely on me for anything – anything." He caressed the outline of her face and without saying more he returned to the easel and started to paint.

Betty was still holding the key to the cottage in her hand as she posed. Martin said that the key was symbolic – it was the key to their freedom to love one another.

CHAPTER THIRTEEN

THE DAY AFTER MARIA AND Anne returned from Paris, Betty could hear voices in Mrs Martinelli's garden and she recognised Tim's laughter.   Standing outside the kiosk to get a better view, she positioned herself so that she could observe Maria and Tim without them seeing her. The couple were holding hands and behaving like love-sick kids. They walked up and down inspecting Tim's newly widened borders, sometimes they would stop and kiss.   "Pathetic, bloody pathetic," she muttered and stormed back inside the kiosk, banging down the counter flap so hard that even the boldest of the seagulls sought safety in flight.   Betty didn't even notice the screaming gulls, she was too busy hatching her plan, a plan to put an end to Tim's relationship with Maria Martinelli.

That evening Marcus and Betty intended to dine at their favourite restaurant. Looking through the window before they went inside, Betty could see Tim at a table with Maria and their friends. Maria leaned towards Tim; she was wearing a midnight blue, silk cheongsam which shimmered as she moved. Her black hair was cut in a fringe to match the fashion of the oriental dress and she looked vivacious and beautiful in a way Betty had never noticed before. When Tim took Maria's hand and pressed it to his lips, she felt sick with envy. Impulsively, she turned away from the window, "I don't feel like eating in this place tonight, Marcus. Let's go somewhere else."

Kellner didn't ask why she had changed her mind, if Betty wanted to dine elsewhere then so be it. "Sure, that's fine by me, darling," he said, "How about that hotel on the front, you know the one? We'll get a table by the window and watch the ships go by. I wish we could sail away, Betty, sail the seas and explore the world together. Just you and me." Betty laughed as if he was joking. "No, I mean it. I'm serious. Think about it, please, for me."

She pretended to be touched by his romantic ideas, "There's nothing I'd like better, Marcus, with you in command I'd go anywhere - do anything.....!" she kissed him on the lips and Kellner thought he was the luckiest man on earth to be loved by the gorgeous Betty. He tucked her arm under his and together they set off for the hotel on the sea front to watch the ships go by.

Meanwhile, in Cecilia and Joseph's restaurant, Anne and Maria's welcome-home party was in full swing and there was an outburst of laughter when Tim told his friends that when he saw first saw Maria in the blue dress he didn't recognise her, "I thought she was a young Chinese girl, giving me the eye."

"Chinese or not," said Anne. "I'll have you know the Anna May Wong look cost Maria a small fortune in Paris."

"Who's Anna May Wong?" Tim's innocent question was greeted by more laughter. "Well, if she's half as beautiful as Maria then she'll be alright," he said.

Maria wanted to tell them all about Josephine Baker's show at the Moulin Rouge but with so much chatter going on she couldn't get a word in edgeways. And now, just as there was a lull, Anne took the opportunity to describe the Sunday mass at Notre Dame Cathedral where she had prayed for the repose of the soul of her dear Jack.

"Rest his soul," said Michael's father, Francis, crossing himself, devoutly.

Maria felt that the moment had passed for chatting about dance revues and asked what Father MacDonald had talked about on the Sunday they were in Paris. "Prayer, my dear Maria, prayer," Francis answered - "The raising up of the mind and heart to God," and having said that he closed his eyes. Maria couldn't make up her mind, had Francis nodded off or was he showing them all how to pray?

Michael didn't attend mass on a regular basis, but he had been there on that particular Sunday and so he was able to pick up where his father had left off, "Father Macdonald told us quite bluntly – "You can't do deals with God.""

Maria, who hadn't been paying a great deal of attention until now, suddenly sat up and took notice. "What's that got to do with the raising of the mind and heart to God?"

"Rather depends on what you raise your mind and heart to Him for, I guess," said Michael patiently.

"How do you mean?" asked Tim.

"Well, suppose I raise my mind and heart up to God and I say to Him, "Hey God, let me back the winner of the 2.30 at Doncaster today and I promise to stop cheating on my wife." Is that clear enough for you?"

Cecilia who was sitting next to Joseph and enjoying being waited on for a change, said sanctimoniously, "Surely people don't pray like that?"

"Maybe they do," said Michael, "You scratch my back; I'll scratch yours. Surely you've met people like that, Cecilia, you know, people who wouldn't lift a finger to help anybody unless they got something in return? Perhaps they try it on with the Almighty as well?"

Michael's explanation troubled Maria's conscience, all those prayers and promises she had made for a small miracle to happen by Christmas so she could marry Tim, wasn't she trying to do a deal with Him as well?

By now most of their gaiety had fizzled out. Everyone was tired and Michael offered to drive his Dad and Anne home. But Anne said she'd like to spend one more night with Maria for company, "As long as that ghost isn't there to haunt us, Maria!"

Anne went off to bed soon after they arrived home, so that Tim and Maria could be alone together. Tim could see that Maria was worried. "You're thinking about what Michael and Father MacDonald said, aren't you?"

"Yes, it makes me angry realizing how stupid I was. Look at me, a grown woman and making all those silly, childish promises. And what I've put you through...."

"All you wanted was a little miracle to happen so we could get married in church and I wouldn't be arrested. How can you blame yourself for that?"

"Well, I've made my mind up. I'm going to do what I should have done right from the start, only this time I'm going to be open and honest about it and I'm not going to be so selfish."

"How do you mean?"

"After Michael's called for Anne and taken her home in the morning, I'll tell Rosie not to bother tidying your room, I'll do it instead, Tim......."

"But what's that got to do with it?"

"I'll come to your room and tidy it up for the last time. We'll pack up all your belongings and bring them up to the house. And when we get here, I want us to live as we would if we were husband and wife. Now what do you say to that, Tim Ryan?"

"I do," said Tim, solemnly.

"In that case I now pronounce us husband and wife," said Maria. "And now you may kiss the bride...."

Tim could hardly bear to part with Maria that night. On the way to his room he said to himself, over and over again, that it was going to be the last time he would have to walk away from her. From tomorrow, and all the tomorrows after that, they would always live together.

He unlocked his door and switched on the light. There was a damp feel about the place so he lit the oil stove and decided to let it burn all night. He opened the window to have fresh air coming into the room while he was sleeping.

Then he locked the door and hung the key on its hook before getting undressed. When he slipped between the sheets they felt as cold as ice, but the room was warming up now and he watched the glow from the stove until he was mesmerised by it and fell asleep.

Just how long he had been asleep before the dream started he didn't know. Or was it a dream? He couldn't be sure; everything that was happening seemed so real. He thought he could see Maria. He could see her in the dim light thrown out by the oil stove. She was standing in the middle of the room naked and her dress was lying in a heap on the floor at her feet. He felt a tug on the bedclothes as they slid off the bed and the night air blowing in through the open window made him shiver. The bed creaked and he saw Maria again in the flickering light of the oil stove, he was lying on his back now, and Maria straddled him, settling herself back on her heels. Silently, she set up some sort of hypnotic rhythm as she began to rock gently forwards and backwards, backwards and forwards. He saw the vague outline of her face just before he felt her lips settle on his lips. Her lips were soft, and the taste of them made him feel dizzy as if he'd been drinking too much wine. He wanted her lips to stay there but she moved away, trailing her fingers lightly down the full length of his body, touching him so gently that he felt he was burning, that he was on fire; he stretched up his arms reaching for her, crying out, "Maria! Maria." The sound of his own voice broke his dream and woke him. A woman kneeled over him, it was – Betty!"

Bewildered and still half asleep, he heard her say, "I want you, Tim. Love me, Tim. Love me." With an effort that made him feel he was saving himself from drowning, he managed to raise himself off the bed and away from her. He stumbled over to the wall to switch on the light, still thinking it must have been a dream. But when he turned back, Betty was there, sitting on the bed, waiting for him.

"For Christ's sake Betty, why, just tell me why you are doing this to me?"

"All I wanted was to make you feel good, Tim. We've always got other people round us, so I came to you here, just to be alone, to make you happy. Don't be angry, Tim."

"I am angry and if you really want to make me happy get up, get dressed and let's get you out of here." He was wide awake now and his voice was harsh. "Just look at the time. It's nearly three o'clock." Betty fiddled around with the bed covers. "Stop wasting time. What the hell are you looking for?"

"My hair ribbon," Betty, produced it from under the covers and held it up for him to see and smiled innocently.

"Okay, but hurry," Tim said. His door key was still hanging on its hook where he had left it. "How the hell did you get in here, Betty?" he demanded. Then he saw a key lying in the middle of the table.

"Where did that come from?"

"It belonged to Jake. He gave it to me. It's a spare."

"And that's how you got into this room on my first day, isn't it? You lied to me when you told me that the door wasn't locked."

"Sorry, I just wanted to get to know you and that seemed to be the best way." Betty shrugged her shoulders. "Nobody got hurt, did they?"

"No, but if Mrs. Martinelli had come into the room just two minutes earlier, neither of us would be here today." Tim pointed to the key on the table, "Jake's spare key stays there," he said, firmly. "Now young lady, get dressed and let's get you home."

"You're taking me, Tim?" Betty sounded surprised.

"Look Betty, it's nearly half past three in the morning and its dark. Of course I'm taking you home. You don't know who could be lurking about outside this time of night." Betty could tell by the tone of his voice that he felt protective towards her and she drew some comfort from that.

They stepped out into the rain and Betty slipped her arm through his. As they walked, Tim forgot his anger and with genuine concern and interest he asked, "What about Marcus Kellner, Betty? He must think a lot of you, I know he gave you a special necklace and earrings, Joseph told me, he saw him give you the present in the restaurant on your birthday."

"Marcus is really sweet. Those diamonds are worth a fortune. I think he's going to ask me to marry him, sometime." But she was careful not to tell Tim about Martin Kershaw and his proposal of marriage, that was a secret between Martin and herself; well, at least for the time being.

They had arrived at the house and Tim was pleased to see that Betty had listened to his advice about key security. She opened the front door and they went into the hall together and stood at the door of her flat. "Well," said Tim "I know Marcus Kellner is older than you, but many a girl would be glad to be in your shoes, Betty, why don't you consider his offer?"

Betty laughed, and there was a touch of scorn in her voice, "I know what you're up to Tim Ryan, you're trying to get me married off, aren't you? You want me out of your hair so that you can be all lovey-dovey with that Mrs. Martinelli. Anyway, I'll be out of everyone's hair soon; Mrs. Martinelli's giving me two weeks holiday." She fumbled in her purse for the key to the flat. "Coming in?"

"I don't think that's a good idea, Betty," he said, smiling at her persistence.

"Suit yourself."

"Have a good holiday, Betty, and look after that grandma of yours. Make sure she gets better. Give her my best wishes, okay?"

"Fancy you remembering my Grandma; you're a kind man, Tim Ryan. Now pull the door closed behind you as you go." Tim closed the heavy door and waited until he heard the key turn in the lock before he walked away.

For reasons that he couldn't understand he felt sorry for Betty and he wondered if she would marry Marcus Kellner - Joseph said the man was crazy about her. Tim thought that Betty couldn't do better than settle down; good for her and good for him too, then she would leave him alone. His thoughts turned to Anne. Lovely, kind Anne, why did she dislike Betty so intensely? Even Maria didn't know the answer to that one.

And Maria, bless her, she always said that there was good in Betty and that given the right sort of guidance she would become a much better person, but not one of Maria's friends agreed with her.

The rain was torrential now, and by the time Tim arrived home, he was well and truly soaked. He flung his coat on a chair and towelled his head dry before getting undressed. Tired out, he left his clothes in a heap on the floor. He shivered and started to cough. The damp night air had chilled him to the bone and his head ached. He pulled the covers up over his shoulders and willed himself to go to sleep just as he had done in the old days when he huddled up in the freezing cold under deck chairs on the beach.

Maria woke him up; she was banging on the door and calling out his name. He opened the door wrapped in a blanket and stood aside to let her in. It was nearly nine o'clock. "Come on sleepy head," she called out cheerfully, "Michael's taken Anne home already and Betty's been to see me, I've paid her two weeks holiday money plus bonus and she's gone away singing and dancing. And here you are, morning's almost over and you're still lying in your bed. Don't tell me you've forgotten what day this is, Tim Ryan?I thought you'd be dressed and ready to carry me over the threshold by now." She started tidying the bed while he washed and dressed, folding the bedclothes and chatting away merrily. Then suddenly, she was quiet, ominously quiet. Tim called out, "What's wrong Maria?"

She was turning something over in her hands, over and over, until she held it up for him to see - a pair of silk stockings! She tossed them on the table and then collapsed into a chair. Tim was horrified; it looked as if life was draining away from her. "Oh God, let me die, let me die. Please God, let me die!" she sobbed. The whole of her body shook; tears ran down her face and fell onto the table beside the stockings.

In a flash Tim realized what had happened. He could see Betty now, rummaging in the bed and holding up the hair ribbon for him to see. The cunning little devil, she hadn't been looking for her hair ribbon at all; she had been smuggling in the stockings and hiding them between the sheets.

Tim felt like crying too, he tried to put his arm round Maria's shoulders to comfort her. She almost spat at him. "Don't touch me. Don't come near me. Keep away from me." Angrily, she pushed the stockings off the table.

"Please Maria, believe me, I haven't done anything wrong. It's not like that. Please listen to me."

Maria's eyes were wild with anger. "No, hypocrite, you listen to me. No wonder you said you could wait for me as long as it takes. Wait for me? You must have been very contented - working your way through all those whores who came to Blackpool for the summer. Been a good season for you, has it? How many have you had in this bed then, ten, twenty?" She saw his wet clothes lying on the chair and on the floor. "Oh my God, even on the last night before coming to live with me, you couldn't wait. You just couldn't wait, could you? You went out in the rain and brought somebody back." Gripping the edge of the table, she stood up. "That's the truth of it, isn't it?" Then exhausted, she sank down into the chair again, and between sobs she said, "I thought you were the right one Tim, I've waited such a long time for you."

"I've waited too, Maria – all my life, not just for a few years."

Maria ignored his answer; she was fumbling with the chain round her neck. She unfastened the clip and flung the engagement ring and the chain away from her.

"Oh no Maria, don't do that. Please, Maria, not the ring..." And he began coughing until he almost choked.

Maria made her way to the door, but hearing his distress, she stopped and turned back, "You can stay until the spring when the weather gets warmer, but after that I want you to go away from here. Don't try to come to the house to see me. I don't want to see you again, not ever!" Tim watched her go up the path; she opened the kitchen door and without a backward glance went into the house. The door slammed shut behind her.

Chapter Fourteen

Michael spotted Tim about two miles out of Blackpool, staggering around like a drunk.   He stopped the car and ran to him, supporting him as he leaned against a wall, retching and coughing. "You'll be okay now, Tim. Come on, get into the car. I'll take you home."

"I can't go back, Michael. I'll explain - something's happened with Maria..."

"I know what's happened, that's why I'm here. Get in the car man, you're ill." He took Tim's arm and helped him to the car.   Tim slumped onto the seat, too weak to resist.

"Where you taking me?"

"Anne's. Get a hot bath, something to eat and then to bed, you look terrible."

"I'm not sleeping at Anne's." Tim was insistent.

"Suit yourself; sleep in your own room at the bottom of the garden then. But no more walkabouts, you're far enough up the creek as it is, okay?"

They travelled in silence until they came within a stone's throw of Anne's, then Michael said with disappointment in his voice, "You didn't say goodbye to Anne or me when you left. I thought we were your friends, Tim?"

"Sorry Michael, I didn't feel well and after that bust up with Maria my head hurt and I couldn't work anything out, except to get away from Blackpool. And I didn't think you'd want to see me, anyway."

"Apology accepted. So what's your side of it then, Tim?"

Michael switched off the engine and listened while Tim coughed and spluttered through the story of Betty's night time visit.

"She's obsessed," said Michael when Tim had finished. "She'll try again you know, she won't give up." He shook his head and then in a sly pretence of puzzlement, he said, "It's no use, I just can't figure out what it is that you've got Tim Ryan, but it sure is something that women go for. Take Maria for instance, despite all the bad things she imagines you've done to her, I know she still loves you. And I'll lay any odds you like she's still in the house crying her eyes out because you've left her." Then he added, "But worst of all, knowing Maria, I bet she's feeling guilty."

"Guilty? Maria's got nothing to feel guilty about."

"She heard you coughing, didn't she? She thinks she's sent you out in the cold to die."

"I don't want her to feel guilty, Michael, but I hope you're right about her still loving me, I don't think I can go on living without her." He sounded feeble and weary now.

"Get better first, that's what Maria would want," said Michael, confidently. "Then you can talk to her. And this time we'll make her listen."

"But don't mention Betty to Anne, okay?"

"For God's sake Tim, why not? Oh, alright," he promised as Tim started to splutter again. "If it's that important to you, I won't mention her."

Anne was waiting for them and so was Michael's father, Francis. Anne took one look at Tim, "Oh, my poor Tim, what's happened to you?" And without waiting for an answer she sat him down in an easy chair and said "I'll pop upstairs and run you a hot bath. Meantime, you talk to Francis and Michael. Then when you've had a bath you can have a meal and then we'll take you back to rest in your own bed. Now don't argue, there's a good boy."

Michael waited until he thought he could hear Anne moving around upstairs, then he said to Tim, "Why didn't you want me to say anything about Betty in front of Anne?"

"Well, Anne's Maria's best friend, isn't she? And if she knew what had happened she'd be off like a shot to tell Maria and then what? Betty might get the sack, Michael."

"Good God! Betty doesn't need the job, Tim, and she deserves the sack. And as for money, she must be loaded, with the prices she charges she could retire today if that's what she wanted. And those diamonds Kellner gave her, they must be worth a bob or two."

"It's not the money, it's her grandma I'm thinking about," said Tim. "Eighty years old and ill and her granddaughter getting the sack and disgraced, what sort of news would that be for her?"

Michael looked at Tim in amazement. "Betty hasn't got a grandma, Tim, her grandparents on both sides are dead, have been for years." Francis, resting in the corner, opened his eyes and nodded his head in agreement.

"She told me she had a grandma and was looking after her." said Tim, lamely.

"Did she now? Well, if she told you that she was pulling both your legs," said Michael. Tim looked over at Michael's father; even the saintly Francis couldn't resist a cynical smile.

After Tim's bath and a meal, Michael took him back with Anne to his room at Maria's and left Anne to do her best for him. She made up Tim's bed and handed him clean pyjamas. Then she busied herself at the sink and filled a hot water bottle for him while he undressed and got into bed. "You'll have to make do with cuddling that for the time being. Keep warm Tim and I'll pop in and see how you are in the morning."Before Tim could thank her, she had closed the door behind her and hurried off to report to Maria.

"I did warn him, Maria, I warned Tim about Betty Williams the first day I met him. She's a devil, that girl." In addition to telling Maria about her warning to Tim, Anne repeated all the information she had gleaned by eavesdropping on Michael and Tim's conversation and by putting two and two together she had pretty well got the whole picture.

Maria was still studying that picture long after Anne left, and the more she studied it the more her feeling of guilt grew. Tim's reason for not wanting Betty to get the sack in case the bad news upset her sick grandmother, now that was typical Tim Ryan, always concerned for others..... the fact that the grandma didn't exist wasn't important, he hadn't known that. All the harsh words she had spoken, her lack of trust in him – her readiness to jump to the wrong conclusion - in the end she couldn't stay away from Tim any longer, she almost ran down the garden path to him.

Half way down the path she paused and panicked, what if Tim told her to leave him alone? What if he told her that he didn't want to see her anymore because she'd said she didn't trust him? She stopped and looked around the garden hoping to feel calm again. It was a dull sort of a day and the light was already beginning to fade. Then she saw "Mr. Tufty," Tim's favourite shrub, growing in the corner of the garden, its blossom glowing golden in the dusk. Convinced that this was a good omen, her mood changed and she ran on towards the old store room. She stood under Tim's window and looked in. Vaguely, in the dim light, she saw him sprawled across the bed. He must have been sweating and taken off his pyjama jacket, it lay on the floor with a heap of bed clothes beside it. He was turning his head restlessly as if he was having a night mare.

Maria pushed against the door, and in her desperate hurry to help Tim she left it open, swinging on its hinges. Tim was lying at an awkward angle and it made it difficult for Maria to lift his head back onto the pillow. His skin was cold to the touch so she piled on all the blankets she could find for him. Then she lit the oil stove and put the kettle on to re-heat his hot-water bottle. Finally she closed and locked the door. The silk stockings, the chain and the engagement ring were tangled together under the table where she had flung them that morning. She noticed a spare door key lying on the table but she paid little attention to it, she had Tim Ryan to look after.

At last she had him warmly tucked up. But he was still restless. In his nightmare, he found himself enveloped in a cloud of black smoke that had drifted across the battlefield; it was choking him and pinned down under the twisted frame of his broken gun-carriage, he couldn't move. "Help me, help me," he tried to cry out, "I'm choking, help me." He woke up then, gasping for breath. "My horses, all dead, all dead," he sobbed, "Save me!"

Maria lay on the bed beside him and she held him close like a child, "Shush, shush my darling Tim. You're safe now; you're with me, Tim, with Maria," telling him over and over again that the war had ended, there was no smoke to choke him, he was safe with her. As she stroked his forehead, she realised that he was feverish; his skin which had felt so clammy was now burning hot. Maria got off the bed and soaked a towel in cold water. She sponged his face to cool him but the heat from his skin almost instantly dried the towel. She found a bowl to fill with water to put beside the bed and more times than she could count she sponged him and refilled the bowl. She felt weary, but she could cope with tiredness, it was when he became delirious and started to babble about the smoke and dead horses that she was frightened and wanted to weep.

About three in the morning, she noticed a change in him, his breathing had become almost normal and his coughing had stopped. "Thank God, he's sweated it out," she said aloud. Relieved and exhausted, she crept into the bed and Tim slept peacefully cradled beside her. When they woke up it seemed natural to them that they should be lying there, together.

"I love you," said Tim.

"And I love you, Tim Ryan."

They lay in each other's arms for a long time before they made love, and then afterwards, for a while, they drifted in and out of sleep.

"Was it alright, Maria?" he asked between kisses.

"Magic," said Maria. "Magic."

"Magic, for both of us," said Tim, sighing with contentment.

CHAPTER FIFTEEN

BY THE TIME BETTY RETURNED from the Isle of Man in late October, the illuminations had ended. The kiosks were all closed and locked; Blackpool was battening down the hatches and preparing for winter.

Tim and Maria decided not to say anything to Betty when she turned up for work, they would carry on as though nothing had happened. Betty started to manage the gift shop in town and Maria agreed to her opening up the kiosk again when the new season started in the spring of 1926. That suited Betty just fine. When Maria asked if she had enjoyed her holiday Betty told her she had, but she didn't mention her grandma and she didn't tell Maria or anybody else where she had been and what she had been up to.

Some interesting things had developed for Betty while she was on the Isle of Man; she had become quite fond of

Martin Kershaw and she had promoted him to number three in the pecking order behind Tim and Marcus, although she really didn't regard him as a serious contender and when he had finished the portrait for Kellner and the special painting for himself, she rewarded him in the only way she knew how and Martin vowed he would do anything for her. He told her she had only to ask, whatever it was, he would do it. He declared his love wildly, passionately, in language Betty hardly understood. Sometimes she wondered if he was mad and that aspect of his personality intrigued and excited her.

Kellner's business on the Isle of Man had come to a successful conclusion. The profits from the venture were enormous and he asked Betty to marry him. Her reaction to his proposal was one of feigned surprise and she lied skilfully, saying it was so unexpected she required a little time for it to sink in before she could give him her answer. When Kellner asked how much time, Betty assured him that he would have her answer by Christmas. Kellner could scarcely believe his luck, Christmas was only a matter of a few weeks away, just a few short weeks to wait and then it would be his best Christmas, ever. He was very pleased with Martin's portrait of Betty, it was perfect. He took it to the cabin cruiser and hung it above the bed, the bed in which Betty always made him feel young again.

But Betty wasn't happy, even though she had now been honoured by two proposals of marriage, the only proposal she wanted was one from Tim. She could see that her plan to make Mrs. Martinelli jealous had failed and Mrs. Martinelli wasn't going to tell Tim to go away and never come back, in fact quite the opposite, they seemed closer and happier than ever. Betty didn't waste much time hatching another plan, she already knew what she had to do. It was important to choose the right day for the plan to be successful and also it had to be a day that would have the greatest impact, a day she would remember forever. She thought about it for a while and then it came to her. Brilliant! It had to be Mrs. Martinelli's birthday, December 23rd. Betty almost hugged herself, the birthday present she had in mind would be totally unexpected. She felt she could hardly wait to see the look on Mrs. Martinelli's face when she delivered it to her personally. Now what could be nicer than that!

A week after Betty started work at the gift shop; Tim, Anne and Francis were just finishing lunch at Maria's when Michael came in bursting with news.

Tim greeted him, "What's up Michael, you won the Irish Sweepstake?"

"No such luck. Can I have a drink first, then I'll tell you, and while you're about it make it a double."

"That's alright, Tim, I'll get it," said Maria and she brought Michael a large measure of Scotch in a tumbler and a jug of water. Michael poured a drop of water into the whisky and returned the jug to Maria. "Don't want to drown it," he said and downed the drink in one. "Oooh! I needed that."

"Another?"

"No, no thanks Maria. That was fine."

"Why don't you sit down and tell us what's making you so excited?" said Maria.

"The editor's bringing out a "special," you'll hear them calling it out on the streets; it's been timed to coincide with folk going home from work."

Francis was feeling sleepy and his eyes were almost closing when he heard Michael mention the word "special." He sat upright in his chair, he knew when newspapers brought out a "special" it often meant there had been some catastrophe and he wondered what the news was this time.

"There's not been another pit explosion, has there?" said Tim, anxiously.

"No, no Tim, nothing like that. Anybody guess what's happened?" Michael paused and looked around to see if there were any takers but there weren't, "It's Jake and Elsie, I found them this morning!"

They were all struck dumb by the news. When they finally got their voices back, they all began to speak at once. Michael had to hold up his hand and ask if they wanted to hear the rest of his story.

"How are they? Maria asked, concerned for Jake and Elsie's welfare. "They're all right, Michael, aren't they?"

"No!" said Michael bluntly.

"Oh my God, they aren't, they aren't ...?" Maria couldn't bring herself to finish the question.

"You found them, Michael? What about the police, I thought they were supposed to be looking for them?" Tim said,

"How I found them was by a stroke of luck, really. I was up early; I wanted to get some stuff sorted out in my mind for my column. Walking always helps me think. It must have been about seven thirty and I'd got as far as the Cuckoo's Nest when I saw these two young lads approaching. They had a small dog with them playing a game, the boys would take it in turn to throw a stick into the undergrowth and the dog would shoot off to find it. It was amazing how clever the dog was, no matter how thick the undergrowth, it always came back with the same stick between its teeth, except for the last time the boys threw the stick it didn't come back. We could hear it barking somewhere in the bushes, and despite everything the boys did to try and coax it, the dog wouldn't come back. The youngest boy began to cry, I heard him say they'd be late for school. That's when I helped them find the dog. I found it digging into a shallow ditch, yelping and barking at what was left of Jake and Elsie. By the looks of things they'd been dead for some time and it was no accident - Jake and Elsie had been stabbed to death!"

Anne shuddered, "Murdered! Oh, my God, poor Jake, poor Elsie."

Francis made the sign of the cross, "God rest their souls."

"What about the children, they didn't see Jake and Elsie's bodies did they?" Maria asked anxiously.

"No, no. They were quite some distance away when I discovered the bodies. I took the dog by the collar and carried it to them. The boys ran off home and I went to the police station." "When school finishes today I bet the Cuckoo's Nest is swarming with kids," said Tim. "My mother always said children make the world's best detectives."

"It'll be out of bounds," said Michael. "Right now, the park's cordoned off and the police are checking every blade of grass for clues."

Maria disappeared for a few minutes. When she returned Tim was surprised to see she was wearing her coat. "Where are you going, Maria?"

"To see Betty at the shop. Her best friend Elsie's dead; can you imagine the shock she'll get if she reads about it in a newspaper? I'm sorry everyone, I've got to go to her. I've got to tell her before she finds out like that."

"Of course, of course you must go," said Anne shaking her head, sadly. "I've never liked the Williams girl, but you are right. Her friend murdered, what's the world coming to? Wait for us Maria, Francis and I will walk part way to the shop with you, it's time we were going home, anyway." Within a couple of minutes she was helping Francis into his coat.

"I'd take you in the car," said Michael, "But I've arranged to receive an important phone call here, at Maria's."

"That's alright. Fresh air will do us good."

"Tim, why don't you stay here with, Michael," said Maria. "I expect you'll have plenty to talk about."

As soon as they were alone, Tim asked Michael about the bodies, "I didn't want to ask in front of Anne and Maria, but what did you mean when you said you found "what was left" of Jake and Elsie?"

"Well, it looked as if bits of their flesh had been eaten away by animals."

"God, no, what sort of animals?"

"Foxes, maybe?"

"Ugh! Enough to give you the creeps," said Tim and he lapsed into silence.

Michael could understand Tim's silence; the grisly picture of Jake and Elsie being eaten by animals was enough to subdue anybody. But that wasn't Tim's reason for being quiet; he needed time to pluck up the courage to ask another question. In the end he came out with it. "Look

Michael, can I ask you something and I won't be offended if you don't want to give me an answer?"

"I can always say no."

"Okay then, it's about Anne. Why does a kind, loving person like Anne hate Betty Williams so much?"

"Well, well, well. So that's why you were quiet. Here's me thinking your mind was still on Jake and Elsie being savaged by wild animals and all the time it was Anne you were concerned about."

"I am. I mean I was concerned about Jake and Elsie, Michael, but this other thing has been gnawing away at the back of my mind for ages. I was going to ask Anne, but something always held me back."

"Thank God you did hold back, Tim. If you had asked Anne it would have caused her a lot of distress. See, something happened once between Jack and Betty. I don't know exactly what, but Anne found out and that's when the hate started. Jack told me about it. Now, this is strictly between the two of us, okay?"

"She forgave Jack but she couldn't find it in her heart to forgive Betty, is that it? I won't say a word, Michael, I promise."

"Seems Anne could forgive, but not forget. But I know Anne and it's not in her nature to hate anybody. One day she'll forgive Betty, you'll see, and when that day comes she'll be very sorry that it took her so long."

The phone rang and Michael went into the hall to answer it. He returned to tell Tim that the police had just had a tip off. "They're on to something, got to go, keep you in the picture, okay?"

"Okay," said Tim, but he was talking to thin air. Michael could move very swiftly when he was on to something important.

Maria was late getting home. Betty had sobbed so much when she heard the news about Elsie and Jake that Maria took her home in a taxi and stayed with her until she thought she'd recovered enough to be left on her own. When she had suggested to Betty she should take some time off work, Betty wouldn't hear of it and said it would drive her nuts to be left in the flat on her own.

"So what did you decide?" said Tim.

"We decided working will help to keep her mind off Elsie and Jake's murder, so she'll be back in the shop, tomorrow."

The following morning, Maria and Tim had just finished breakfast when Michael arrived on the doorstep demanding tea and toast, saying he would collapse and die in front of their very eyes unless they fed him. Between mouthfuls he explained that he had been up all night staking out police headquarters. At six o'clock in the morning he had seen two police officers come out of the building, get into a car and drive away. He followed, keeping a discreet distance between them, hoping they didn't notice they were being tailed. In just a few minutes the police car stopped outside Betty's flat.

Michael said he pulled into the kerb and turned off his lights. He watched the policemen get out of their car and ring Betty's bell and she opened the door and they went inside. He thought he might be in for a long wait so he switched off his engine, his legs were freezing cold and he wished he'd borrowed one of Anne's warm travel-rugs. The police stayed at Betty's flat for about an hour.

Michael gave them a few minutes to get clear and then he rang Betty's front door bell.

She didn't invite him in, said she was getting ready for work and talked to him on the doorstep.

"How did she look?" asked Maria.

"Awful, she'd been crying by the look of her. I asked if she wouldn't be better off spending the day at home. She wouldn't have it, said that she preferred to be at work rather than stay in the flat on her own."

"That's what she told Maria," said Tim.

Michael nodded. "Elsie's death seems to have knocked the stuffing out of her. The girl I was talking to on the doorstep, didn't seem like the old Betty at all. She was like a little girl lost. And that's when I warned her to be careful....."

"Warned her? What's there to warn her about?" asked Tim and Maria.

"Well, she could be in terrible danger, couldn't she? I mean, whoever killed Elsie and Jake might think she was part of the same blackmailing gang and be out to get her as well."

"Oh, poor Betty," said Maria, "I'll go to the shop and stay with her and work full time until the danger passes. Well, you never know, it might help."

"And I'll be watching to see you're both safe," said Tim.

"I don't think you'll have to work there for more than a few days. I've got a feeling that things are coming to a head," said Michael.

"Thank God for that," said Maria.

"Although Betty didn't invite me in, I had the feeling that she was glad to have me there to talk to."

"You can't help being sorry for her, can you," said Tim sympathetically. "I mean losing your best friend and then to be told that you might be the next one to be murdered? Did she tell you anything about the police visit, Michael?"

"First, they asked if they could search her flat and then they searched Elsie's rooms."

"And?"

"They took something away from Elsie's flat. Betty was watching and she said they were whispering about it as though they had found something important."

"Wonder what that was?" said Tim.

"Don't know," said Michael, "But I intend to find out. Oh, and by the way, Betty heard one of the police officer's say that they were going to search Jake's room. So if that's the case they could be here at any time. You keep out of the way Tim, leave the talking to Maria and me, okay?"

The police arrived about nine to search the old store room, "Just a routine check," they assured Maria and to every one's relief they found nothing.

Early the following morning, Michael phoned. "I'm booking breakfast with you again, Tim, and I'm bringing the morning paper. You'd better warn Maria because she'll be in for a shock when she sees the headline."

Tim groaned. "Michael, what time is it?"

"Just after six. Hey! By the way, you took your time answering the phone didn't you?"

Tim said, "Come here before seven and I'll shoot you."

"See you in an hour then, give Maria my love."

Maria was preparing the breakfast when the doorbell rang. She called to Tim, "If that's Michael bring him in here, it's cosier in the kitchen."

"You sound happy this morning, Maria," said Michael. "Sorry if I'm the one to spoil it." He slapped the newspaper down on the table, "Front page again, folks. Don't say I didn't warn you." Maria was the first to read the headline. She uttered a cry of disbelief, "It says here that the police have taken Mr. Beswick in for questioning. You wrote that Michael; is it true? Surely you don't believe that he has anything to do with Jake and Elsie's murder? Mr. Beswick's not a murderer, he couldn't hurt a fly. I can't see him killing or threatening to kill anybody."

"No, I don't believe he had anything to do with it at all and I know for sure that Tim doesn't either. But the police must have a reason, Maria. They didn't invite Berwick down to the station just to have a cup of tea and a pleasant chat did they? We know they took something away from Elsie's flat; perhaps that's what they want to talk to him about?"

It was all too much for Maria. "I'll get the breakfast," she said. "Tell them to find the real murderer."

Tim and Michael looked at one another. How could they tell the police they'd got the wrong man? All they had was a hunch that Beswick didn't do it and they had no evidence to support their hunch.

Maria had cooked ham and eggs but Michael's news dampened their spirits and they ate without enjoyment. Tim broke the silence, "I think we should tell Maria all we know about Beswick," he said to Michael.

Michael agreed and Tim told Maria about the episode in the Cuckoo's Nest when he had to rescue Betty, who claimed Beswick had assaulted her. Then Michael repeated the story about Beswick's brief affair with Elsie and how Jake photographed him when he was having sex with her. "Fifty pounds, that's what Jake and Elsie were demanding before they would hand over the negative of Jake's photo. Just before they ran away, Elsie asked Betty to get the fifty pounds from Beswick saying that the money was something to come back to if things didn't work out with Jake. When Betty asked Beswick for the fifty pounds, he thought she was in on the blackmail racket with Jake and Elsie and she must have the negative. Betty swore she didn't have it...."

"Maybe it was hidden in Elsie's flat," speculated Tim, "I wonder if that's what the police found and took away with them? It could be the evidence they're using against Beswick. Poor devil, he's had such a lousy life, Maria, and I've got a feeling things are going to get a whole lot worse for him."

"Perhaps the police think that he killed them to put a stop to the blackmail," said Michael.

"But why didn't you tell me all of this before?" Maria was close to tears.

"Tim and I agreed not to. We didn't want to say anything to upset you or Anne, and what was the point, Maria, with the police after them we thought it was the last we would ever hear of Elsie and Jake. Murder never crossed our minds."

Maria seemed to accept this explanation. "Despite the blackmail, I don't believe Mr. Beswick murdered them, the man couldn't hurt a fly."

Michael shrugged his shoulders and made a move to the door. "Where are you going? asked Maria.

"Get some shut eye, for a start," said Michael.

"And after that, what?"

"Try and find the answers to a few things that are puzzling me."

"Can I ask what they are?" said Tim.

"Why not? The thing that bugs me most is this. Why did Jake and Elsie go to the Cuckoo's Nest when they'd packed their bags and were in a hurry to get away? It doesn't make sense to me. What do you think, Tim?"

"I agree. And what about the money and their bags, Betty said they had stacks of cash, enough to start up a business in any place they chose. They must have taken it with them, they were running away remember? So where's their luggage and their money, none of it's been found, has it?"

"That's what I've got to track down next and more besides, look, I'll phone you later this evening and let you know the score."

At eight o'clock in the evening the phone rang. "You answer it Tim," Maria said nervously.

Tim lifted the receiver to hear Michael say emotionally, "They've found the murder weapon - it was hidden in a toolbox in Beswick's garden shed! The police have officially charged him with the murder of Jake and Elsie!" Michael hung up and Tim broke the news to Maria.

CHAPTER SIXTEEN

NOVEMBER DIDN'T SUIT TIM, HE thought of the month as the saddest time of the year and All Souls Day marked the start of it. This year, the damp, chilly weather affected his chest and made him cough again. And just when he hoped the month couldn't bring any more misery, Michael had told them Mr.Beswick had been charged with the murder of Jake and Elsie. Tim was convinced this mild, unhappy, little man was not capable of committing such a terrible deed.

"I expect they're satisfied now they've got somebody locked up for it," said Maria, cynically.

"Michael's sure to help him, he'll come up with something that'll surprise everybody and get Beswick off the hook. Rely on it," said Tim, confidently.

Maria looked doubtful, "I hope you're right about Michael. Mr. Beswick needs all the help he can get."

Michael's editor had sent for him and he sat facing his boss across a somewhat battered, old oak desk. John Pickersgill was a big man with a ruddy complexion and iron-grey hair. He had a deep rough voice and spoke with a local northern accent. "No guesses as to why you're here eh, Michael? It's about those bodies you found. Now, I don't believe John Beswick killed that couple any more than you do. Beswick is my friend, known him ever since he came to Blackpool after the war. The police have got it wrong; all that rubbish about him murdering people, the man's incapable of hurting anybody." He paused and Michael wondered if it was an invitation for him to say something in defence of Beswick. He wasn't sure, so he remained silent.

Pickersgill lit a cigar, inhaled and then breathed out a cloud of smoke which seemed to fill the room before it mingled with the smoke from the open fire and disappeared up the chimney. "Now see here Michael, if anybody can solve this case, you can. But it's all a question of time, you'll be leaving us at the end of the year, and I can't help wondering if there's enough sand left in the glass to give you the time to do it? What do you think lad? Can you do it?"

"Yes sir," said Michael.

"Great!" Pickersgill slapped a hand on his desk. "Great! That's all I wanted to know. You want help? Just ask. You've got it."

"Okay sir, I will but I hope I'll manage on my own."

"I thought you'd say that."

Michael was John Pickersgill's protégé, and he had great confidence in him. There was no doubt about it, when Michael cracked the case, it would be the scoop of the year, maybe the newspaper's finest scoop ever, and his favourite reporter would go out in a blaze of glory! Oh, the pleasure of it, the editor scrunched up his toes inside his brogues just at the very idea. "Perhaps now's the time for me to tell you how sorry I'll be to lose you Michael, but I guess you know how I feel about that already. Look son, I've said it before and I'll say it again, a brilliant future awaits you out there, just remember when you're at the Manchester Sentinel you'll be working for the tops - the best. But first, I want you to find the murdering bastard who put my friend in jail. Will you do that for me Michael?"

Michael vowed to do that; it would be a small "thank you" for everything his boss had done for him. They shook hands and Michael left the office with all the assurance of youth to find the person or persons who had murdered Jake and Elsie.

Maria and Tim were concerned about the effect of Elsie's death on Betty. She rarely spoke unless spoken to and when she did reply her voice sounded flat, without interest. Maria worried about her. "You know, Tim, since Elsie died, Betty's forgotten how to smile."

Marcus Kellner was also concerned about Betty; it grieved him to see how unhappy she had become. Over and over again he tried to find ways to help Betty recover from the trauma of Elsie's murder. He tried the theatre, taking her to the best restaurants, dancing, cinema, but none of the outings changed her mood. Then Marcus remembered how exhilarated she had been at the wheel of the boat, sailing at full speed towards the Isle of Man. He arranged for a buoy to be placed about two hundred yards outside the entrance to the marina and another buoy placed a couple of miles further out to sea and with the help of some friends and approval granted by the coastguard, he organised timed solo races from the inner marker buoy round the outer buoy and back again. As a deliberate ploy, he didn't try to persuade Betty to compete. Instead he handed her a clipboard, a pair of binoculars and a stop-watch and asked her to record the timings. Betty accepted without demur and watched Marcus get ready to make the first solo run.

The races were a huge success and more and more boat owners decided they wanted to join in. As word spread around town a large crowd of spectators gathered at the marina to enjoy the fun and shout encouragement. After Betty had recorded a number of races she handed back the clipboard, binoculars and stopwatch to Marcus, "I'd like to have a go now," she said. Kellner nodded his agreement and without any farewell gesture Betty kicked off her high heels and boarded the cabin cruiser, she didn't even give Marcus a backward glance. So far his plan was working perfectly.

He made sure that she stayed within his sights as she cautiously manoeuvred her vessel through the lines of moored boats towards the inner marker. He watched her make the final turn towards the buoy, silently encouraging her, "That's it Betty, slowly now, slowly now, take your time, take your time. Marcus smiled, it was incredible, it seemed as if she could hear every word he was saying and was acting on his instructions. When the nose of the cabin cruiser reached the first buoy Betty flung the throttles wide open. Kellner pressed the button on his stopwatch. The roar that came from the twin Austin engines stilled the voices in the crowd for a few seconds, then the prow of the boat rose up out of the water and someone cried out, "Look! Look! It's flying!" The crowd took up the call, "Go girl! Go! Fly girl, fly!" They were still chanting as Betty and her vessel became a tiny dot on the horizon.

When Betty returned she was laughing. She hadn't made the best time, but that didn't matter, she was laughing at last. Kellner was jubilant!

Interest in solo racing around the markers soon waned, there were a few more days of competitions and races and then the sport was abandoned. But that didn't matter; it had achieved what Kellner had intended. Betty was no longer depressed. To his delight she seemed to enjoy his company again.

Maria was pleased to find Betty much more cheerful when she went to the shop to give her instructions before leaving for Glasgow to help Bernadette during the last days of her pregnancy. Bernadette's call had come sooner than expected and Maria quickly made arrangements for the business and then asked Anne to move into the house to stay with Tim until she came back.

Tim decided now would be as good a time as any to start some detective work and the first thing he wanted to investigate was the business of the missing suitcases. He didn't believe for one minute that Elsie and Jake had carried them all the way to the Cuckoo's Nest. The word was that Jake was lazy; Tim guessed the suitcases had been deposited somewhere safe, somewhere handy and ready to be collected later for their journey. And where else would they leave them, but in the railway left luggage office? Maybe he could crack the case himself and beat the experienced Michael Topliss to it! He would visit Betty at the gift shop to make sure she could identify the suitcases if she saw them and he'd try to persuade her to go to the left luggage office with Michael to search for them.

Through the shop window Betty saw Tim at the far end of the street. When he crossed the road her heart skipped a beat, perhaps he was coming to see her? The door opened and in he came. "What's this you're up to then, Tim? A case of when the cat's away, is that it?" she said teasingly.

Tim told Betty about his plan but it wasn't what Betty wanted to hear. She managed to swallow her disappointment and said that a policeman in plain clothes had been to see her a few days ago and asked the same sort of questions. She had actually gone with the policeman to the left luggage office and together they'd turned the place upside down and inside out without finding a trace of Elsie or Jake's cases. Betty tried her best to persuade Tim to stay and chat, but all he wanted to do now was go home and work out another plan. Betty waved to him as he left the shop, "Don't forget, come back anytime Tim, anytime."

In the evening, Michael came round to the house and Tim explained the disappointing outcome of his visit to see Betty. Michael sympathised, he was having a problem with the missing suitcases too. What he wanted to talk to Tim about was the murder weapon. Tim groaned. "God,

Michael, if there's one thing that's going to put the noose around Beswick's neck, it's that knife."

"The knife was a plant," Michael said, calmly. "The murderer put it there to implicate Beswick and, if my informant tells me right, that's what the police are beginning to think as well."

The possibility of the knife being planted in Beswick's shed had never occurred to Tim; perhaps he wasn't cut out to be a detective after all.

"Where's Anne?" asked Michael.

"Gone to confession, she'll be back soon."

"I wouldn't count on that," said Michael. "I know Anne. Once Father MacDonald kicks her out of the box, she'll be scouring the town for the latest news updates. I can't wait any longer for her, Tim, so when she comes back will you ask her a question for me?"

"What's that?"

"Ask Anne if Elsie had a Scottish grandmother. You can give me the answer when I call round tomorrow."

"Elsie, you did say Elsie?"

"That's right."

"Is it important?"

"Yes," said Michael. "Hope to tell you more tomorrow evening."

Michael was right about Anne being home late, Tim was getting ready for bed when she came in. They called goodnight to one another and Tim decided to leave the question of Elsie's grandmother until morning. He fell asleep with his mind full of speculations about the suitcases, the murder weapon and the missing money, perhaps the money had been the motive for the murder?

At two a.m. he was woken by Anne banging on his bedroom door. He switched on the light and she stumbled into the room.

"What is it Anne, you look as though you've seen a ghost."

Anne sat on the edge of his bed. "I have, I have. I didn't believe in ghosts but I've seen one now!"

"Come on Anne, let's go down to the kitchen and have a cup of tea and a chat, shall we?" Tim put on his dressing gown and helped her down the stairs.

Anne described what had frightened her. "Something woke me - it must have been the noise of the bedroom chair being knocked over. And then I saw the ghost, Tim, dressed all in black. I couldn't see its face, though it must have been standing right over me, watching. Then it seemed to run through the open door of my room and vanish, just vanish! When you went to bed last night, did you close your door?"

"Yes."

"Well, it was wide open when I came to wake you just now. The ghost must have been in your room as well, watching you while you slept."

Tim poured Anne another cup of tea and to reassure her he went off to inspect the doors and windows. There was nothing amiss. All the doors were locked and windows closed except for a window in his room which he had left open for fresh air and that was too small even for a child to crawl through. Somehow, he managed to convince Anne there was no way the ghost could come back. Gradually she relaxed and chatted about Bernadette, trying to guess whether the baby would be a boy or a girl and what first name would sound best with their surname, Bruce? Tim found the opportunity at last to slip in the question about Elsie; did she have a Scottish grandma?

"Of course she had, when she died last year she was over eighty. And a grand old lady she was, her name was Maggie Tulloch, famous for her knitting! Why did you ask about Maggie?"

"It was Michael who wanted me to ask you. It's something he needs for the paper."

Anne was pleased to think her information could be helping Michael. Relaxed and sleepy she was ready to go back to bed. "Time I had some shut-eye," she said and Tim went up the stairs with her. He did a final check of the doors and windows before he closed his own bedroom door.

Anne woke him up at eight o'clock next morning, handed him a cup of strong tea and asked if, after breakfast, he would help her put up the Christmas tree and decorations. "I promised Maria it would be all done by the time she got back."

They were hanging tinsel and baubles on the tree when Tim suddenly fell silent. "What are you brooding about, Tim?"

"Nothing," he said.

"It must be something. You were all right a minute ago and now you're all worried looking."

"Well, I was thinking about Mum and Dad. It must be nine or ten years since I spent Christmas with them. Maybe they think I'm dead. Maybe they're dead....?"

"Oh, you poor boy," Anne put her arms around him and hugged him. "Why don't you send them a Christmas card? At least you can let them know that you're alright."

Tim looked startled. "The Blackpool postmark, the police could trace me through that!"

"For goodness sake Tim, how could they? But if it makes you feel any better we'll get Michael to post the card from Manchester."

"Thanks, Anne, that would be great....."

Anne produced a Christmas card from her handbag, found a bottle of ink and a pen and sat Tim down at the table to write to his family.

Michael called in the evening as promised. "Hey, somebody's been busy since I left here yesterday," he said, "I like your tree and decorations, Tim." He noticed the holly. "Lot of berries this year, people say it's the sign of a cold winter."

"That's what they say in Yorkshire, too,"

"Must be right then! Anyway, the decorations look splendid. It'll make a bright homecoming for Maria, that's for sure."

"It was Anne's work, mostly."

"Where is the lovely Anne?"

"Gone to the pictures."

"Don't tell me, I know who she's gone to see, it's Rudolph Valentino and Bebe Daniels in "Monsieur Beaucaire."" He sighed. "Women, are nuts about this guy, Valentino. Remember the dance, Tim, with your hair sleeked straight back? You were his absolute double! It's true, I mean it."

Tim laughed. "Michael, don't you think I've enough trouble on my plate already without asking for more?"

"Talking of trouble, did you ask Anne the question about Elsie; did she have a Scottish grandma?"

"Yes, Maggie Tulloch."

Michael was excited, "I knew it, I knew it."

"What's the big deal? What's so important about Elsie's grandma?"

"Well, it solves one of the problems I had on my mind. I mean, it wasn't Betty who had a grandma, it was Elsie wasn't it? Doesn't that tell you something about Betty Williams?"

"Nothing we didn't already know - when it suits her, Betty tells lies. She lied about having a grandma and lied about the phone call when we were celebrating her birthday. She said a neighbour had phoned and told her that her grandma had a fall. All lies."

"Right, and the knitting, Tim, the knitting you saw on her settee, I'll wager she lied about that too. That was Elsie's knitting, not Betty's. I'd bet my last penny that Betty couldn't even cast on a stitch, never mind knit!"

"Okay so she makes up stories. What does that prove?"

"Tell me, what was it she said to you the first time she talked about Elsie and those suitcases? Can you remember?"

"She told me Elsie had decided to run away with Jake and then she packed her suitcase and went off to join him." Tim shrugged his shoulders. "That's all......."

Michael smiled. "That's what Betty told us and we believed her and the police believed her because they thought Jake had twigged they were onto him and so he'd packed his bag and scarpered."

"But you don't believe that?"

"No way, Betty tells lies; your words, Tim, not mine. Did she lie about them running away? I think she did. Suppose Jake and Elsie weren't running away? If they weren't running away they wouldn't need suitcases, would they? Suppose they'd gone up to the Cuckoo's just for a quick roll in the grass. They could have, just like anyone else ......"

"Okay, so you're saying Jake and Elsie went up to the park and got murdered?"

"Yes."

"But their rooms were cleaned out, their clothes, suitcases, everything they possessed, gone! If they didn't pack those suitcases and dispose of them, who did?"

"Who else but the person who wanted everybody to think they'd run away?"

"For God's sake, Michael, you can't mean, Betty? I know she's a liar, but I can't believe she's a killer."

"I can - I think she killed Elsie and Jake. Perhaps she got greedy; perhaps she wanted the extra money to run away with you, Tim? Think about that...."

Tim tried to shift the focus away from Betty. "Well, what do we know about Kellner, what about him? It could be him, couldn't it?"

"Oh, he didn't arrive on the scene until after Jake and Elsie were murdered. Come on, I know Maria and you want to believe there's some good in Betty, but this is murder we're talking about. You're clutching at straws. Betty's the one - she did it, give me a couple of days and I'll prove it!"

Tim said sceptically, "So for reasons best known only to her, Betty followed them up to the Cuckoo's Nest and killed them. After that she went to their rooms, packed their clothes and valuables, put everything into their suitcases and hid them. Is that it?"

"Correct. But because she was in a hurry she had to find a temporary home for the cases until she could find a permanent hiding place. I'm still convinced the temporary home was the left luggage office at the railway station."

"But Betty told me she accompanied the police to the railway station, they turned the place upside down and didn't find a trace of what they were looking for."

"Because, when she took the police to the railway station, she had already removed the cases and hidden them somewhere else," said Michael.

"Oh, had she? So where's the missing money then?" challenged Tim, "And where are the photos that Jake took and where's the list of the people he was blackmailing?"

"That's for us to find out. I'm convinced none of it's in the suitcases; Betty would have found a very special hidey hole. She's just biding her time, waiting for things to settle down, and when she thinks it's safe she'll be back in business again. So, if you're still keen on being a detective, find her hidey hole and when you do, tell me because I'm damned if I can find it."

Tim was determined now to prove Betty's guilt or innocence, one way or the other. "Okay Michael, maybe I've been a bit slow but I'll think of something." Michael made a move to leave. "Don't go yet Michael, stop and have a drink. We might come up with some new ideas?"

"Thanks Tim, but I've got a busy day tomorrow, I've arranged to interview all the staff at the railway left luggage office and then after that, at eleven o'clock, I'm going to see Marcus Kellner. He's the man who organised those races from the marina and I've promised to write an article about them."

"I can see the reason for the railway visit, but what can Kellner tell you?"

"It's just a hunch I have. You never know, the Marcus Kellner interview might help us find another piece of the jigsaw." And Michael left Tim wondering how Marcus Kellner could possibly provide a clue to the murders?

Tim tried to project himself into Betty's mind to work out what sort of secret hiding place she'd use. He was still trying to puzzle it out when Anne came back from the pictures. Tim told her Michael had been very impressed with the Christmas tree and decorations. Anne was delighted, and Tim settled back while she told him all about the film at the Casino. "You know something Tim, you're that man's absolute double, you could pass for Rudolph Valentino any day." Tim was about to say, "Twice in one day....." when the telephone rang and he went into the hall to answer it. Maria was phoning to tell them the baby had been born, a girl, six and a half pounds in weight, with beautiful jet-black hair and mother and baby were fine. When she paused for breath, Tim managed to say how much he had missed her. "I'm coming back on December the 22nd, the day before my birthday, missed you too."

"Love you darling," Tim said, before passing the receiver to Anne.

Tim thought the two of them would never stop talking. At last Anne ended the conversation and came to share her news with Tim. "They're going to call the baby, Maria Anne. It was Bernadette who wanted the baby to have my name, too." Anne was almost weeping. "Thanks to Bernadette, little Maria Anne will be part of my world as well."

That night as he got ready for bed, Tim remembered Anne and Michael's remarks about him looking like Rudolph Valentino. "Slick your hair back and do something with your voice and you'll be his double." Tim decided to do a bit of hair slicking and see for himself. It was just a lark really; vanity wasn't even a small part of Tim's nature. He took a tumbler of water from his bedside table and doused his hair with it, then he combed and brushed it back it until it shone as sleekly as if it had been dressed with Colene, the stuff that his sister Polly's husband, Owen, used on his hair. He looked in the mirror; there was no doubt about it his face did bear a resemblance to those glossy photos he'd seen of Valentino. But what about the voice, Michael said he had to do something with his voice? He adopted the most romantic looking pose he could muster and tried to say in what he imagined was a Valentino sort of voice, "Darling Maria, I love you." He tried it over and over again, every time with varying emphasis, but no matter how hard he tried, it didn't sound right. The face was okay; the hair was okay, but the voice was still unmistakably Tim Ryan's, the Yorkshire man from the pit village four miles from Doncaster! He thought again about his Mum and Dad, hoping his Christmas card would arrive soon. At least when they received it, they would know he was alive and the thought of that made him feel he was still part of the family.

Chapter Seventeen

It had been raining heavily all night but now the sun was out and the wet pavement outside the offices of Marcus Kellner shone like a polished mirror. Michael saw a seagull pecking at one of the upper windows but he didn't give much thought to it at the time. He entered the building and climbed the stairs to the top floor.

Kellner's secretary opened the door to the office suite just as Michael was about to knock. She showed him into a room at least three times the size of Mr. Pickersgill's, the furnishings looked expensive and compared with this, his editor's office was more like a second hand junk shop. Michael felt his feet sink deep into the carpet and as he walked towards Kellner's desk he saw that the walls were lined with paintings. Shaking Michael's hand, Kellner invited him to view the pictures more closely. "But if you're thinking of asking me questions, Mr. Topliss, don't, you'd be wasting your time, art isn't my strong suit. My wife, Joan, is the expert. If she were here she'd give you chapter and verse and talk your head off." Having dismissed the paintings, he asked Michael to sit down with him at a coffee table in the middle of the room. The secretary reappeared with a tray of refreshments; Michael murmured his thanks for the coffee and complimented Mr. Kellner on his timing. "You should thank the seagull for that," said Kellner, smiling. "The winged vandal, that's what I call him, he comes here every morning, eleven on the dot without fail, and if there's no food on the ledge he uses his beak like a hammer and threatens to crack the window pane. I look forward to his daily visit. Seagulls are such intelligent birds, don't you think, Mr. Topliss?"

Michael remembered looking up at the windows from the street. "I understand how you feel sir; I saw your seagull putting on a first class performance just as I arrived outside."

Kellner was pleased with his response. Michael knew that he had made a good start to the interview.

Kellner poured their coffee and while they drank they talked about the solo boat races. Michael took notes and promised a full report in his column the week after Christmas. Kellner nodded his satisfaction; he was looking forward to reading the article, "Reliving the action," as he put it.

Things were going so well, Michael managed to steer Kellner onto one or two items of national interest, such as the coal industry and industrial relations. He was rewarded by Kellner's grasp of the subjects and found his views balanced and fair. "Sad isn't it? These conflicts will be head to head in '26 and nobody's doing anything to stop it.

In fact just the opposite, they're all digging trenches! Of course, these are my private views, Mr. Topliss, I've been happy to share them with you, but they're strictly not for printing, you understand?"

Michael assured him he could rely on his discretion.

Kellner took this opportunity to end the interview, "If there's anything else you think I can help you with, just say the word."

After a brief pause, Michael asked, casually, "Oh yes, Mr. Kellner, it would be helpful if I could have the timings, individual timings of the races, but perhaps you haven't kept those records?"

"No problem with that." Kellner took out a clipboard from his desk drawer and handed it to Michael. "The timings are all there, let me have them back when you've finished, Mr. Topliss, I'd like to keep them to remind me of a special occasion."

Fifteen minutes later Michael was back at his desk in the newsroom reviewing his morning's work. From the very beginning it couldn't have gone better. His first appointment had been with Mrs. Beswick at the Beswicks' house. She had shown him the shed where the murder weapon had been found and confirmed that the shed was never locked, anybody could have gained access to it from the street without being noticed, particularly at night. Michael was more convinced than ever that the knife had been planted and Mr. Beswick was innocent.

He had gone from the Beswicks' to the railway station to interview some of the staff and had shown one of the porters a photograph of Betty. "Yes, that's her," he said, "She was wearing a head scarf, it slipped off and then I recognised her face and hair – that's the girl, she collected the cases and took them away about a week ago, I'm not exactly sure of the day. Works in the candyfloss kiosk, doesn't she?" He leered at the photograph, "Who could forget her?" Michael quickly tucked the photograph away in an envelope and reminded the man that he may have to repeat what he had said to the police.

Finally, he had gone to see Kellner and been able to obtain the timings of the races. The list made very interesting reading; it showed that Betty was up amongst the leaders in all of the races - except one. Michael double checked and yes, he was right, in one of the races she was out by almost one and half minutes compared to all of her other timings and there was no explanatory note to account for it. "That's it," he exclaimed, "That's when she must have slung the suitcases overboard!"

Michael was sure now that Betty was the killer although his conclusion was based on conjecture and he knew he would have to come up with something more convincing before reporting to the police. As for the missing money and the photographs, he guessed she must have them hidden away with the rest of her cash; if he could find them, he would have all the proof he needed. Somewhere, in the back of his mind the answer was there, if only he could just dig it out. Angry and frustrated he stabbed at his notes with his pencil, stabbed too hard and the pencil snapped. Sweeping his hand across the desk he brushed the broken bits into the wastepaper basket. He'd had enough puzzling for one day, it might be more helpful to find out about Betty's past and he decided to go and see Betty's previous employer, Anne Johnson, at the dress shop.

As he prepared to leave the office, he became aware that someone was standing beside his desk. He turned to see Nancy, the editor's secretary. "How long have you been there, Nancy?"

Nancy blushed, "Oh, just arrived," she said shyly. "We'll miss you when you leave us, Michael, but best of luck at the Sentinel."

"Thanks and I'll miss everybody too, you especially. You've just caught me, Nancy, I was about to buzz off to do an interview."

"Buzzing off is strictly verboten, Mr. Pickersgill wants to see you in his office – now! Sounds important. And another thing, he wants me to type up your interview with Mr. Kellner. Are those the notes?"

Michael pointed to the papers on his desk and Nancy picked them up together with Kellner's clipboard of the boat race timings.

"No, not the clipboard Nancy, I haven't finished with that yet."

Michael waved a grateful hand to her as she went off to transcribe his untidy shorthand notes. He had always enjoyed working with her and always enjoyed her company and had hoped to get to know her better. The new job in Manchester would probably rule out any chance of that. He sighed, there was always a downside to everything, wasn't there?

"Afternoon Michael," Pickersgill greeted him. "Dug up any more new evidence, you know, missing blackmail pictures, that sort of stuff?"

He sounded cheerful enough, but his face bore the signs of someone who hadn't been sleeping well, he looked drawn and pale. Regretfully, Michael said he hadn't dug up anything new yet, but tried to assure him everything would be resolved in a few weeks..

"Oh, good to hear you say that, Michael," Pickersgill lowered his gaze, he seemed to be embarrassed. "There's something I have to tell you, something I should have told you from the start." He hesitated. "Remember, Michael, I said I wanted you to find who'd implicated Beswick?"

"Yes sir, I remember."

"As I said, he's a good friend and I'm genuinely concerned for him but I should have told you then that I'd also been, er .. visiting, Elsie. Jake photographed me, too, and until the time they disappeared I was paying him five pounds a month to keep quiet about it. I'm sorry about Elsie, but I think Jake got what was coming to him." His voice fell to a mumble, "I could be implicated, Michael."

Michael was shocked. "If you repeat all that to the police they'll definitely question you as a suspect."

"I'm aware of that, but I didn't murder them, Michael. You've got to find the negative, otherwise I'm finished – find it and destroy it." He looked at Michael directly, "You don't believe I killed them, do you?"

"I know you didn't kill them."

"I should have told you the truth from the start and I'm deeply ashamed." He raised his eyes appealingly, "I'm not a bad man, Michael, never done a bad thing until now, not ever! I know I will have gone down in your estimation, I deserve it. I'm human, imperfect, make mistakes ...."

Michael saw the pain on Pickersgill's face and pitied him. "Don't worry sir, I'm determined to get there first, nobody will know about you and Elsie, I promise you."

"Thank God! We're still friends, aren't we?"

"Always," said Michael.

On the day Maria was due home, Michael invited himself to breakfast with Tim and Anne.

"So, this evening you'll pick Maria up at the station and bring her straight home?" checked Anne.

"Yes, and she'll be tired, I expect she'll need a quiet night in with Tim. Tomorrow night Cecilia and Joseph want us to be at the restaurant at nine o'clock to celebrate Maria's birthday, is that okay with you, Tim?"

"Yes, but what about Francis?"

"Dad's looking forward to it; I'll drop him off first and then call for you and Maria."

Anne could tell by the faraway look in Michael's eyes that he had something on his mind. "Penny for 'em," she said.

"Tell the truth, I was going over my visit to Betty's old employer, yesterday."

"Why did you go to see Anne Johnson?" Anne asked, sharply.

Michael told her a white lie, "I wanted to see what sort of an employee Betty was, that's all."

"Hmm. I know Anne Johnson, I know her well. You could have asked me what Anne thought about Betty Williams, it would have saved you a visit. Anyway, what did she say?"

"Said Betty was the best of all her employees."

Anne snorted. "I just knew she'd say that. Anyway, I'm fed up with all this talk about Betty Williams; so if you two will excuse me I'll be off upstairs, I've got a bit of tidying up to do before Maria comes back tomorrow. And when I come down, I don't expect to see any dirty cups and saucers lying about or you'll be for it." Tim and Michael pretended to take her threat seriously and cringed away from her. Anne laughed, "You two, why don't you go to the Central Pier and join the rest of the comedians, you're wasting your talent here." On her way up the stairs, she began to sing,

"Sounds happy," Tim said.

Michael laughed. "She's happy for you, Tim. She's singing because by this time tomorrow you and Maria will be back together again."

"She thinks what's happening with me and Maria is a bit of a miracle, doesn't she?"

Michael nodded his head, "Know something Tim, that's exactly what I think, too!"

They heard Anne pottering about upstairs. "Coast's clear now, Michael, you can tell me the rest of the story about seeing Anne Johnson at the dress shop."

"First, cast your mind back to the day you started to work for Maria. Early that morning Betty arrived on Maria's doorstep and told her Elsie had run away with Jake and pleaded with Maria for Elsie's job. Right, Tim?"

"Right."

"Maria had doubts about employing her, Betty persisted and finally Maria agreed to let her have the key to the kiosk and she started work the same morning?"

"Yes, so?"

Michael repeated, "She started work the same morning. How come she was able to do that, surely she would have to have given notice to the dress shop before she was free to work somewhere else? But listen to this, Tim, she had already left the dress shop, she had given her notice to quit two weeks before Elsie and Jake ran away, two whole weeks before the murder!   Now what was she doing in those two weeks?"

"Knowing Betty, she'd have been planning ahead," said Tim.   "And, assuming she is the killer, in those two weeks she must have been watching Jake and Elsie, stalking them, waiting for the right opportunity to come along and then........ It doesn't bear thinking about....."

"What I can't understand Tim, is why?   Why kill them?   They were all supposed to be best friends, especially Betty and Elsie, why would she want to kill, Elsie?"

"How do we know they were best friends, it was Betty who told us that?   Anyway best friends can fall out ...."

"Perhaps she was after their money?" said Michael, "Maybe she saw the blackmail business as a dripping roast - her pension?   I don't know."

Tim shook his head. "I know Betty likes money, but surely not money to hoard for some far off pension. Money's simply for spending, as far as she's concerned."

"How do work that out?"

"From personal experience," said Tim. "If Betty's told me once she's told me at least ten times, she's got plenty of money, and it's all mine if I'll just run away with her. She doesn't care a damn about money, it's the person she imagines she's in love with that counts. You've seen what she did to try and drive a wedge between Maria and me, she'll do pretty well anything to get the man she wants. So, if it wasn't for money, why would she want to kill Jake and Elsie?"

"I give up for now, Tim; I'm going home, tell Anne I couldn't wait.   See you later.   Perhaps we'll have come up with some answers by then?"

Tim washed up the breakfast dishes deep in thought, trying to figure out where Betty could have hidden the money and the blackmail evidence. He was startled by a dull thud on the ceiling. Maybe Anne's knocked over a chair, he guessed, then, in a flashback, he remembered the night Anne came to his room convinced there was a ghost in the house. Tim didn't believe in ghosts, but didn't Betty once have a spare key to his room and did she have a spare key to the house as well? Betty could have been the ghost, she'd have thought it a great joke, coming and going at will – keeping an eye on them all. Did she roam about in the night watching them? Suppose she had hidden the missing money and the other evidence right here in Maria's house? It was just the perverse, mad sort of thing Betty would do.

He was about to go upstairs to see if Anne was alright when she came down and announced she was going home. "I'll be back later with Michael and Maria," she said, "and I'll prepare something for us all to eat then." She gave him a hug. "You're a lovely man, Tim Ryan, and you'll make Maria very happy, it'll be good to have you two together again."

Tim was alone at last to search the house. He searched from top to bottom but without finding anything Betty might have hidden there. He quickly finished tidying up the kitchen, put fresh flowers in the living room and waited with growing excitement for Michael and Anne to bring Maria from the station.

Maria's birthday dawned, but it was long past dawn when Tim and Maria woke up. Tim went to make her a cup of tea and drew back the kitchen curtains to see if the sun was shining.No such luck, through a veil of rain, he could see the Mahonia doing its best to brighten up Maria's special day, its blossom seemed to be glowing more golden than ever.

Maria sat up in bed and sipped her tea. "What's the weather like?" she asked, dreamily.

"It's wet and it's going to get worse rather than better." Seven years on the run, mostly outdoors in all kinds of weather, had made Tim an expert. "Mark my words, Maria, when it comes to party time it'll be blowing a gale, one to remember." She patted his pillow, "Come back to bed, its ages before we have to get ready for the party....."

The rain fell all afternoon and by four o'clock the sky was dark. A sudden gust of wind rattled the bedroom window pane, Maria didn't notice, she was busy trying on the tiara Tim had bought for her birthday.

"Which way do you like my hair?" she asked.

"Up," said Tim, "I like your hair when you wear it up."

"Not too old looking?" said Maria.

"Never," said Tim and he kissed her.

Maria had laid several dresses out on the bed and was trying to make up her mind which one to wear. "They're all lovely and all from Anne Johnson's," she said. "Fancy, Betty giving up her job in that gorgeous gown shop to work in a draughty old kiosk selling cheap post cards. Doesn't make sense to me. Do you know, Tim, she even turned down my offer of manager's job at the gift shop? You'd think that kiosk was Aladdin's cave, the way she talks about it."

She paused and waved a dress in front of his eyes, "What about this one, Tim, d'you like it?"

Tim chose his favourite, the blue silk cheongsam. "What's that you said just now about the kiosk?"

"I said Betty talks about it as if it were some kind of Aladdin's cave, why?"

Tim didn't respond, he was halfway down the stairs, calling out to her, "Sorry love, got to phone Michael, something urgent."

Maria stood on the landing straining her ears to make out what Tim was saying. She heard him asking for Michael, there was a moment's silence and then, "It's me, Tim. Yes, yes, it's great to hear you too, Michael. Look, don't ask questions. Meet me at the kiosk right now, okay? I think we'll find what we are looking for."

Tim replaced the receiver and raced upstairs to tell Maria that he had to meet Michael. "Haven't time to explain now, but something's cropped up which might help Mr. Beswick. Tell you everything when I come back. Shouldn't be more than half an hour at the latest..."

"Okay, if you must go," said Maria, "Remember your chest though. It's still raining, wrap up and don't get wet."

"I promise, Maria, promise I won't get wet."

She couldn't help laughing, he sounded like a little boy. "All right Tim Ryan, make sure that you don't, or you'll get into trouble!"

Tim took his raincoat from the stand in the hall, put the kiosk key safely away in his pocket and grabbed an umbrella. He stopped briefly to lock the kitchen door behind him and then, unfurling the umbrella, he set off towards the kiosk, head down against the rain. He didn't want to keep Michael waiting.

Chapter Eighteen

Michael had already arrived and was waiting for Tim in his car. He had parked on the promenade only a few yards away from the kiosk and left his window slightly open to stop the glass from misting over. Through the gap he could hear music coming from the direction of the Central pier. The Salvation Army band was playing "Oh come all ye faithful," Michael had already hummed his way through two verses of the carol when he saw Tim approaching, his face obscured by an umbrella. Michael recognised Tim by his walk, deserter or not Tim still walked like a soldier. Michael got out of the car to greet him, he held a torch in his hand and showed it to Tim, "Just in case," he said.

Tim unlocked the kiosk and groped about for the light switch, a flick and it was on. "There you are Michael, as bright as day."

The hunt was on and they started to rummage through some cardboard boxes. They cleared a space and Tim found a small metal ring fitted flush into the floor boards. Michael handed him the torch, "You'll need more light, you're in your own shadow there."

"Thanks Michael." Tim pulled at the metal ring and a piece of the flooring about eighteen inches square came away in his hands, he pushed the wood aside, groping in the hole until he felt his fingers touch something solid. He yelled with triumph and within seconds he was thrusting a parcel into Michael's hands, "Christmas box for you Michael, from Santa, hope it's what you wanted?"

"Oh you beautiful, beautiful Tim, if it's what we think it is, it's going to be our best Christmas ever. Come on; let's have a look see."

The parcel was wrapped in a piece of dirty yellow oilskin. Michael tore at it with his fingers until he managed to rip it apart. "Looks like remnants of a cyclist's cape," he said, "I wore one as a kid, yellow just like this."

Tim spread the contents of the parcel out on the floor of the kiosk and for a minute or so they knelt over them without speaking. Then they began to sort through the pile of material; it was all there, the photographs, the negatives, a list showing the names of people who were being blackmailed and a record of their payments. And the money – there was a lot of money, too much to be counted at the moment! There was a daily diary of appointments Elsie had kept and a change of handwriting showed where Betty had taken over the entries. But it was Betty's own personal diary Michael was most interested in and he began to flick through the pages. Suddenly he stopped reading. "For God's sake Tim, get home to Maria," he looked horrified. "Betty's on her way to the house..... !"

"What do you mean on her way to the house?"

"It's in the diary, Tim, Betty's going to the house to deliver Maria's **last** birthday present! I think she intends to kill, Maria! Go on. Go. I'll take this stuff to the police – catch up with you as soon as I can."

Tim didn't need to be told twice; he rushed out of the kiosk and raced as fast as he could to Maria's.

The silk cheongsam lay across the bed, Maria had made up her mind, this was what she would wear, this was the gown Tim said he liked best. She took off her blouse, stepped out of her skirt and ran her hands critically over her figure before pulling the dress over her head. She reached for the comb lying on the dressing table and combed her hair up on top. Satisfied, she tried on the tiara and was admiring her reflection in the full-length mirror when she thought she heard someone coming up the stairs and called out, "Is that you Tim?" No reply. Maria thought she was imagining things. She busied herself tucking an unruly strand of hair back into place when she heard footsteps again, this time from the landing.

"That you, Tim, back already?" she called.

"It's not Tim; it's me."

Maria turned, "Good heavens Betty, you startled me. Who let you in?"

"I let myself in." The words sounded like a challenge and there was a smirk on Betty's face as she held up the key for Maria to see. Betty's voice frightened Maria, but the sight of her standing there smirking and being in possession of a key to the house roused her anger and anger overcame fear. She rounded on Betty, "So, it's you is it? You're the one who's been roaming around the house at all hours frightening people. You ought to be ashamed of yourself. As far as I'm concerned, we're finished – it's the end for you my lady, get out of this house right now. Go on, give me the key and get out! I never want to see you again!"

Betty's tone was derisive, "Don't try to order me about, Mrs. Martinelli. I'm the one in charge now. Christ, just look at you, you're scared absolutely bloody shitless. And in case you haven't tumbled to it, I'll tell you, it's the end for you my lady, not me – just like it was for Jake and Elsie!" She pulled out a knife from an inner coat pocket, grinning as she showed it to Maria. "My birthday present, dear Maria, now where would you like me to put it, I can think of three places, can you guess just one?" She moved forwards, and in retreat Maria stumbled backwards onto the bed. Recovering her balance quickly, Maria made a dash for the door, but Betty caught her and forced her against the bedroom wall.

In desperation she cried out, "But why Betty, why did you kill Jake and Elsie, Elsie was your best friend? I've been a good friend to you as well?"

For a moment Betty relaxed her grip on Maria, "You still don't get it do you? That time I told you that Jake and Elsie were at it, it wasn't Jake and Elsie, it was me. Me! Have you got it now? Then Elsie got her fucking claws into him, didn't she. I watched them. I followed them. I followed them when they went up to the Cuckoo's Nest; she was laughing and shouting to him, encouraging him, so I stabbed him in the back and that's what stopped him. Elsie screamed her head off, she couldn't move. Jake was on top of her, so I stabbed her throat, that made her shut up. I hid them in the bushes, but I hid the knife in Beswick's tool shed – that was a laugh. I told everybody they'd run off." She changed the knife from one hand to the other, "Now you can clear off, too."

"But what have I done to hurt you?"

The question amazed Betty, "Christ! You must be thicker than I thought if you can't work that out. Elsie took Jake from me and he let her do it, so I killed both of them. You've taken Tim from me, so you have to die. But not Tim, he'll want me when you're dead and then we'll run away together."

Maria was terrified, she tried to call for help but her mouth opened and closed without a sound. Betty was gloating now; she waved patterns in the air with the knife inches from Maria's face."Oh yes, Tim and me, we'll go away together." She moved closer to Maria and held the point of her knife against her throat. Maria closed her eyes and silently prayed, "Holy Mary, mother of God, pray for us ....." and waited to feel the thrust of the knife..... "Drop the knife, Betty. Drop it, do you hear me?" Tim's sharp command startled Betty and she turned around to face him. For a moment she stared at him and then whimpered, "Tim, Tim, I was doing it for us. It was for us Tim. I was doing it for us."

Maria slipped from behind Betty into the safety of Tim's arms. Betty screamed at her, "Keep away from him bitch, leave him alone," as she raised the knife to Maria's back. Tim pushed Maria behind him, placing himself between the two women, "If you intend to kill Maria, then kill me first, Betty, is that what you want?"

"Kill you, Tim? Never! I love you. You never lied or deceived me...." she pleaded.

Tim reasoned with her, "Please Betty, no more killings and give me the knife. The police will be here in a minute....."

"Now you're lying. They don't know anything about me."

"I'm not lying, Betty. I've never lied to you. You know that. We found all the evidence in the kiosk. Michael's taken it to the police. They'll be more lenient if you give yourself up."

"No way," snapped Betty. "Don't try to stop me, Tim Ryan, or she'll get it, I mean it." She backed towards the bedroom door and fled down the stairs. Tim and Maria clung to each other as they heard the kitchen door slam shut behind her and Maria sobbed with relief.

Running, stumbling, the rain stinging her face, Betty cursed the luck that had helped Michael and Tim find the stuff she had hidden under the kiosk floor. It was Jake's hidey-hole; Jake was the one who'd made it. If only they hadn't found it, if only Tim had been a few minutes later arriving at the house she would have had time to kill Maria, and she could have run away with him. But now she'd lost everything – her freedom too, if she wasn't careful. Through tears of bitterness, she smiled at her own rotten luck; it seemed she'd spent a life time making plans that failed. Her plan now, her last resort, this had to work, Martin Kershaw had said he'd do anything for her, absolutely anything, now she was going to give him the chance to prove it.

She made her way as quickly as she could to the marina. The sky was black with rain clouds and the wind was whipping up to gale force. She hadn't thought about the weather until now, but there was no turning back. She climbed aboard Kellner's boat, put on her lifejacket and took the stout belt from her coat, tied one end to the wheel and the other end she strapped round her wrist as an anchor, just in case. She manoeuvred the craft slowly out of the marina and into the swell of the Irish Sea. Exhilarated now by the challenge of her voyage and the prospect of her latest plan she threw open the throttles.

The belt from her coat saved Betty from being swept overboard, not once but twice. Twice she was flung to the heaving deck by the force of the waves, each time she dug her finger nails into the woodwork and hung on until she found the strength to haul on the belt so she could stand on her feet by the wheel again. Blood ran from her torn fingernails as she adjusted the throttles, but the experiment paid off and she found that the boat was more stable if she set them to deliver a slower speed of between eight and ten knots. The waves were getting bigger now and the boat was tossed between them, the wheel spun and her arms ached with the effort to control it. She started to sing, hysterically, "On the road to Mandalay where the flyin' fishes play ..." She laughed and cried and with tears streaming down her face she called out, "Listen to me Marcus, listen to me Tim, "An' the dawn comes up like thunder outer China 'crost the Bay!"" ....

At times it seemed she was riding a giant roller coaster on the pleasure beach, only this was a thousand times more scary and she screamed out when a huge wave struck the craft and lifted it up as if it would never stop rising. At last the boat teetered for a second and hung there on top of the wave just long enough for Betty to see the lights of Douglas twinkling in the distance. Then the wave collapsed and the boat dropped into a seemingly bottomless dark pit. A wall of water surged down into the void and pounded the craft with such force that every joint in every timber groaned in agony. Betty gulped water and feared she would drown and then, miraculously, the boat surfaced, and Betty clawed her way to her feet again. There had been damage to the prow, but it was difficult to see the full extent of it because of the darkness and the driving rain. Almost immediately another wave crashed against the prow and this time it took Betty by surprise and she lost her footing on the wet deck, slipped and struck her head against the wheel. She lay unconscious as the boat ploughed on towards the shore.

When Michael arrived at the house he found Maria and Tim downstairs in the kitchen. Maria was still in a state of shock and she was gripping Tim's arm as if her life depended on it. "Tim saved my life, Michael, Betty Williams had the knife at my throat, Tim stopped her. I really thought she'd kill me." She began to sob again. Tim drew her close to him, "Hush darling, you're safe now."

"Yes, I feel safe with you. But, remember the way she threatened me? She said I hadn't seen the last of her, Tim."

"I don't give much for her chances of escape," said Michael. "The police are everywhere, bus station, railway station. There are roadblocks everywhere."

Tim asked about Marcus Kellner, could he be hiding her?

"The police have gone to see him and …" Michael let out a yell, "Christ! Tim, I should have thought of it before - the marina! That's where she'd be making for; she'll try to get away in Kellner's boat. Tell the policeman at the door, Tim, and I'll phone the police station."

When the police alerted Kellner, he insisted on accompanying them to the marina. They arrived too late, the boat was missing and they knew Betty must have taken it. Kellner felt dizzy, silently he despaired, "I loved her more than any other woman in my life and now she's going to die." Aloud he said, "Those waves, the boat won't take it." He wandered aimlessly away from the police, muttering, "She didn't learn how to swim. Why didn't I teach her how to swim.........?"

A young policeman followed him and then reported back to his sergeant. "He looks ill serge. Shall I go and talk to him?"

"No son, he's just had more than his share of bad news, that's all. Best leave him to his own thoughts, but don't let him out of your sight, mind he does nothing daft? Know what I mean?"

"Yes serge, I'll stay close."

After her ordeal at the hands of Betty Williams, Maria wasn't in the mood for celebrating, so they decided to put off her birthday party until January. And although she was feeling much calmer, Maria didn't feel well enough to go either to Midnight Mass or to church on Christmas day. It seemed as though Christmas Day was going to pass without any festivities until, like the good fairy in the Pantomime, Anne put in an appearance. She was accompanied by Michael, Francis, Cecilia and Joseph and they brought Christmas dinner with them, calling, "Surprise! Surprise!" and Anne the good fairy must have brought some magic with her too, because by the end of the day Maria declared that she felt as fit as a fiddle.

Putting off Maria's birthday celebrations had suited Michael because it gave him time to sift through everything Tim and he had discovered in the kiosk. The day after Boxing Day his task was complete and he asked Tim if he could use the garden incinerator to make a bonfire of Jake's blackmailing photos. "I know it's wrong to destroy evidence," said Michael as he struck a match and they watched a plume of smoke rise high into the air. "This smoke's taking a whole lot of misery with it, Tim. I gave the police Betty's diary, the money and some of the other stuff, but they don't need this muck." And he flung the last bundle of envelopes containing photos and negatives into the flames. One envelope Michael didn't burn. "I promised somebody I'd deliver this to him in person," he said.

Tim didn't ask who it was for, "Go ahead, take it now, the sooner the better!"

Mr. Pickersgill was waiting in his office and Michael handed the envelope to him. "It's the only one, I've checked and there aren't any more."

John Pickersgill opened the envelope, got up from his chair and walked across the room to the fire. He threw the negative and photo onto the coals and watched them curl up and burn. As the last charred remains fluttered up the chimney taking the threat to his reputation with them, he heaved a long sigh of relief, "Thanks Michael, I'll be eternally grateful to you." He paused for a second and then in his brisk editor's voice demanded, "Now my boy, you can fill me in and tell me the rest of the story."

When Michael had finished bringing him up to date he said "I know it's your story Michael and you deserve to have the final word, but my advice is that Kellner has had enough for the time being, I think that he deserves a break, don't you? What say we phone him and tell him that we won't publish that piece about the boat races because it might link him with Betty Williams? I don't want to hurt a decent man and have it on my conscience, Michael; I've had enough of that already. Okay, maybe we are only a small newspaper, but when we're searching for news we don't have to go scraping in the gutter to find it, do we?"

Michael gave his editor a nod and watched as he dialled the number, wondering what Kellner's reaction would be. When Pickersgill put the phone down, he said, "He knows about Betty, he knows everything that's happened. Upset? He could hardly speak. He mentioned you though, and asked me to tell you how grateful he is to you for not writing about the races."Pickersgill felt very satisfied with the way things had turned out; Michael had saved his reputation, had discovered the real murderer of Jake and Elsie and established the innocence of Beswick. Not bad going, all things considered! But who was the one who had made it possible? He smiled, wasn't he was the one who had set the ball rolling for Michael to take it up and run with it, he pulled on his cigar and breathed out again slowly and contentedly, things were back to normal.

Nancy said goodnight to Michael as he made his way to leave the building. She had been waiting for him at the door, hoping to have a word with him, but Michael didn't stop, "Goodnight Nancy" he called as he hurried away. He was deep in thought giving himself a mental pat on the back, convinced that in the right hands, his hands, the press could be a power for good.

So Christmas 1925, came and went and after seeing in the New Year with Tim and Maria, and promising faithfully to return for Maria's birthday party, Michael packed his bags ready to start a new life in Manchester. As he folded away the last of his shirts he envisaged all the things the world needed him to do and he just couldn't wait to make a start on them.

CHAPTER NINETEEN

IN JANUARY TIM AND MARIA prepared to celebrate their joint birthday party. Now, recovered completely from her encounter with Betty, Maria looked radiant and when Tim saw that she was wearing his special birthday present, his happiness was complete.

There was no news about Betty, she was tactfully forgotten for Maria's sake and as friends and family gathered at the restaurant conversation turned instead to rumours of a General Strike, everybody wanted to discuss how seriously the strike could affect Blackpool businesses. Michael assured them there would be enough holidaymakers from the affluent new car making industries in the Midlands and London to keep Blackpool's trade going. Tim's thoughts were on families like his own in the mining villages of Yorkshire, he knew what a strike would mean for them, it had all happened before, no money, no food and men and children scrabbling about on frozen pit top wastes scavenging bits of coal for fuel to keep their homes warm.

Michael's sympathies were with Tim. "Blackpool will survive, it's the poor devils on strike I feel sorry for," he said.

Joseph and Cecilia saved the evening from descending into gloom by suggesting they finish off the party having a "knees up" at The Tower ballroom. Michael danced with Anne and Tim and Maria demonstrated the tango with their "deadpan face, head jerk" technique and when Francis saw Maria fling herself backwards across Tim's knee in the last passionate movement of the dance, he wished with all the fervour in his soul that he could be young again!

Before they got into their taxis outside the ballroom, Michael managed to have a quick word with Tim, "I've heard that driftwood from a boat wreck has been found at Portpatrick - from the description it sounds like it could have come from the cabin cruiser. I've told Kellner and he wants me to take him up there. I'm staying here the night with Dad, so that Kellner and I can make the journey to Scotland first thing tomorrow."

"What about petrol, it's a long way to Portpatrick?"

"I'll take a spare can just in case and there's definitely a petrol station at Gretna. I'll phone and let you know if the wreckage turns out to be what we think it is."

Kellner wasn't a talkative man, he usually waited until he considered he had something important to say and then he expected to be listened to   It had been well over an hour since they left Blackpool and he had said no more than "Yes," or "No." Michael thought he was carrying his quiet man reputation too far, by this stage of the journey surely he could have spared a few words of conversation. They were going over Shap when Kellner noticed several abandoned vehicles on either side of the road and at last he spoke spontaneously, "I wonder what happened here?"

"Haven't you read the newspapers, Mr. Kellner?" Michael's voice sounded querulous, he was thirsty and hungry and a bit hung over from the night before.

"Yes Michael, I have, is there something I've missed?" Kellner's voice sounded calm and pleasant and immediately Michael regretted being irritable.

"Sorry, I didn't mean to be off hand Mr. Kellner, up to three days ago Shap was completely blocked by snow, heavy rain cleared it so we're lucky. A few days earlier and we could have been among that lot."

Kellner shuddered, "I don't like snow, sunny and warm's the way I like it. That's why I bought the cabin cruiser you know. We were going to..." he broke off, realizing that perhaps he'd said more than he intended. He changed the subject. "When you are ready, choose a spot Michael, we'll get out and stretch our legs. I see you've brought a picnic with you – looks tempting!"

Within minutes Michael had stopped the car, spread a rug over the nearest patch of level ground and opened up the picnic basket. The ground was still damp from melted snow and they could feel the chill through the rug. They ate in silence, Kellner deep in thought and Michael overawed by the massive beauty of the mountains.

"Call me Marcus," said Kellner when they were on the move again. "I hope you feel you know me well enough to call me by my first name?"

"Yes, er - Marcus, I think I do," said Michael, expecting Kellner to continue talking, but a glance at his face showed Michael that he was still preoccupied.

There seemed to be no end to the twists and turns in the road and Michael was kept busy changing gear. Kellner mightn't have been talking but he had been watching, "One day they'll invent a car that changes gear without all that fuss and palaver," he said at last, "Automatic," he predicted. "Just wait and see."

Michael stopped the car at Gretna petrol station and while the garage attendant filled up the tank and chatted about the weather, Michael checked the wheel hubs. The hubs were hot, he wasn't surprised, the brakes had taken a hammering on the steep downward slopes, they waited to give them time to cool before they set off again for Portpatrick.

"How much further?" asked Kellner.

"We're about half way."

"It'll probably be dark before we get there."

"Do you want a turn at driving; this last leg's not so hilly?"

"I can't drive," said Marcus flatly, and they finished their journey in much the same way as they set out – in silence!

At the hotel, however, Marcus relaxed and began to confide in Michael. During dinner he said, "I was in love with Betty you know, I really loved her."

"I realized that Marcus, months ago, the first time you and I talked together."

Kellner pushed his meal around the plate, picking at it. "I was lonely you know," he explained, "My wife wouldn't leave London; all she did was supply me with those paintings for my office.   We didn't really get on, hadn't done for years, had no interests in common and yet I was lonely without her.   Oh, business was fine, couldn't have been better, so good I wanted to celebrate and that's how I came to meet Betty."

Michael nodded, encouraging him to continue.

"A friend told me about her and I went to see her at the kiosk, I was quite nervous really. Know what she said to me?"

Michael shook his head.

"First you must buy some cards and then you can tell me what it is you want me to do for you." Kellner laughed. "I ask you? First you must buy some cards from me and then …" He stopped laughing, and Michael thought he was about to cry. "I know she did some terrible things, I reckon it was due to the way she was brought up. I'm not making excuses for what she did, but I don't think she stood a chance of making a different life for herself. On the other hand, what Betty did to Mr. Beswick was rotten and I feel sorry for him. In fact, poor Beswick didn't stand much of a chance either, did he?"

"No, he's had it pretty rough," said Michael.

"You can say that again.   I'm going to try and put that right for him. I've instructed my personnel team to offer him a job in the finance department at head office.   Not charity, absolutely not. I need a good man in London and I've asked about and found that Beswick's highly qualified and very well thought of. So, with a good salary, a flat only a stone's throw away from the National Gallery, he's very keen on art you know, maybe he'll take the job. What do you think, Michael?"

Michael didn't want to discuss Beswick's private life, "It'll be a change of career for him," he said discreetly."

"Career! Give me credit, Michael," said Marcus. "I know all about his wife and daughter. I know the rotten life he's had with them. I think he's looking for more than a new career!"

"I'm sure he'll accept the job," said Michael.

Kellner felt tired now and wanted an early night, he thanked Michael for listening to him; it had been a relief to talk openly about his relationship with Betty.

Michael told him he'd arranged a meeting at the local police station for ten o'clock the following morning, afterwards they should be able view the wreckage.

"All's arranged for tomorrow then," said Marcus opening the door to his room. On the threshold he hesitated and turned back, "I find it hard to bear, Michael; despite everything Betty did, I love her."

After breakfast they went to meet the local police sergeant who took them to the lifeboat station on the seafront. The skipper showed them the wreckage stored in a small enclosed pound behind the building and Kellner recognised all that remained of his dream. They were back under shelter when the wind started to blow heavy grey curtains of rain swirling in from the sea. Visibility was reduced to less than a hundred yards and it grew cold, much colder than yesterday. "Looks like we could be in for a bad storm," said one of the lifeboat crew checking around for the umpteenth time that morning to make sure that everything was ready – just in case!

Despite the rain, Kellner asked if somebody was free to show him where the wreckage had been washed up.

The men consulted amongst themselves; there seemed to be some difficulty in deciding who should take him.

"Best if I take you," the police sergeant said. "I think the lads want to stay here. By the look of the weather, they might be needed."

Sergeant Morrison drew his cape around his shoulders and led the way along the promenade. Kellner and Michael followed; heads down against the wind and rain. Two hundred yards away from the lifeboat station, Morrison swung his bulky frame over a low wall and trudged a few yards through the wet sand. "It was around here we found it," he said pointing to the wall. "See, we marked the place with yellow paint."

The beach was deserted and desolate under the grey sky and the wind whipped up spray from the waves at the shores' edge. Despite his warm clothing, Sergeant Morrison was beginning to shiver, he thought about his kettle and teapot at the police station. "I'll have to be getting back to the station soon, Mr. Topliss, I've done all I can for you here."

"Yes, yes of course, thanks, sergeant, you've been most helpful," said Michael and he called out to tell Kellner who had wandered off down the beach towards the sea. In the distance Michael saw him bend over to examine something and then pick it up, it looked like a tattered rag hanging from old sticks. Suddenly, clutching the rag to his chest, Kellner fell face down in the sand.

"I'm coming, I'm coming Marcus," yelled Michael. With each step he took his feet sank deeper into the wet sand and his shoes felt as heavy as divers' boots. No matter how much effort he put in, he seemed to be running in slow motion. At last he reached Marcus and knelt beside him. "Wake up Marcus, can you hear me? Wake up!" He turned Marcus' head towards him and was shocked to see his eyes wide open, lifeless, staring blindly at the sky.

Sergeant Morrison arrived, puffing and panting under the burden of his heavy cape. He stooped to feel for a pulse in Kellner's neck. "We're too late, he's dead, Mr. Topliss." He closed Kellner's eyes and then pulled out the broken picture frame from under his body and handed it to Michael, "This is what your friend was looking at when he collapsed," he said. The tattered canvas was Martin Kershaw's portrait of Betty Williams, the portrait Kellner had hung so proudly above his bed in the cabin of his boat.

When Michael phoned to tell Tim about Kellner's death at Portpatrick, Tim couldn't believe how a man as fit and active as Kellner could die so suddenly. He found it easier to accept Betty's death, the violence of the storm in the Irish Sea the night she had tried to escape and the wreckage washed up on the beach at Portpatrick were surely proof enough that she had gone down with the boat and drowned.

CHAPTER TWENTY

MICHAEL SAT AT HIS DESK brooding about Marcus and all the deaths of the past few months. First there had been the shock of Uncle Jack's death, then his discovery of Jake and Elsie's bodies and now Betty Williams was presumed drowned. Tragically Marcus had died with Betty's portrait clutched in his hands.Sergeant Morrison's words came back to him, "This is what your friend....." And Michael found himself repeating those two words over and over again, "Your friend, your **friend** ...." And that is how Michael felt this loss - he had lost a friend. Their first meeting, followed by the journey to Portpatrick and the conversation over dinner, was all it had taken to create a bond of friendship.

One of the editor's secretaries spoke to him as she dropped a memo onto his desk and brought him out of his reverie. He read the memo several times before he fully understood what he read; starting in March, he was to work alongside Paul Elkington, the political editor. Michael forgot his sadness, a feeling of great elation swept through him, his feet were on the ladder and he was on his way up! Michael was sure this move coming so soon after he had joined the paper, must mean there was something important lined up for him. Rumour had it that Paul planned to retire in '28. Did it mean he was being groomed to fill Paul's shoes, was he going to be the Manchester Sentinel's next political editor? With all the confidence of youth, Michael whispered to himself, "Yes!"

Meanwhile in Blackpool the 1926 season got off to a shaky start. There was trouble brewing between the government and the unions and there were a lot of gloomy faces to be seen on the streets of the town. Strikes and rumours of strikes abounded and people were nervous in case their own livelihoods would be affected. When the Samuel Report came out in March and recommended a cut in miners wages Tim worried more than ever about his family in Woodlands and there was worse to come; the mine owners demanded longer hours at the coalface in addition to a cut in wages. Tim was bitter; "A lot of kids will go hungry to school this winter if the government allows them to get away with that."

"Michael was right," said Maria, "He said this would happen, they must have been scheming and planning this for months."

Tim was only one of thousands who thought the Samuel Report had been cruel; workers in several major industries made the decision to strike. When the General Strike began at the beginning of May the clarion call of the miners became, "Not a penny off the pay, not a minute on the day."

Michael had also predicted their action would be doomed to failure right from the very start. He was convinced that the Samuel Report had been released only when the government were fully prepared and convinced they would win and it didn't take the T.U.C. more than a couple of days to realize they were backing a loser.

After just nine days the other unions called off their support for the miners and business people in Blackpool sighed with relief, perhaps the season would turn out to be better than they expected. And it actually was better because workers from the new car manufacturing areas in the Midlands came to Blackpool for their holidays and the absence of the miners' and their families was barely noticed. The sun shone, the days were pleasantly warm and the season gathered pace, Blackpool proved it was the place to be in the summer of '26. Tim, Maria, Anne, Joseph and Cecilia were all kept equally busy. In the midst of this activity there was the odd free moment when Tim found himself looking over at "Betty's kiosk." He listened for the noise of the counter flap being smashed down and remembered with a shudder how she had used it to express her annoyance. Sometimes he imagined she had managed to escape from drowning and was still alive, but when Maria asked him what he was thinking about he always said, "Nothing - nothing at all...." The last thing he wanted to do was frighten Maria with memories of Betty.

One blazing hot day in July Tim went to buy paint from Mr. Nightingale. The ironmonger had pulled out the awning over the south-facing window and the shade made his shop refreshingly cool inside. Tim leaned against the counter and waited his turn to be served. Mr. Nightingale's shop fascinated him; it was bursting at the seams with everything a handyman could wish for, it was like a treasure cave. There were nuts and bolts of all sizes housed in neatly labelled easy pull out drawers and there were saws of all types hanging on a board next to a warning notice that said, "BEWARE OF THE SAWS, THEY HAVE SHARP TEETH!" Spades, pick-axes, shovels and brooms were in the middle of the floor stacked in neat rows – ready for instant action! But it was the cocktail of heady smells, a blend of paraffin, firewood, soft soap, candles and creosote wafting through the air that Tim enjoyed most and he breathed it in contentedly.

Mr. Nightingale enjoyed Tim's company and pretended to have difficulty in finding some of the paints on Tim's list so he could pause for a chat. Tim didn't mind his delaying tactics, it was relaxing to listen to Mr. Nightingale's chatter, he adjusted his stance against the counter and prepared himself for a long wait.

"Which way are you going home?" the ironmonger asked.

"Prom, I've got to look at one of the kiosks."

"If you head for the North Pier, there's a young couple there doing their own show, you can't miss 'em, raising money for the miners, attracting quite a crowd. They're not bad, not bad at all and the girl's a real sight for sore eyes."

As soon as Tim turned out of the side street and onto the prom he saw the crowd. There must have been at least twenty or thirty people and, if the volume of laughter was anything to go by, the couple were giving them their monies worth. Before he mingled with the crowd he stopped to see if the coast was clear. No police, no redcaps, but even so he pulled the brim of his hat down low over his forehead. Now he dared to stop and take a closer look. He heard music from a gramophone, it sounded foreign – sort of Eastern - and someone standing in front of him called out, "Shuffle, Mustapha. Go on, we Mustapha shuffle," and people responded with good-natured laughter to the man's wit.

Tim slid further into the crowd to see the show for himself. There was a man with heavy tan make-up on his face and a fez of red cardboard perched precariously on his head. He wore a nightshirt about ten sizes too big for him and was shuffling about the sand strewn prom in ill fitting boots, doing a comic version of an Egyptian sand-dance. A beautiful young woman wearing a glittering head-dress and wrapped in swathes of gauzy, coloured scarves was busy collecting money from the crowd. "That's Princess Zoe," a woman whispered. Then Tim spied the placard placed against the sea wall, MUSTAPHA COPPA AND PRINCESS ZOE, HERE TO ENTERTAIN YOU AND RAISE MONEY FOR THE MINERS.'

In the heat of the blazing sun, sweat had mixed with Mustapha Coppa's tan make-up turning it into a thin brown sludge which trickled down his face and into his false moustache. Slowly the colour of the moustache began to change from black to brown. The make-up lubricated the moustache and it began to slip about, moving round between nose and lip like the fingers on a clock face! At the position of six o'clock exactly, the moustache stopped moving! The crowd applauded wildly, by accident or design the moving moustache had won them over completely. A sudden gust of wind lifted the man's nightshirt to his knees; the sight of his brown face atop long white legs made him look more like a toffee apple than an Egyptian dancer and brought extra laughter from the crowd. When the hem of the nightshirt fell back into place it settled just an inch or two above the old pair of pit boots the man wore. His boots and his white skin were a dead give-away, Tim thought. The man was obviously a miner. And there was something else, something vaguely familiar about him but Tim couldn't figure out what it was.

The music stopped. It was the end of the act and the man in the fez smoothed down his nightshirt and bowed politely to the audience. Money showered into the collection baskets, with a good sprinkling of three penny bits and sixpences added to the copper. Then Princess Zoe restarted the gramophone and one by one discarded her gauzy scarves as she swayed into the rhythm of her belly dance. Her ample bosom quivered and strained under the restraint of her bra and the crowd was hypnotised by the red jewel set in her navel; her body seemed to gyrate around it. And as she danced so the crowd grew, she seemed to be drawing people to her like a magnet. Soon, there must have been more than fifty people watching and they began to clap their hands to the rhythm of the dance. Inspired by the clapping, Zoe swung her hips faster and faster until the gramophone record spun to a halt and the music stopped.

Mustapha had taken off his fez and wiped some of the brown sweat from his face onto his sleeve. He was passing round the collecting baskets when his moustache fell off. As he bent down to pick it up, he smiled. Without the fez and moustache Tim recognised him instantly, it was his elder brother – Jim!

Tim's single thought was to get home as fast as possible and bring Maria back to meet his brother. He felt a tremendous excitement as he tried to imagine the expression on Jim's face and he wanted her to be there to share the joy of their meeting.

Maria was working in the garden when he arrived, he urged her to leave everything and run with him to the prom. Laughing, she pointed to the soil on her shoes and her hands but when Tim explained what was happening she didn't care how she looked, she was off like a shot and left poor Tim trailing.

Despite all their rush they were too late. The crowd had vanished and so had Jim and Princess Zoe. A man sat gazing out to sea and Tim recognised him as the comedian from the crowd.

"Where did they go?" Tim asked, "The man in the nightshirt and the girl dancer?"

"You mean Mustapha Coppa and Princess Zoe? An older man, grey hair, came in a big car - took them away."

Tim was bitterly disappointed and as he walked back to the house with Maria he was overcome by a feeling of homesickness and longed to see his family again.

It wasn't until the end of the season that Tim and Maria found out what had happened to Jim. It was Anne who brought them the news. "I was passing that bit of waste ground," she said, "You know, where they have the travelling fair every year. They were all packed up and leaving town, when I saw Sid Silver just about to get into his big car. Like a flash it came to me, he must have been the man with the grey hair who took Jim and his girl friend away that day."

"You know him? Did you ask him about it?" said Tim.

"O' course, I asked him."

"And he remembered them?"

"Remembered? Yes, Tim, he did. He'd collected them from the sea-front to work for him. Well, not so much Jim, Sid only wanted him for odd jobs, it was really the girl he needed for a few days to fill in for one of his "Hawaiian" dancers who had been taken ill. Sid wanted her to stay longer, but she wouldn't and they went back to Doncaster."

Anne had brought them such welcome news, they couldn't thank her enough. "If you hadn't been quick enough to put two and two together when you saw Sid Silver getting into his car, we'd still be worrying about what happened to them." Maria said.

"Well, they must be okay and that's all that matters. But look, I have to go. Mrs. Childs will be champing at the bit, I should have been at the ice-cream kiosk ten minutes ago, it's her lunch break."

"Wait a tick and I'll come with you, I've got to go to the gift shop."

Tim watched as they left the house and called, "I'll be working in the garden when you get back, Maria." She blew him a kiss, Tim didn't know whether she had heard him or not. He was well on with his tidying up when he heard the garden gate open and looking up saw John Beswick striding up the path. "Well, surprise, surprise," Tim greeted him. "Good to see you, John. What brings you back to Blackpool? Shall we go up to the house for a cup of tea and a chat?"

"Thanks, but I haven't got time, Tim, I've a train to catch to London, there's something that's been on my mind for a while though and I had to come and see you to tell you about it - get it off my chest." He looked towards the house. "Maria, is she ..?"

"She's out," said Tim.

"Just as well," said Beswick. He pulled out a newspaper from his pocket and was about to hand a page of it to Tim when he changed his mind. "Ah," he said. "Perhaps before I show you this, maybe I ought to tell you about Joan, Marcus Kellner's widow. She and I have become very good friends, by coincidence a mutual interest in art brought us together."

Tim had no idea where all this was leading, but he could see the Beswick of today was a different man, brimming over with confidence, and he seemed to have grown at least two or three inches in stature!

"To cut a long story short, Mrs. Kellner and I were in New York visiting art galleries. At one of the smaller, private galleries we stopped to look at a painting by an English artist from the Isle of Man, a Martin Kershaw, neither of us had heard of him before.His figure painting of a girl was excellent, attracting a lot of attention; we could hear viewers speculating about the significance of a key the girl was holding, was it symbolic? Then I discovered that Kershaw himself was in the gallery, so I asked him directly about the key."It means what you want it to mean," he said abruptly and walked away....."

Tim interrupted. "Look, John, I don't know anything about art - at the school I went to, we got the three Rs and that's all."

"Be patient for a second, Tim, I am getting to the point. The painting was untitled but the girl who posed for it, I swear to God it was none other than Betty Williams!" If Beswick thought this pronouncement would surprise Tim, he was mistaken.

"It could be her," said Tim. "Betty did go to the Isle of Man with Kellner. And that artist Martin Kershaw, Kellner paid him to paint a portrait of her. Michael thinks the portrait was the one in the wreckage from the boat......"

"The one he found before he collapsed?"

"Yes. And, knowing Betty, she could have persuaded Kershaw to do other paintings as well as the portrait......"

"Very likely, and perhaps modelling and painting wasn't the only thing she and Kershaw shared in the Isle of Man?"

"What d' you mean?"

"The story didn't end there, that's what I mean."

"Well, it couldn't have gone much further could it? Betty's dead."

Beswick shook his head in disagreement. Kershaw had married and his wife had travelled to America with him, he told Tim - very few people there seem to have met his wife and apparently she hated being photographed. He handed the newspaper to Tim. "Take a look at that photo - the woman has short black hair - imagine if it was longer and blonde. Now, doesn't that remind you of someone you know?"

Tim looked closely, "Yes, she's like Betty Williams."

"There you are then." John Beswick sounded triumphant. "If it is her then she survived the storm in the Irish Sea, changed the way she looked and married Kershaw. I believe Betty Williams is alive."

Tim wasn't convinced. "Michael said the boat was completely wrecked; surely she must have drowned when it went down?"

"Betty was always cunning, suppose, just suppose she did make it to the Isle of Man, she'd want everybody to believe she had drowned, stop the police looking for her."

"Sounds the sort of thing Betty would do, but it doesn't explain about the boat," said Tim.

"Assuming she reached the Isle of Man and providing the boat wasn't too badly damaged, it would have been a simple matter for someone like Betty to lock the wheel, open the throttles and send the vessel speeding back to crash on the mainland. When the wreckage was found at Portpatrick she must have clapped her hands with glee, she had provided proof that Betty Williams was dead and now she could invent an alias and start living again."

"And become Mrs. Martin Kershaw; is that what you're saying? But knowing she was a murderer, how could Kershaw even think of marrying her?"

"She'd probably convince him that in the case of Elsie and Jake it was a question of her life or theirs – had to kill them in self-defence – something like that. As for Maria, Betty would tell him Maria was lying, jealous because she thought Betty was trying to take you away from her. Kershaw would believe her alright, Betty Williams could be very persuasive....."

Everything Beswick said about Betty rang true, although, Tim still wasn't sure he was right. "I don't want to offend you, John – somehow it all sounds a bit too far-fetched for me."

"Not really." said Beswick, "And if Mrs. Kershaw is Betty Williams then its Kershaw I feel sorry for."

"Why?"

"Because Kershaw is the only one who knows the truth about her and maybe one day Betty will consider that's a risk too many."

"You mean she might kill him?" At last Tim sounded surprised

"Don't know why you sound surprised, she's done it before hasn't she? And you, my friend, if you've got any sense, you'd better watch out for your back and Maria's.... Better to be safe than sorry. Anyway I've done what I set out to do, I've warned you, the rest is up to you. By the way, I almost forgot to tell you, I've been writing a book about my prison experiences, Michael's kindly done the editing for me and the publisher says it will be out next summer. Look Tim, I've got to be off, I'm late enough as it is."

Tim was so bemused by all Beswick had said about Betty, he almost forgot to offer congratulations, he called after him, "Great news about the book, John, Maria and Anne will be so pleased to hear about it!"

Tim stayed on and worked in the garden for a long time laboriously pulling weeds and puzzling over what Beswick had said about Betty Williams. It was probably all conjecture, there were too many if's and buts for it to be real. He would just tell Maria, Beswick had called to let them know he had written a book; the photograph of the woman in the American newspaper did look like Betty Williams, but only he and John Beswick had seen it and Tim decided to keep that to himself.

CHAPTER TWENTY ONE

BLACKPOOL'S BUSINESSES BOOMED IN 1926; even when the government, blaming coal shortages at the power stations, restricted the period of the Illuminations to a meagre three days, money didn't stop flowing into the seaside tills. Maria's accountants predicted that the next financial year was going to be just as good, if not better.

Making money didn't make everyone happy, however, and in the spring of 1927 Maria noticed Tim's lapses into silence were becoming more and more frequent. Was it something she had done to upset him? "No, no, this isn't about us," he reassured her, "It's Mum and Dad, I keep worrying about them, they're old, Maria - and the strike - Lord alone knows what that did to them. I know it's still risky but I'll have to take a chance and go to see them. So when it comes to the end of the summer, if everything's okay with you, Maria, that's when I'll go."

"Of course everything will be fine here, Tim, it's a lovely idea and I'll go with you." Tim sighed with relief, those few encouraging words made all his worries vanish and he chided himself for not telling Maria earlier about his troubles. As for making arrangements for the journey they agreed that September was soon enough for that. In the meantime, Tim vowed to himself that between now and September he would work harder than ever to help Maria.

At the beginning of August Bernadette phoned to tell them she was pregnant again -several months pregnant. Maria was delighted and began to make plans for a family reunion at Christmas, plans for herself and Tim to go to Glasgow in December to celebrate Christmas with Bernadette, Robert and little Maria Anne. Hopefully, the trip to Doncaster would go well and Tim would gain enough confidence to travel again.

Before August had ended, and before she had begun to discuss her Christmas plans with Tim, a sad and anxious letter arrived from Robert explaining that Bernadette had miscarried. She was ill and very weak, unable to care properly for Maria Anne and none of his family, living locally, could help, they were all busy with work and their own children. Could Maria please come to look after Bernadette and the little one so he could go back to his job at the shipyard? Maria phoned immediately to say she was coming and that evening she was packed and ready to catch the next day's train to Glasgow.

Once again Tim was alone. Fortunately, this time he was too busy to feel lonely and although the load was heavy,

Anne, Cecilia and Joseph all helped with the running of the shop and kiosks and their companionship always cheered and reassured him. Maria wrote and phoned with reports of Bernadette's gradual recovery and entertained him with accounts of little Maria Anne's baby talk and growing independence. As the months passed, Tim realized that there was no hope now of visiting his parents until next year and at Christmas, Maria and he reluctantly decided that it would be best if Maria stayed on in Glasgow until January. Tim would celebrate Christmas and New Year in Blackpool with Anne and Francis and possibly Michael if he could get leave from the Sentinel.

Michael did come home for Christmas and was home again before the end of January to join Tim, Maria, Anne and Francis for Tim's birthday party at the restaurant. Maria was chatting to Anne and Cecilia when Tim confided to Michael that he wanted to make the journey to see his parents alone. He said he'd work with Maria through the holiday season and then set off on foot over the Pennines to arrive in Doncaster for Leger week. The idea was to travel mostly by night, better by shanks pony and safer!

At first, Michael laughed and when Tim told him he was serious, Michael said he was crazy to be even thinking of walking. "Know what year this is? Nineteen twenty eight, the war's been over for ten years! Nobody's looking for you now and, apart from that, Blackpool to Doncaster's too far, it could take weeks not days to get there on foot....."

The women were listening, "Weeks to get where?" said Maria

"Haven't you discussed this with Maria?" asked Michael

Tim hesitated, "Well.... we did discuss it last year, planned to go together by train – then Bernadette took ill – I changed my mind - I can't risk putting Maria in a situation where she could be implicated if I'm caught......."

Michael interrupted angrily, "Tell him Maria, tell him he must go by train and take you with him."

"His mind's made up, Michael. I know how stubborn he is," Maria tried to hold back her tears.

"Some people! Unbelievable," said Michael. "Well, if we can't persuade you to change your mind, let's see if I can help." He flicked through the pages in his diary. "Here we are, St. Leger's on September 12th this year. Now listen to me, Tim, and I don't want any argument, I'll pick you up early on Sunday the ninth and take you as far as I can on the road to Penistone and Barnsley. But after that you're on your own, I've got to get back to the office because on the tenth I'm leaving Manchester for Germany."

"Germany! Did you say you were going to Germany?" If Michael had said he was about to fly to the moon, Anne and Maria couldn't have looked more startled.

Michael shrugged his shoulders, "There was political trouble in Bavaria a few years ago, never stopped really and now it's getting worse. My editor was intrigued to notice that in all the news reports, whenever trouble flared, the same name cropped up with it - Adolph Hitler! Paul wants me to go to Germany and find out what the man's up to. Don't look so worried, be happy for me – it means I'm going to be promoted - the Sentinel's new man in Germany!"

So, in January, 1928, as well as celebrating Tim's birthday, they celebrated Michael's future promotion and when Michael left for Manchester early the following morning he promised to return for Tim's journey to Doncaster in September. "And no changing your mind," he said to Tim with mock reproof as he was leaving.

On the 9th of September, Michael called for Tim and they set off on the first stretch of the journey to Doncaster.

"We're making good time," Michael said as they drove through Tintwistle, "Think I'll press on a bit further before I let you out, okay?"

"Further the better. Thanks Michael."

They drove on without speaking until Michael broke the silence to tell Tim how much he was looking forward to the job in Germany. "Sure, I'll miss everybody but it'll be a big step up for me you know."

"Sounds right up your street," said Tim, "Investigating, playing detectives again."

"Huh! And what about you, you had a bash at being a detective, didn't you?"

"Not exactly Sherlock Holmes though, was I?"

"I wouldn't say that, Tim. You were the one who discovered where Betty's loot was hidden."

"Just lucky," said Tim, "Chance remark from Maria that did it." He was wondering whether to tell Michael about Beswick's American newspaper photo, when Michael said, right out of the blue, "By the way, the wife of that artist fellow, Martin Kershaw. You know, the one John Beswick thinks is Betty Williams.....?"

"Beswick told you about that?"

"Yes, he told me when he came to thank me for helping with his book. And he told me something else as well. He said the woman's no longer Martin Kershaw's wife."

"How's that?"

"Because she's his **widow!** It seems they were celebrating the sale of his painting when he had an accident, fell from the balcony of their hotel room, died instantly. He's left a very rich widow, apparently the painting sold for a fortune! Of course, John Beswick's convinced his death wasn't an accident."

"Don't listen to him Michael, John's got too much imagination. Betty's dead, she was drowned - you saw what was left of the boat. How could she survive?"

"You don't have to convince me that she's dead," said Michael.

Tim was pleased to find he had an ally. "I can't understand Beswick, unless it's because of the awful experiences he had – maybe he's still frightened? Anyway, the artist's widow, where is she now?"

"Disappeared after the funeral and no one's seen her since. Could have returned to England for all I know, or she may have gone to Paris on a shopping spree." Michael grinned. "All this news you're getting Tim, I hope you're taking it in, I don't suppose you'll be reading many newspapers for a day or two once I've dropped you off?"

"Don't suppose so. Thanks for telling me about Kershaw, Michael, but don't mention any of this to Maria, will you, she might believe what Beswick's saying and it would really scare her?"

"Me scare Maria? Never, Tim, you can count on that."

They reached a crossroad and Michael looked at the signpost. "This is as far as we go, Tim. But we're over the top and now it's a straight run for you down the Pennines and all the way to Barnsley. From Barnsley, I guess you've about a twenty mile hike to Sunny Donny."

"Thanks Michael. Thanks for everything." As they got out of the car together Tim noticed a bundle of newspapers on the back seat. "Are they old papers? Do you want them?"

Michael had forgotten they were there. "What do you want them for?"

Tim pointed upwards. "Clear sky, it's going to be cold tonight. A few newspapers stuffed up front and back and I'll sleep as snug as a bug in a rug. I'll miss your company, Michael....."

"Miss you too, Tim. And I really wish you weren't doing this." They hugged and Michael climbed back into the driver's seat. "Take care, Tim - for Maria's sake most of all - and I hope you find your mum and dad are well." As he turned the car round, he opened his window to call goodnight.

Tim returned the call, "Thanks again for everything. Good luck with your new job and you take care in Germany." Michael switched on the headlights before pressing his right foot down hard on the pedal, the back wheels threw up smoke, protesting as they spun around on the gravel; it was Michael's way of saying a final goodnight before speeding back to Manchester. Tim kept his eyes on the car's tail light until it disappeared round a bend in the road.

There was a moon around somewhere, but it had hidden itself behind a cloud and if there were any sheep roaming about there wasn't enough light to see them. It was all too dark and quiet for Tim, he called out at the top of his voice, "Hello Mum, it's me, Tim. I'm on my way to see you. Be with you soon. Love you Mum, love you Mum, love you Mum....." His cry echoed and re-echoed in the hills and the echo brought him some comfort. Feeling less lonely, he set off at a brisk pace down the eastern Pennine slope. The cloud had drifted away now and the sky was shining with stars and moonlight. The night air was cold, very cold, so Tim swung his arms as he walked to keep warm. He decided he would walk 'til dawn if he had to and then he would find a safe place to lie down and sleep before the morning traffic started.

The sun had just risen when he saw the sign for White House Farm. He opened the farm gate and made for a grey stone barn to the left of a gravel path leading to the farm house. The barn was locked, but Tim found a well hidden spot beside the west wall where he would be sheltered from the wind. He stuffed the old newspapers under his jacket and lay down at last. In next to no time, he was fast asleep.

Maria had asked Anne to stay with her while Tim was away. Although they had talked long into the evening on Sunday, Anne felt quite refreshed when she woke up next morning at five. She decided she'd had enough sleep and went down to the kitchen to make a cup of tea. Maria was already there. "Holy Mother, Maria, what's wrong, you look awful?"

"I didn't get much sleep last night. I had a bad dream about Tim and then I couldn't get back to sleep."

"What did you dream, can you remember?"

"Men were chasing Tim and he couldn't get away, he fell down and cried out, I tried to reach him, then I woke up."

"Oh, my poor love," said Anne. She poured out a cup of tea for Maria and one for herself. "There now," she said, "I'll put a drop of whisky in yours, perhaps you'll feel better after that."

Maria took a sip of her tea. Carefully she returned her cup to the saucer, "I didn't tell you everything last night, Anne. I meant to, but I didn't."

"What didn't you tell me?"

"I'm pregnant Anne"

"Oh my God, how far on are you?"

"A month."

"A month! Perhaps you're just a bit late?"

"I know I'm pregnant. I feel pregnant."

"Did you tell Tim?"

"Not yet."

"Why not?"

"He was set on seeing his mother, Anne, if I had told him he wouldn't have gone - he might never have gone, I didn't want to have that on my conscience."

"I understand, but it was a brave decision, Maria, I don't think I could have done it. Typical of you but I'm sure you did the right thing. Come on, finish your tea, try not to worry and let's see if you can get some rest."

CHAPTER TWENTY TWO

POLICE CONSTABLE ARNOLD SIMPKINS LEANED his bike against the gate of Whitehouse Farm, took off his helmet and hung it by its chinstrap on the handlebars. After giving the helmet a little tug to make sure it was secure, he took out a handkerchief from his trouser pocket and wiped the sweat from his brow. He had biked six miles uphill clad in his heavy tunic and it had been pretty tough going. It was two o'clock on Monday afternoon, a good time he hoped, for visiting Josie the farmer's wife. He settled his thoughts on her and that made him feel better.

He looked across at the farmhouse windows, if the curtains were closed it meant that old Amos, Josie's husband, was out for the day and the coast was clear. Good, the curtains were closed, but to be on the safe side he decided to wait for a couple of minutes before he opened the gate. Amos was a friend; he didn't want to hurt him. It was best to be cautious.

The sun beat down. Even within the thick walls of the farmhouse it must have been hot. Arnold was becoming fidgety, a whole week had passed since he and Josie had been able to lie down together and the dull ache in his groin told him that he couldn't bear to be away from her much longer. Taking hold of the handlebars of his bike with one hand, he gave the gate a push with the other and deftly manoeuvred his bike through the gap.

A casual glance to his left almost made him trip over his front wheel. He saw two feet sticking out from behind the west wall of the barn encased in a stout pair of boots which were in a far better condition than his own. Careful not to make any noise Arnold lowered his bike onto the soft grass beside the path and went to investigate. For the moment Josie was forgotten, it was duty first, Arnold Simpkins was a policeman!

Tim was in the deep sleep of the exhausted when a smart kick on the soles of his boots awakened him He sat up with a jerk and rubbed his eyes. When he saw the policeman standing over him his heart began to sink. "Oh God!" Tim thought, "This is the end of the road."

Arnold put on his tough policeman's voice, "Get on your feet and tell me who you are and why you're trespassing. Come on, gerrup sharp, or you'll feel the weight of my boot up your arse!"

Tim obeyed instantly, stammering in his haste to explain that he wasn't a vagrant, that he worked for Mrs. Martinelli in Blackpool and he produced the box of presentation clay pipes to prove it. "My name's Ryan, Tim Ryan," he said, "Ring Mrs. Martinelli and ask if you want.

She'll tell you," and he pointed to the telephone number on the box……..

Josie Appleyard couldn't understand why Arnold was so late and when she looked out of the window and saw his bike lying on the grass, she came out of the house to find him. She stopped when she reached the bike, the pedals had propped the back wheel clear of the ground and the wheel was still turning. It was then that she saw Arnold; he was holding a man by the scruff of the neck, backed up against the wall of the barn. The man looked terrified. Josie said sternly, "Arnold, what on earth's going on? You're hurting him, let go of him this minute!"

Arnold released Tim immediately. "Don't worry Josie, he's not hurt." Turning to Tim, to seek confirmation, he asked "Have I hurt you Mr. Ryan?"

"No constable, you haven't."

What Arnold wanted now was to get rid of Tim as quickly as possible so he could get into the house with Josie. "There you are then, Josie," he said, "I told you that he wasn't hurt, Mr. Ryan's on his way to Doncaster and he's walking all the way. He's doing it for a wager. Thing is, he's in a hurry to get there. Can't stop. Can't wait a minute, can you Mr. Ryan?"

"Yes, constable, I mean no constable, I mean I've got to get on my way." Tim straightened the collar of his coat and turned to Josie, "Sorry if I caused you any trouble, lady."

Josie's heart melted, she wasn't used to such consideration. "No, no trouble, no trouble at all Mr. Ryan." She thought that the trespasser was a nice looking young man, quite well dressed too and with such good manners. She watched him walking to the gate and called after him, "Did Arnold say you were going to Doncaster?"

Tim waved to her, "That's right missus, Doncaster."

Josie called out again, "They say it's going to be good weather for the St.Leger,"

Tim didn't hear, distance and the click of the gate drowned out her words. He hurried down the road on the last stages of his journey.

Josie and Arnold watched for a few seconds and then they turned to walk up the gravel path to the front door of the house. Arnold quickened his step and began to draw away from Josie. She tried to keep up with him, she knew why he was in a hurry and felt flattered, but Josie had something she must to tell him before they reached the house. "Wait, Arnold, wait. Listen to me, it's very important."

Perhaps Arnold didn't hear because he was already in the house before Josie had reached the door. He wheeled his bike into the hall and leaned it against the wall. In front of him was the staircase to the bedrooms. Arnold's heart beat faster and he was conscious again of the ache in his groin. He shot up the stairs, his fingers already busy undoing the buttons of his tunic. He tore it off and left it where it fell; he heard the faint sound it made as it landed on the stair-carpet behind him. Braces and trousers were next. Off they came and now Arnold was ready!

He had reached the landing when he heard Josie come into the hall. He called down to her, "Are you coming up, Josie?" There was no reply from Josie, she had tried to warn him but now it was too late. Arnold was about to find out just what it was she had wanted to tell him.

Arnold entered the bedroom and almost collapsed; lying on the bed was old Amos, his face as pale and still as if it had been carved out of marble, a large white handkerchief was looped under his chin and tied in a knot at the top of his head and a round dark penny closed each of his eyes.

Jose waited for Arnold at the foot of the stairs. "I tried to tell you, but you wouldn't listen," she said when he came down and she led him into the kitchen. His face was almost the colour of the corpse laid on the bed upstairs.

"But our signal, Josie, our signal, the curtains were drawn," moaned Arnold.

"I know Arnold," said Josie patiently, "But when somebody in the house dies, what do we do? We draw the curtains. You know that."

Arnold mumbled his response and Josie couldn't hear what it was he was saying. When he sat down she noticed that he was trembling.

"I did try to warn you Arnold, I did," said Josie, sympathetically. She pulled up a chair and sat in front of him and took his hands in hers. "Look at me Arnold," she said. "Look at me, there's a few things I've got to get straight with you. You are listening to me, Arnold?"

Arnold raised his head. "Yes," he said his voice still shaky.

"Right, well, first things first - the first thing I've got to tell you is that Amos knew what was going on between us. Right from the start he knew and we had his full approval."

"He knew? He approved?" Arnold almost lost his voice completely, the most he could manage was a whisper and his face was a picture of complete bewilderment.

"Yes, approved. I'm a young woman, Amos knew I had needs. Amos couldn't meet them; he suggested you were the man to do it ....."

"**Suggested me!** I can't believe it," Arnold roared now, his words rolled round the kitchen angrily, like thunder.

"Well, it's true," said Josie, calmly, "And sometimes when you thought he was away at Doncaster market, he was here, fast asleep in the barn. Amos thought that if you knew he knew about us, you wouldn't come here again, so that's why we didn't tell you."

"Oh my God," said Arnold, "Well, he was right about that. Is there any more you've got to tell me?"

"Only that Amos appreciated all the help you gave him with the farm work when he was getting frail. He said that you always did more than he asked you to do. He told me what a good man you were. Amos always said that you'd make a better farmer than a policeman. He said that when he died there was nothing he would like better than you and me, as husband and wife, running the farm together. And that's what I've got to talk to you about, now."

Arnold was mumbling again.

"Can't tell a word you're saying," said Josie. "No matter, I want you to listen to me, Arnold, because what I've got to say to you is important. Are you listening to me?"

"Yes, I'm listening."

"Good, 'Cos two months after the funeral you and me are going to get wed. Tell that mother of yours when you go home, today. You can't be her baby boy forever, Arnold. Promise me, you'll tell her?"

"I will. I'll tell her, I want to marry you Josie, I do. It's all come as a shock though, finding Amos dead in his bed and now you telling me that all the time he knew about us, it's a shock. It's a right big shock, Josie."

"Tell your mother she can come here and live with us on the farm or stay where she is. It's her choice. Promise you'll tell her, today!"

"I promise, today, Josie. It's you I want to be with."

"Right then," said Josie.

Arnold made a move to collect the trousers and tunic he had abandoned on the staircase. Josie stopped him. "No, Arnold, you won't need your uniform yet and we'll have something to eat, later...."

They didn't see Tim outside the window. He had doubled back to the farm because he was starving; he left behind the sandwiches and bottle of milk Maria had given him in Michael's car. Seeing no sign of the bike, he hoped that the policeman had left, in which case he would try to persuade the farmer's wife to sell him milk and perhaps something to eat. No such luck! As he crept up to the open kitchen window he heard Arnold and Jose's raised voices. A large jug of milk stood on the sill inside the open window. Tim reached out, took the jug by the handle and drained it dry. The lovers, in a world of their own, didn't see or hear him. He left a three penny bit on the window sill for the milk and hurried away before his luck ran out!

CHAPTER TWENTY THREE

TIM HAD WALKED BARELY FIFTY yards from the farm when he heard the sound of rushing water; he crossed the road and a grass verge to a section of dry stonewalling. Sure enough, at the bottom of a deep grassy bank ran a swift flowing stream. Tim was over the wall and down the embankment within seconds. Sweating in the hot September sun he stripped off, waded into the clear water and soon felt cool and clean again.

As the stream cascaded over pebbles and boulders it sparkled in the early afternoon sun, dazzling his eyes. A shady tree invited him to lie down and Tim couldn't resist the offer. His thoughts drifted to Whitehouse Farm, he guessed that by now Arnold might be fancying a cup of tea and Josie would discover the empty milk jug! Tim didn't dare contemplate the possible outcome of that little discovery, he dressed in a hurry, climbed to the top of the embankment and half running, half walking, put as much distance as he could between himself and Constable Simpkins.

About half a mile along the road he rounded a bend and found a lorry blocking his path. The driver was out of the cab, angry and frustrated, swearing and kicking at a couple of heavy crates that had fallen from the vehicle. One of the crates had been damaged by the fall; some of its contents had spilled out and lay strewn across the road. A broken rope dangled from the vehicle and Tim guessed the driver had taken the bend too fast and the rope had broken under the strain. He called out, "Looks like you need a hand there mate."

"They're too heavy for me on my own." grumbled the driver.

"So what happened?" asked Tim.

"Coming round the bend and the bloody rope broke, didn't it? Those two crates came off. Well, you can see for yourself."

Tim took a look up the road, "Better get them back on quick, or you might be in trouble. Police might come asking questions about overloading. I saw a copper at a farm not a mile back - could be here any minute."

"Yeah, I know the one you mean. I do this run a lot and the bugger never seems to be off duty - up and down this road all hours." He kicked again at one of the crates. "Well, if you want to help, give us a hand with this one first, it's the lightest." Between them they manhandled the crate and lifted it back without too much effort. The driver jumped up onto the floor of the lorry to examine the broken rope.

"While you're fixing the rope, shall I get the lid of this crate back on? Lid's damaged and loose, another accident like the last one and all this stuff will end up on the road."

"Okay, go ahead," said the driver, "I'll see how much rope we've got left to play with."

Tim picked up a large stone to use as a hammer. "What you got in this crate then, there's a lot of foreign writing on it?"

"Bottling plant spares – made in Germany."

Taking hold of the lid, Tim caught his hand on a sharp nail and drew blood. "Shit!" he stopped what he was doing to suck the dirt out from the wound.

"What's up?" shouted the driver.

"It's nothing - just caught my hand on a nail that's all. How are you getting on with the rope?"

"Nearly finished."

"I'll have this lid back in a minute and then you'll be on the road again." Tim was putting the last of the spilled items into the crate when he saw pistols mixed up with the bottling plant spares. He recognised them as Luger pistols; he had seen so many on the battlefields clutched in the hands of dead German officers'. Instinct warned him not to let the driver know he'd seen them. He lowered the lid, slammed it down hard on the crate, and banged away with the stone until it was fixed back firmly into place. Then he flung away his makeshift hammer, "Right, mate, I'm ready when you are," he called

Together they lifted the crate onto the lorry and tied the load down securely.

"Where you going, then?" the driver said, gruffly

"Doncaster," Tim replied.

"Well, if this ain't your lucky day, mate. That's where I'm going. Hop in. Come on and let's get going. We don't want to be here when that copper comes along with his questions, do we?"

He drove a few miles in silence before he asked, "Got anything to drink, mate?" The smell of stale whisky wafted from the man's breath as he spoke and when Tim said no, sorry he scowled and lapsed into silence again. Tim was convinced the driver suspected he had seen the guns, there was something about this man that Tim hadn't liked from the start and he began to feel uneasy. He moved over in his seat towards the cab door, widening the distance between them. Maybe he should open the door and make a jump for it? He dismissed the idea as too risky – he wouldn't get to Doncaster with a broken leg!

Tim made up his mind to humour the man. In a friendly manner he introduced himself, "My name's Tim Ryan, mate, what's yours?"

"Ron Goodwin," was the surly response.

Silence again and then Goodwin said, "I've been watching you, Tim Ryan. You're on the run, aintcha?"

Tim spluttered, what could he say?

"Oh, you're on the run all right. I can tell. Looking around all the time, you never stop. Head's never still. I've had plenty like you in this cab. Don't worry mate, I'll not shop you. I've been inside myself - twice – I hate the law."

"I'm a deserter," said Tim and immediately regretted telling him.

"Christ, is that all?"

"Bad enough if they catch me," said Tim.

"Yeah, 'spose so. Look, where you staying when you get to Doncaster, mate?" The question was asked casually enough, but Tim detected some craftiness in it. Did Goodwin want to keep tabs on him?

"Depends   Why?"

"Oh, I was just thinking, my boss will want to thank you for helping with the load."

"Don't bother about that," said Tim. It was dusk now and they were passing over the North Bridge, a couple of minutes from Doncaster town centre. "This'll do fine Ron; drop me off here." He tried his best to sound casual.

Goodwin drove on. "We're almost at the yard, now. A word of thanks from the boss and a nice cup of tea and you're on your way, now what could be better than that?"

They pulled up outside locked gates. The light was fading, but Tim could see several brick buildings in a compound surrounded by a high wire fence. He made out the letters, STAR TRADING COMPANY, on a board above the fence. Goodwin kept his engine running, gave a couple of blasts on his horn and a sleepy-eyed night watchman stumbled out of his cabin to unlock the gates and they drove in. Two men came out of the main building and in response to Goodwin's request they helped to unload and carry in the crates. The watchman relocked the gates behind them.

Tim and Goodwin followed the men down a passage and into a storeroom where theystacked the load alongside some older-looking boxes. "Thanks mate," said Goodwin when the job was finished, "Hold on for a minute or two while l go and see about the tea.   I'll let the boss know you're here."

Tim looked about the room, it wasn't big as far as store rooms go but the ceiling was high, Tim reckoned it was about twelve foot from floor to ceiling. A single bulb hung down from a beam above, the light it gave was poor and instead of brightening the room it created shadows. In the centre of the room there was a small wooden table with two old kitchen chairs beside it. Tim shivered as he sat down to wait for his cup of tea.

Goodwin popped his head round the door. "That's right mate," he said, "Take a load off your feet, I've put the kettle on - won't be long now."

Tim heard the click of a key turning in the lock as Goodwin closed the door. He tried the locked door and cursed himself for being so stupid. Goodwin was evil, he'd known it as soon as he first set eyes on him, and yet he had been daft enough to let the man dupe him.

He heard voices in the next room and calmed himself while he concentrated to make out what was being said. The walls were thin, he heard Goodwin mention "deserter" and then, "They shoot deserters, you know. He could tell on us to save himself. Tell them what he saw in the crate. What do you think we should do with him, Barnsie?"

"Kill 'im! Safer. Tomorrow take him back where you found him. Dump him. Job done. End of story."

Barnsie's voice was flat, without any emotion, as far as murder was concerned it was obvious that he considered it to be routine!

Now someone with a Scottish accent was speaking, "But what about Mr. Frost and Herr Schulz? Herr Schulz won't stand for it, you know." The voices were louder, they seemed to be arguing. Then he heard the Scottish accent again, quite clearly this time, "We're agreed. We kill him tonight. Tomorrow Goodwin dumps the body. We don't tell Frost or Schulz. Right?"

Tim was scared out of his wits. "Those bastards are coming to kill me!" For a moment he panicked and almost knocked over one of the chairs. Then he moved quickly and methodically. He hauled the heaviest of the crates against the door hoping it would hold them back a bit. The only window was high, almost near the ceiling and narrow; he positioned the table underneath it and placed a chair on top of the table. He climbed onto the table and up onto the chair but he wasn't high enough to reach the window! As he jumped down he saw an empty box to add height to the pile and trying again he reached the window. The catch was jammed! Somehow he stayed calm, steadied himself on his makeshift ladder and fumbled in his pocket for his old penknife. He prised the rusted catch open and pushed the window outwards only to find the gap was too narrow for him to get through. There was a noise in the passage and then heavy thuds on the door as the men tried to force it open against the weight of the crate. Tim tore off his bulky coat and jacket and pushed them through the open window, his strong fingers found a grip on the sill and he pulled himself up onto the ledge. Slimmer now, he managed to squeeze through the window like thread through the eye of a needle. His discarded clothes broke his fall but he was winded and it took a few seconds for him to recover before he got to his feet. He grabbed his coat, jacket and hat and ran for the wire fence!

An hour later, scratched and bleeding and with most of his top clothing in tatters, he reached his mother's house in Woodlands. His sister Martha came to the door. It took her a few seconds to recognise him and when she did she flung her arms around him and smothered him with kisses. She called to her husband, "Tom, it's my brother Tim. Tim's come home!"

Chapter Twenty Four

"And Mum, how is she?" said Tim when Martha stopped plying him with questions.

"Oh, Mother's fine Tim, but she's asleep just now, you'll have to wait 'til morning to see her. You don't want to wake her up, do you?"

"No, let her rest. What about Dad?"

Martha took his hand. "We didn't know where you were to let you know, but Dad had a stroke six months ago ..... he died, Tim."

Tim grew quiet and Martha, recognising he needed some time to be on his own, said she'd have to get to bed now, there would be more time to talk in the morning. At the door to the stairs she turned back, "We got a Christmas card from you," she said, "Post mark Manchester - about three Christmas's ago? It meant a lot to Dad."

That night Tim slept on a rug in front of the fire in the living room. There was no bed for him and no spare blankets either. Martha had apologised and explained that she'd shared most of the blankets between the children, in the winter they made do by throwing old coats on their beds. "And when it gets really freezing cold," she said, "there's always the oven plate, isn't there?" Tim knew very well what she meant by that. He remembered the large, flat cast-iron oven plates being drawn from their grooves in the hot oven and wrapped in old cloth remnants so they wouldn't scorch the precious bed sheets. When the beds were given the oven plate treatment, there were no complaints; they were all snug as bugs in a rug!

Tom, Martha's husband, had banked the fire half way up the chimney before going to bed. "Should keep you warm all night, Tim, but I'll put some more coal on if it needs it when I leave for the early shift."

Tim picked up the poker and gave the fire a gentle stir and instantly the room became bathed in a warm cosy glow. He stretched out again on the rug, warm and comfortable and safe! In the light from the fire he was able to pick out familiar objects that had been in the room years ago, before he went on the run. The two large pot-glazed lions still guarded each end of the side-board and on a table in an alcove next to the door leading to the front room was **the** gramophone. It was the same gramophone that had provided Princess Zoe with music to dance to on that sunny day in Blackpool! Martha had told him about their rehearsals in the house – Mum and Dad laughing at their antics until they gasped for breath.

Martha seemed so composed and mature, a young girl before he ran away now with a family of her own, two children, Margaret and Tommy. Tim reflected happily that he had a niece and a nephew; he had a lot of catching up to do. He remembered his own childhood –remembered happy times spent with his father and he wanted to call out, "Dad's dead, Maria, I was too late; I was too late after all."

At seven o'clock in the morning Martha came down stairs with young Tommy and Margaret. She flung a clean tablecloth over the plain deal-topped table and Tim and the children sat around it together on shiny, black-varnished wooden chairs. As they ate their breakfast, Martha reminded Tim that this was the same furniture their parents had piled onto the cart in the snow and brought from Sheffield all those years ago when Dad came to work at the new pit in Brodsworth.

Tommy and Margaret looked up from their bread and milk to steal shy glances at Tim and for a while he tucked into his breakfast pretending not to notice them. Then suddenly he caught their gaze and pulled faces until they giggled helplessly and forgot their shyness.

Martha chatted about the family, waiting patiently until Tim was ready to tell her his news. Eventually he told her about Maria. Martha was overjoyed. "Not hearing from you for such a long time we thought that you were -" and she lowered her voice to a whisper – "dead." She thought that the children wouldn't hear her. That was a mistake of course; children can hear a pin drop at over a hundred paces! Tommy and Margaret gazed at him with renewed interest! "Then we got your Christmas card telling us you were alright and now, thank God, you're here. And you look so fit and happy. And you know something Tim, as you've grown older you've become quite good-looking. Honestly, you have. In fact, you're quite hand-some."

Tim was embarrassed. He turned to the children, "We want to talk about Blackpool and the donkeys, don't we, Tommy and Margaret?"

"Yes, the donkeys and the sea and the sand," the children chorused. "When can we go?"

Martha had to call a halt to it in the end. "Give Uncle Tim a rest so he can go and talk to Grannie upstairs."

The children went out to play while Martha prepared a breakfast tray for her mother. "Ten minutes for breakfast, a few minutes to do her hair, then add a bit more time for a wash and freshen up and Mum's all yours. Okay, Tim?" Before he could reply she had balanced the tray on one hand and climbed the stairs. He heard her call out, "Morning Mum. Its early breakfast today and there's a great big surprise waiting for you, after."

When Martha came back into the living room, Tim fished about in his sock for the ten-shilling note he had hidden there and offered it to her. She didn't want to take it but he insisted. "Please take it. Don't be offended. I can afford it, Martha."

"Don't think we're starving Tim, we're not. It's Mum who helps, she must have a secret mint hidden in that room of hers. When things are really bad, I'll come down in a morning and find a nice shiny half crown or even a half sovereign on the table. I told her I think she's a witch."

"I've always known Mum was magic," said Tim. "About Blackpool, Martha, next year, you and Tom and the children, will you come and stay with us for a holiday? It's a big house, room for everyone. The children have never been to the sea-side have they?"

"No," said Martha wistfully. "And I suppose it will be a long time before they do."

"Next year they will and that's a promise."

Martha thanked him graciously but secretly she doubted Tim's promise, what if he disappeared and they didn't hear from him again? "You can go and talk to Mum now," she said.

After all the hugging and kissing was over Tim sat on the edge of the bed and took a good look at his mother. She was almost seventy and still beautiful. Her small oval face was framed with thick, white hair which Martha had brushed and tied back with blue ribbon. The wrinkles round her eyes and lips creased more deeply as she smiled at him.

Tim told her about Maria and his mother plied him with questions until she was satisfied. "Every woman needs a good man to look after her," she said. "I say, every women needs a good man to look after her," And then, as if realizing the significance of what she had just said, she lapsed into silence.

"What is it, Mum?" said Tim anxiously.

"Oh, it's your Dad, Tim. Six months he's been dead, but I don't seem to be able to get over it. I miss him. It comes over me terribly, sometimes. The loneliness just comes over me, I can't stop it." Tim held her in his arms while she wept and slowly, slowly, a change came over her. She drew her head away from him and tried to smile, "Oh, I'm sorry Tim. Look at me, miserable creature feeling hard done by when I should be thanking God for **you**. I thought I'd lost my husband and my son, but now He's given you back to me." Tim held her again, "God's good, I say, God's good, Tim. Why should I ever have doubted?"

She reached under the pillow for her rosary beads and Tim strained to hear her prayers, "I know, Mum, I know," he whispered.

And then their chatter began all over again. This time she was telling him the family news. She told him how Sheila, the wife of Tim's elder brother Bernard, had met a quack doctor in Doncaster market and run away with him to America and taken their baby daughter with them. Poor Bernard, thought Tim, he'd been through the Boer War and the Great War and now he'd lost his wife and his child.

"But you can't blame Sheila entirely, not really," his mother said. "Our Bernard and those two daft friends of his, Long Andy and Short Andy, are convinced there's going to be another war with Germany. They're on about it all the time. Bernard doesn't seem to be able to talk about anything except war. He was like a sergeant major with Sheila, had a flagpole stuck up in their front garden and morning and evening he used to order Sheila to raise and lower the flag!"

Tim tried to change the subject. "What about our Jim and that girl who came to Blackpool during the strike, to raise money for the miners. They took the gramophone with them - remember?"

"Oh, that's Bethany Hughes. Lovely girl, we call her Beth. Didn't our Martha tell you what happened?"

"Tell me what?"

"It was in the local paper. The local paper was full of it. Go over to that wash stand. That's it, the stand with the big bowl and jug on it. Now open that little drawer underneath, there's a newspaper cutting in the drawer. Can you find it?

Tim nodded.

"Bring it to me, son."

She unfolded the newspaper carefully, smoothed it out and handed it back to him. "There now, read that and tell me what it says."

"It says here that Jim fought off three men who were attacking and trying to rob a Frau Weisskopf outside her house, Millbank."

He lowered the paper and looked at his mother, "Millbank.....?"

"Yes, Millbank, that big house by the millstream. Surely you remember that place, Tim? And the millstream, you and your pals used to bathe in it when you were a boy. The young ones still bathe in it now."

Tim remembered bathing in the buff because they didn't have swimming costumes. He laughed, "I remember just like it was yesterday, Mum. But seriously, those robbers, they must have got a fright when Jim came on the scene. Regimental boxing champion, our Jim was."

"There's a picture on that cutting. Have a look."

Tim looked at it and read the caption aloud, "Congratulations - a lucky escape for Frau Weisskopf!" The picture showed a small group of people smiling and raising their glasses to a young woman. The group were named – to the left a man called Joachim von Ribbentrop and to the right, Herr Schulz and his wife, Renate. There was only one Englishman in the group, Jack Frost and he stood next to the young woman. Tim caught his breath. Herr Schulz, Frost, weren't they the names those thugs mentioned when he was locked in the room at the Star Trading Company? Tim began to sweat. If ever he needed advice from Michael, it was now.

"Frau Weisskopf, she's beautiful, isn't she?" his mother said.

Tim agreed and his mother continued with her story, "Jim's left his cottage and gone to live with her in Millbank. Poor Beth, he's broken her heart and if that's not enough the poor lass has got the sack and she can't teach at the school. That's Sir Henry's doing, I say that's Sir Henry's doing."

Before she could explain further, they heard voices at the foot of the stairs. "Quick Tim, that's Doctor McKenzie. Best if he doesn't see you. We don't want anybody to know you're here. Go in Tom and Martha's room next door an' be quick about it!"

Tim crouched beside Tom and Martha's bed. He had left the door slightly open, if there was anything seriously wrong with his mother's health, he wanted to hear about it.

"Mary Ryan, how many times do I have to warn you," Doctor McKenzie admonished, loudly - "One of these days you'll strangle yourself with those Rosary Beads."

"Scottish heathen," Mary Ryan scolded. But she was joking and her scolding changed to laughter.

"All right Mary. Come on then, let's lift you up a wee bit higher so I can listen to that chest of yours."

He put his stethoscope back into his bag, "Good, good, you seem much better today, Mary. Maybe you should try getting up for a bit? Got to keep those legs moving, you know."

"I will, I will. I'm starting today; I say, I'm starting to-day."

"That's the spirit Mary. And talking of spirit are you still taking a dram of the Bell's morning and evening? Have you had a wee drop this morning?"

"Not yet, I was waiting for you, Alistair. There's two clean cups on the mantelpiece, Martha washed them this morning."

"Good."

Tim heard them chink their cups together and he could imagine them smacking their lips and whispering conspiratorially. Then he heard his mother say, "By the way, Alistair, tell me truthfully, did you do it on purpose?"

"Do what on purpose?"

"You know perfectly well. My St. Theresa statue, the one you accidentally knocked off the mantelpiece, when you stuck her head back on again, you put it on back to front, you heathen. You did it on purpose. Come on now, admit it."

"I didn't do it on purpose, Mary. Why don't you keep the statue with the head the way it is - say there's been a miracle, people will be most impressed!"

"Nonsense! When are you coming to see me again?" she asked.

"A week today."

"Well, when you come make sure you bring that glue of yours. And do a proper job on it next time; I say make sure you do a proper job next time."

"I will Mary, I will," the doctor said contritely, "And you won't even see the join."

Tim waited until the doctor was at the foot of the stairs before he slipped back into his mother's room. He stood at the bedroom window looking down at a laburnum tree. "Where did the tree come from?"

"Jim. Your brother Jim, he planted it years ago. Oh Tim, you should have seen it in May, '26. It was dripping with blossom. Golden! A sign of hope for the strike and the future, that's what our Jim said it was. Turned out to be a false hope, didn't it? But the tree blossoms every year and every year it brings us fresh hope. That's the only thing we've got left now – hope and prayer. Never give up hope, Tim."

She reached for her rosary beads again and whilst she was preoccupied Tim copied his Blackpool telephone number onto the newspaper cutting and returned it to the drawer in the washstand for safekeeping. When his mother had finished praying, he told her what he had done. "I've put my telephone number on the newspaper cutting, Mum, in case you or Martha should need it. Martha can phone from the post office. I'd like Martha and Tom to bring the children to us next summer for a holiday. What's Martha's married name, we had so much to talk about, I forgot to ask her?"

"It's Fallon, Tom's from Ballinasloe, County Galway."

"They're all coming from Ballinasloe," murmured Tim, thinking about Maria's father.

"What's that?" said his mother.

"Nothing, Mum - just something about Ireland...."

They heard the tread of heavy footsteps on the stairs. "Bernard, it's your brother Bernard," she said, "His feet tell you most about him, you always know when it's him on the stairs."

Bernard filled the bedroom doorway. He took one look at Tim and shouted, "You! What the hell are you doing here? Bloody deserter! Not content with bringing shame on the family, you're back to cause trouble for Mother, is that it?"

"No he isn't, Bernard, and it's lovely to see him," protested Mary, gently.

Bernard lowered his voice but he was still scowling. "Lovely to see him? He's out to bring you trouble. Listen to me Tim, brother or not, if you've not gone by Leger Day I'll shop you to the redcaps myself. I'm not having you worry our Mother. Savvy?"

"That's up to you, Bernard," said Tim, sadly. It didn't seem so many years ago that he'd sat beside his elder brother enthralled as he listened to him telling stories about Africa. Now Bernard was abrupt and aggressive, a different man. Tim didn't like this new man at all but he forgave him instantly, a lot of cruel things had happened to Bernard, it wasn't his fault that he'd changed. Ignoring Tim, Bernard spoke to their mother. "I'll come back Leger Day. He'd better be gone then. It'll be in the evening and I'll let you know how Jim got on after his fight with Buster Bates. Is that alright with you, Mother?"

"That's alright Bernard, but before you go, may I ask you a little question?"

"What's that?"

"It's something that's been puzzling me for ages," she said. "And I thought that perhaps you could give me the answer. What I want to know, Bernard, is this, why is it that a young man who fought for his country for four years........." Bernard had already turned towards the door, "Are you listening to me Bernard?"

"'Course I am."

"Well, what I want to know is this, why is it that a young man who fought for his country for four long years -

and him only a boy remember – why should he get treated so badly? Fighting all that time, is it any wonder his nerves were shattered? And what did all those important people do for him when that happened? Did they thank him and reward him in some way for what he had done? Did they offer to give him doctors' advice, take him to a hospital and try to help him to get better? No, they didn't do any of those things. Those important people – our so called betters - they tried to hunt him down like an animal so they could tie him to a stake and shoot him. And as far as I can make out, they're still at it." She paused to catch Bernard's gaze, "What sort of a reward is that? But they gave him a title though – "Tim Ryan, Deserter." Now, isn't that a grand title for somebody who has suffered and given so much for his country?" Bernard lowered his eyes and examined the shine on his boots. - "We're supposed to be civilised, Bernard. The people who order these wicked deeds, what sort of people are they? I say what sort of people are they?"

Bernard defended himself. "Our way is the army way, Mother, and the army way is the right way," and with that he stomped down the stairs, calling, "Be gone before I come back on Leger Day, Tim, I'm warning you!"

"Poor Bernard," said Mary.

Tim diverted her, "What was all that about a fight between our Jim and Buster Bates?"

His mother sighed and told him the story. "It all started with Freddie Payne. You remember Freddie Payne the milkman, don't you?"

"'Course I do."

"Well, there was an old lady, a customer in trouble with her rent and kind hearted Freddie fought Buster Bates at the fairground to try and win five pounds to get her out of trouble."

"Freddie? I know he's big, but he couldn't knock the skin off a rice pudding. So, what happened?"

"For three rounds that heavy-weight Buster fellow played cat and mouse with him. Cruel they say he was. Cut poor Freddie to ribbons and then knocked him clean out at the end of the last round. Jim says he's going to put things right – even things up. And he will, you know what our Jim's like. Tim, it will be best if you leave before Bernard comes back on Leger Day. If you're still here he will tell the redcaps and from the bottom of his heart he'll think that he's done his bit to try and save England!"

Chapter Twenty Five

Leger day, September 12TH 1928, arrived. It was a bright, sunny morning and Mary got out of her bed her mind made up, she was the one who was going to cook the dinner, it would be something special for Tim to enjoy before he set off for Blackpool.

"No!" she said to Martha, "I don't need you to help me to get ready, I can do it myself." And although it took her over an hour, she managed to dress and come down the stairs unaided.

The meal Grannie Twiceover cooked was a labour of love and she timed it exactly to coincide with Tom's return from the pit at four o'clock. Margaret and Tommy gobbled their food so they could run outside to play. Tom ate slowly, relishing the meal Mary had cooked but he looked worn out and after saying goodbye to Tim he went upstairs to sleep. Mary sat on the sofa under the window while Tim and Martha stacked up the dishes, took them into the kitchen and washed them in water that had been simmering away on the living room fire. Their mother heard them talking in whispers for a while then she dozed off and dreamed about them as children.

Martha put the last pot away, "I think it's time you were getting ready, Tim."

"What time is it?"

Mary had woken, "Just turned six," she called.

Tim went through to her in the living room. Stretching, he let out a deep groan of satisfaction, "Some meal, Mum. Some cook, eh, Martha?" He patted his stomach. Martha smiled; she disappeared for a minute and returned with his jacket and heavy coat. He put on the jacket but decided to carry his coat, the evening was warm. Martha fussed with his collar and handed him his hat, "There now," she said, kissing his cheek.

His mother led him through the parlour and opened the front door. "Go out through the garden, there's nobody about, they're all away at the races." A final hug, a last kiss and they parted. He paused to reach out and touch the laburnum tree; the words his mother had whispered as she lay in her bed came back to him, "Never give up hope, Tim."

He decided to return home by the same route he had taken when he first set out from Blackpool, maybe it wasn't the shortest way back, but it was the one he knew. The day must have been one of the hottest days of the year; Tim loosened his jacket and shifted the weight of his coat to his left shoulder. He thought about taking off his hat, but instead pulled the brim down lower over his eyes – he felt safer with his face hidden and soon the evening air would be cooler.

The road back to Blackpool started at a pub with a thatched roof called the Sun Inn. The pub was sited where the road turned westwards almost midway between Woodlands and Doncaster and in less than half an hour Tim was there. Outside the pub a crowd were celebrating Lord Derby's fourth St Leger winner, Fairway, and it seemed they had gone through the rest of the card as well. They were in the money!

Tim stood at the apex of the triangle where the road to the Pennines branched off from the Great North Road leading north and south. Should he turn right and head for Barnsley, Blackpool and Maria, or should he continue straight on southwards through the town to the fairground to find out how Jim got on with the fight? The detour would add a couple of hours to his journey but it would be worth it just to see Jim again and maybe to help him. Although his brother had been a champion boxer at his own weight, Buster Bates had more than a two stone advantage and a much longer reach. With those odds, Jim could get seriously hurt, he remembered his mother's account of what had happened to Freddie Payne and made up his mind to walk on to Doncaster and find Jim.

The thugs from the Star Trading Company, Barnes, Goodwin and McLeod were waiting for Tim at the fairground. They knew he would come, McLeod, the soft-spoken Scotsman had guessed so and he was always right. They spied Tim rubbing his eyes as he stumbled into the blinding lights of the fairground and Barnes immediately made a move to go after him. McLeod grabbed Barnes jacket and hauled him back.

"What d'yer think you're playing at? I could have had him then."

McLeod released his hold and hissed, contemptuously, "For Christ's sake use your head, laddie. With all those people around, you wouldn't have stood an earthly. Can't you see that?"

Barnes glared at McLeod; he made no attempt to disguise his hatred. Their eyes met, but McLeod's unwavering look unnerved him and Barnes was the first to blink. Muttering to himself he lowered his head and slunk away to join Goodwin at the rear.

McLeod pointed to Tim. "I think he's looking for somebody. Any road, we'll tail him for now and see." He moved ahead and they followed.

Barnes complained in Goodwin's ear. "He's always calling me laddie and telling me what to do. Who the hell does he think he is?"

"He's Jack Frost's right hand man mate, that's who he is and you'd best remember that, Barnsie."

Barnes didn't reply, one day he'd get his own back on McLeod. He ran a hand over his face and winced. The bruising was still tender from the beating he'd received at the hands of Jim Ryan at Frau Weisskopf's. "Ryan's a bastard, first chance I get he'll be dead before he knows what's hit him!"

The marquee for Hagan's boxing booth stood next to the one housing Sid Silver's Hawaiian Paradise, pitched at the far end of the fairground they were the two largest tents on the site. Tim made a beeline for the boxing booth only to find that he couldn't gain entry - the fight was still on!

Keeping one eye on Sid Silver's marquee and the other on Hagan's boxing booth, Tim waited anxiously for the contest to end.   Sid Silver stood, immaculately dressed, megaphone in hand, silver hair glistening under the bright lights.   Now halfway through his spiel, he drew the crowd to him - controlling the crowd made him feel powerful! He looked at his watch; there were several minutes still to go before the spectators came out from the tent next door. He would "hook and reel 'em in," along with the rest of 'em, meanwhile there was time for a bit of fun with this lot. On cue three girls in grass skirts came out from the shadows and positioned themselves behind Sid, swaying gently to the sound of Hawaiian guitar music.   Sid gave them a wink to indicate that the game was on; they winked back and with smiling faces waited for his signal. "Ladies and gentlemen," shouted Sid through the megaphone," All the way from Hawaii and here tonight for your special entertainment are the most talented, the most beautiful dancing girls in the world." The girls swished their skirts and wiggled their hips madly to show the crowd how much they appreciated Sid's compliment.   Sid's back was to the girls and he pretended that he didn't know what had happened.   The crowd roared with delight.   As soon as Sid turned the girls resumed their gentle swaying, their faces pictures of innocence. The crowd loved it, they were waiting for more!

Sid flicked some dust off his jacket and took a quick look at his watch. Any minute now the audience would be streaming out of Hagan's tent. He picked up the megaphone again,   "Ladies and Gentlemen. Tonight we're in for a treat. It's something special the girls want to do to mark this glorious St. Leger Day. Believe me, Ladies and Gentlemen - it's a real winner! For the very first time in this country, the girls are going to perform the Hawaiian fertility dance - the dance the missionaries banned! The dance they tried to ban – forever! Why did they want to ban it? Well, if you want to find out, just step into the tent. You can see for yourselves...."

From inside the tent the sound of gently throbbing drums had taken on a wilder beat, the music grew louder and the movements of the dancing girls behind him became more and more enticing. Sid was giving the crowd a taste of what they might see if they entered into his Hawaiian Paradise - and it would cost them only sixpence! The boxing booth crowd came streaming out and a good many - hearing Sid's comments about the missionaries - joined onto the queue for the Hawaiian show.

A man with a limp, leaning heavily on a walking stick, left the boxing booth and hobbled towards the fairground exit without giving Sid or his Paradise in Hawaii a second glance. Tim saw him and anxious to find out what had happened to Jim, hurried to intercept him. "Excuse me mister, I saw you come out from the boxing just now. Mind if I ask; who's won?" He had to shout in order to make himself heard because the fairground steam organ had been turned on and the noise was almost deafening.

Cupping his ear the man replied, "Pity you didn't see it mate. You missed a great fight. Jim Ryan won."

"Great! Great news," said Tim, relieved and excited at the same time. "Anybody get hurt? I've heard stories about Bates, likes inflicting pain. I heard about that fight with Freddie Payne..."

"Huh! 'Spect he thought he'd do the same to Jim. But he had another thought coming, didn't he? For two rounds Jim hammered away at Bates midriff. He took a bit o' stick getting through, but it paid off in the end. When the last round started, Bates could hardly draw breath and that's when Jim waded in and gave him a dose of his own medicine - and when Jim dropped him at the final bell you should have heard the crowd roaring and cheering."

Tim was pleased to hear the news; it wasn't so much the reaction of the crowd it was finding out that his brother hadn't been hurt.

"But that Buster Bates, you should have seen him, mister, know what they call him now?" the man chuckled, reliving the fight, "Busted Bates! That's what they call him now. **Busted** Bates! Get it?"

"In one. Is that why you're looking so happy?"

"Yeah. I had a bet Jim would win and I've got a couple of pints waiting for me at the local. Mind you, that's not the only thing Jim's won for me ..." He gave his left leg a hefty crack with his walking stick. "Meet Tin Lizzie, Jim won her for me after a pit accident, and a bit o' compo extra, helps to pay the rent. What do you think of her, tough, eh?" and he gave his false leg yet another crack to demonstrate the point.

"She sure is," said Tim. "Judging by the sounds of her she'll take a lot of **beating – get** it?"

"In one," said the man. He grew quiet, lowered his head and poked the ground with his stick remembering the nightmare shift when he had lost his leg.

"You all right?"

" I'm okay. But **he** didn't like it you know."

Tim looked puzzled. "Who didn't like it?"

"Sir Henry o' course."

"Oh?"

"When he found out that Jim was representing me he decided to fight the case. Jim won and he lost, simple as that. Mind you, it wasn't so much the money or me for that matter; it was Jim Sir Henry was fighting. And I'll tell you something, win or lose Sir Henry enjoyed it; it was like he was fighting the unions and the strike all over again. When the strike ended the first thing he did was to sack Jim. Said he was a trouble maker and he'd see to it that Jim never worked in a mine again." He shook his head, "Funny thing happened at the fight just now though and I can't understand it."

"What's that?"

"Sir Henry's niece, Henrietta, she was in the boxing booth. I was standing close to her, I couldn't help seeing. When Bates drew blood she went white as a sheet and I'll swear to God she felt every blow that Jim took. What do you make of that then?"

"What's to make of it? Maybe she doesn't like to see men trying to hurt one another? Perhaps she only went there to please Sir Henry?"

"Yeah, well, maybe," said the man, shuffling his feet. He was staring at a fashionably dressed group of people who had left the boxing booth and were talking to Sid Silver. Sid was smiling, this was his catch of the day - they paid him their sixpences and Sid triumphantly led them into his Hawaiian Paradise. Tim had recognised most of the people in the group, Sir Henry and his niece for a start. The tallest man in the group he didn't know, nor did he know the handsome looking woman who was with him but Herr Schulz he recognised from the photograph in the newspaper cutting. So this was Schulz, the boss of those men who had held him captive at the Star Trading Company. Tim shivered. Images of McLeod, Barnes and Goodwin swept away all the good news he had heard about his brother, the music from the steam organ, so jolly before, now seemed to have taken on a sinister note, blaring out a warning, "Get out! Get out of the fairground Tim. Go now, before it is too late!" In the space of just a few seconds his nervousness had changed the fairground into a place of menace. Feeling cold, he put on his coat and pulled up the collar to hide more of his face. The sooner he got out of the fairground the sooner he would feel safe. Urgently he thought of finding a phone and letting Maria know he was on his way home to Blackpool.

McLeod and his men were watching him, they hadn't let him out of their sight from the moment he had first entered the ground. They were standing no more than twenty yards away mingling with parents behind a kids' carousel, grinning and waving to the bobbing children as they whirled around.

"It's getting late, nice to have talked to you, mister," said the man with the tin leg. He scuttled away quick as a Blackpool crab chased by a kid with a bucket and his abrupt departure took Tim by surprise. Left on his own, Tim's fear grew, but more acute than his fear was the ache that had started up in his bladder, the pain was excruciating. He ran for the cover of the big traction engines parked in a patch of waste ground on the edge of the fairground.

Save for the odd shaft of light penetrating from the stalls and carousels it was too dark to see clearly and Tim had to tread warily to avoid tripping over lines of thick black cable that snaked in all directions amongst the grass. The traction engines hissed and spat out clouds of vapour as he looked around to choose his spot. He undid his flies and once he started to relieve himself he thought he would never stop. A rat watched him through bright, beady eyes but when the high steaming arc thudded into the ground just missing it by inches, the rat fled to find sanctuary elsewhere. Tim didn't notice; no pain now, only bliss!

McLeod picked up a piece of thick black cable, a cut-off discarded by one of the fairground fitters. He handed it to Barnes. "Here laddie, hit him with this, not too hard mind, just enough to send him to bye-byes until we get him back to the yard for questioning."

Barnes almost snatched the cable from his hand. He wanted to strike McLeod with it, "Laddie this and laddie that." The cable was a nice weight; he liked the feel of it. He gripped it in his right hand and smacked it against the palm of his left hand, it felt good. Turning away from McLeod he muttered under his breath. "Laddie, I'll give you laddie. So you want him for questioning do you? Well, dead men don't tell no tales, how's that for a laugh, laddie?" The thought that he was about to put one over on McLeod made Barnes happy for the first time in ages and there was more, not only would he be getting his own back on McLeod by having the deserter for desert, he would be satisfying his overwhelming desire to kill! "Deserter for desert," he couldn't help smiling, sounded clever, pity he couldn't tell the others what a wit he was. Barnes slapped the cable against his left palm again and crept up behind his quarry.

Tim had started to button up his flies when Barnes struck him, he saw a blinding flash of light and then everything went black. Barnes left him where he fell and made his way to the truck. McLeod waved Goodwin aside as he stooped to lift Tim's shoulders and drag him through the grass. Goodwin raced ahead after Barnes. "You're in for it Barnsie," he said, "You hit him too hard. Mac knows. You should see his face."

"Who gives a shit? What can he do? He can't tell Frost or Schulz about it, can he?" Barnes was feeling powerful now – it was a great feeling!

"You deliberately tried to kill that deserter, just like you would have killed Frau Weisskopf if Jim Ryan hadn't stopped you."

Barnes scowled. "Don't think I've forgotten about him. He's next on my list."

McLeod caught up with them and ordered Goodwin to help him load Tim's body onto the truck. He looked around for Barnes, "Where is he?"

Goodwin pointed, "Christ, Mac, look!"

McLeod couldn't believe his eyes. He saw Jim Ryan with three companions walking towards a charabanc parked further down the road and Barnes was running after them swinging the heavy cable.

"He's out to kill him, Mac."

"Get in the cab and start her up," said McLeod and cursed Barnes for being a mad dog, there was nothing more he could do until Barnes came back.

Joby Ford, the charabanc driver, was waiting wearily outside his vehicle, Leger day seemed to get busier every year. Four more seats to fill and then he could go home and put his feet up. The seats were for friends of his, Jim Ryan, Jim's brother Bernard and the two game keepers, Long and Short Andy. At last he saw the group approaching but there was someone else too, a man chasing them swinging something that looked like a club. Quick to sense danger, Joby heaved his bulk from the side of the cab and yelled out a warning as Barnes raised his arm to strike, "Behind you, Jim! Look out!"

The blow from the heavy cable would have caved in Jim's skull had it landed, but Joby's call came just in time. Jim dodged out of harm's way and countered with a left hook that caught Barnes on the chin and sent him sprawling across the road into the path of an approaching tram. Barnes didn't stand a chance; the tram dragged his body several yards down the track before the driver could bring it to a halt.

McLeod sprang into the cab to find Goodwin spewing out of the side window. "Bloody hell, Goodie, you stink!"

Goodwin wiped his mouth on the sleeve of his jacket. "I couldn't help it. I saw the tram hit Barnsie. They'll have to scrape him up. What'll we tell Mr. Frost?"

"Never you mind about Mr. Frost, laddie." McLeod pushed Goodwin further away from him, "Don't get any of that shit on me. Let's get a move on and get out of here before the cops come!"

McLeod wasn't softly spoken now; his voice cracked like a whip and stung Goodwin into action. A touch on the accelerator and they were away and within seconds Goodwin had manoeuvred the truck into a line of southbound traffic. McLeod was impressed. Once clear of the scene Goodwin first took a westerly route, then with a few more misleading twists and turns he was back in town again, heading for the depot. McLeod didn't interfere and his silence gave Goodwin time to think about the man they'd thrown in the back of the truck. He knew perfectly well that when Barnes had struck him with the loaded cable he meant to kill. If the deserter was dead McLeod would be the loser and Barnsie the winner – except now Barnsie would never know whether he had won or not.

Goodwin was glad it was Barnes and not McLeod who had been killed, at least you knew where you stood with McLeod, do as you were told, don't make a fuss and he left you alone. Yeah, Mac was okay. With Barnes you'd needed eyes at the back of your head, especially when he was in one of his moods. They reached the yard, Goodwin switched off the engine and helped McLeod unload Tim's body and carry it into the building.

CHAPTER TWENTY SIX

ANNE COULDN'T UNDERSTAND WHY MARIA was looking so miserable. Tim was on his way back to Blackpool and they would be hearing from him shortly, so why wasn't she happy? Anne had been expecting to have a pleasant evening's chat with Maria. There was plenty to talk about, the nursery for one thing and how to tell Tim that he was to become a father, but all Maria did was sit there with her eyes fixed on the clock, staring and looking anxious.

"Is there something troubling you, Maria – something you want to tell me?"

Maria grasped Anne's hand for comfort. "Tim promised to ring me today - Leger day - to let me know he was on his way home, but so far I've heard nothing. D'you think he'll come back?"

Anne hugged Maria and reminded her that the day was still young, the sun was shining and Tim would probably think it safer to wait until after dark before setting out for Blackpool.

"Once he's on his way, he's bound to find a public phone box and give you a ring to let you know where he is." Maria was reassured, Anne was right of course; Tim would definitely choose to travel by night. Dear Anne, how would she manage without her, she had been both friend and mother to her for so many years. Maria tried to find something cheerful to chat about as a way of thanking Anne, but she failed.

Again it was Anne who came to her rescue. "Michael's back from his flying visit to Germany, did he phone, he said he would?"

Maria nodded, "Yes, this morning, early. Said he was meeting up with John Beswick. It's something to do with John's best seller – you know...."

Anne didn't want to waste the opportunity of emphasising Michael's contribution to the book's success. "Oh, you mean the book Michael helped him with?"

"Yes. Michael promised he would pop in and see us." Maria looked at the clock. "I thought he would have been here by now."

Anne didn't see that as a problem, all they had to do now was wait for Tim's phone call and then they would arrange for Michael to pick him up. She paused to calculate the time it would take for him to reach Tim. There and back, five hours, six at the most and Tim would be home. She was beaming. "I can't wait to see his face, Maria, when you tell him about the baby."

Maria laughed. Relaxed at last, she waited patiently for things to work out nicely, the way that Anne said they would.

Tim lay without any movement. Goodwin, who had been trying to find a pulse in Tim's neck, stopped probing with his fingers and looked at McLeod to see what they should do next. "It's no use, Mac. You're right. He's dead."

"Of course I'm bloody right, there wasn't as much as a smudge on the mirror was there?"

"So what do we do about him then?"

McLeod had it all planned. "Well, now he's dead he can't hurt us can he? Anything he saw or knew, he'll carry to the grave with him. But we can't leave him here that's for sure: Frost and the others will be back tomorrow. Look Goodie, you've another load waiting to be picked up at Liverpool docks in the morning, right?"

"Right."

"Okay, that fits. I'll tell Frost you've gone tonight very early so that you'll be first into the dock's queue in the morning. D'you remember the spot where you shed the load and picked him up?"

"'Course."

"So dump him there, over the wall by the river."

"What about Barnsie, what will you tell Mr. Frost about him?"

"The truth, tell him that he got killed trying to settle old scores with Jim Ryan."

"But ..?"

McLeod interrupted. "No more questions. No time. Come on; let me give you a hand with this body before it gets too stiff to handle."

Together they swung Tim's body over the side of the truck and it hit the deck with a thud. Goodwin winced and was about to throw some empty sacks over Tim but McLeod said, "No, don't do that, the colder he is the better."

Goodwin shot an anxious look at him. "Why, you don't think that he might still be alive do you?"

"Even if he had the slightest spark left in him it would be out by the morning," said McLeod. He pointed to the sky, "Know what they say in Donny about the weather, Goodie? They say that winter comes in hanging on the tail of the last horse in the St. Leger and they're right you know. See, no cloud to keep the heat of the day on the deck, it'll be cold as winter tonight." Goodwin collected the empty sacks and put them beside the driving seat, there was no heating in the cab and he might need them for himself.

He'd only been on the road for half an hour when he was shivering; he reached for the sacks and arranged them over his thighs and knees to keep the cold out. When he reached the other side of Barnsley he recognised the bend in the road where he'd first met Tim. He slowed down, any minute now and the stone wall should come into view. Goodwin strained his eyes to make sure he didn't miss it; he wasn't going to take any chances. Once he got there, it would be over the wall and into the river with the body and when that was done they'd all be as safe as houses – "Well done, Goodie," he congratulated himself.

His headlights picked out the exact spot. He left the engine running and doused the lights. The body was heavier than he thought and on his own he had a struggle to get it out of the truck, he slipped on the grass verge and decided to take a breather before attempting to heave it over the wall. Then he saw a faint light weaving unsteadily up the road towards him – somebody on a bicycle! No prizes for guessing who that was! Goodwin panicked, he left Tim's body lying on the side of the road, leapt into the cab, released the handbrake and put boot to pedal. Good job the night was bright enough for him to drive without lights because he must have covered a good couple of miles before he had the nerve to switch them on again. What would he tell McLeod when he got back to the depot? He daren't tell him the truth; he'd tell him that he'd dumped the body as he'd been told - just that and nothing more.

Arnold Simpkins almost collided with an obstacle on the road. At first he thought it was another dead sheep, hardly a night duty passed by without him coming across one, but not this time, this obstacle had human form. He dismounted quickly and laid his bike on the grass verge while he went to take a closer look. Straight away he recognised Tim. Abandoning his bike, he picked him up and carried him like a baby to Whitehouse Farm.

Josie looked after Tim while Arnold telephoned for help. She felt Tim's forehead – cold! Almost as cold as death! When Arnold came back from the phone she had Tim covered in blankets with a hot water bottle at his feet. She was rubbing his hands vigorously, trying to get some heat into them and her face was flushed with the effort.

"Well?" she said.

"Stroke o' luck, Josie. There's an ambulance on its way from Barnsley to Manchester Infirmary - could be passing here any minute. I'll stop it and get them to pick him up. Once he gets to the hospital he'll be in good hands ..... Any change?"

"Not so's you'd notice,"

"Keep trying, luv – he's far too young to be keeping Amos company."

"I'll do my best, Arnold," said Josie and once again, and with more vigour, she started to rub Tim's hands and chest.

CHAPTER TWENTY SEVEN

IT WAS AFTER ONE O'CLOCK in the morning when the phone rang at Maria's house and Maria had the receiver off the hook before Michael or Anne had stirred in their chairs. They could hear the faint mumble of her voice in the hall, then silence. Within seconds she came stumbling back into the room, she swayed and would have fallen if Michael hadn't caught her in his arms and carried her to the settee.

Anne knelt beside her. "What on earth's happened my love, what's wrong, was it Tim?"

"Not Tim," Maria whispered, "It was a policeman."

"A policeman! My God! He's not been arrested, has he?"

There seemed to be a long pause before Maria responded, then she said weakly, "No, he's not been arrested, he's been taken to hospital in Manchester, he's poorly Anne, very poorly." Michael wanted to know why the policeman had phoned Maria, how did he get her name and telephone number? He was very gentle with his questioning and gradually Maria was able to tell him about the presentation box inscribed with her name and telephone number.

"The policeman found Tim lying on the Pennine road leading out of Barnsley," she explained. "He carried Tim to Whitehouse Farm - the farm belongs to the Appleyards and Mrs. Appleyard nursed him."

"Did he say how Tim had come to get injured?"

"He didn't know for sure, but he thought it might have been a car or lorry, "hit and run,"" said Maria.

Michael suggested they should try and get a few hours sleep before ringing the Infirmary, "Give them time to find out what's wrong, then I can drive you there to see him."

Anne didn't quite know how to put this to Maria in case she might find it distressing, but distressing or not it had to be said. "When we visit Tim, don't you think we should take Father MacDonald with us as well, Maria? You know – in case …. " she left the rest of the sentence unfinished.

Maria knew perfectly well what Anne was talking about, "I know, I know, Anne. You're right. I'll get in touch with him after we've phoned the hospital. I'm sure he'll come with us if he can and Tim likes Father MacDonald ………" This time she couldn't halt her tears and there was nothing Michael or Anne could do to console her.

When Anne tucked her up in bed, Maria lay awake; her head ached until she thought it would burst. She tried to pray but couldn't. Surely a just, loving, all seeing

God would have taken care of Tim? What had Tim done to deserve this?" She repeated the questions over and over again until eventually, overcome by exhaustion, she fell asleep.

In the morning she felt strong again both emotionally and physically, two or three hours sleep had made all the difference to her and when Michael came upstairs half an hour later with a cup of tea he was pleased to find her calm and wide awake. He had already been in touch with the hospital. Tim had concussion from a severe head wound and was in a deep coma. The news was grave but Maria's heart leapt – Tim was alive – and today she would see him!

At the Infirmary a consultant explained to them that Tim had responded to light and appeared to react to noise in the ward, these were good signs and he was optimistic about Tim's progress. After all the bad news, these words were like music to Maria's ears. Anne put her arms around her and whispered excitedly, "Hear that Maria, Tim's going to get better." Michael needed further reassurance, "But when will he recover full consciousness?" he asked. The consultant shrugged his shoulders, "Perhaps today, maybe tomorrow, with these cases it's difficult to predict exactly when ...."

While the others were talking to the consultant, Father MacDonald had sat by Tim's bed and was bowing his head to pray when he noticed Tim's eyelids flicker. Slowly Tim's eyes opened and he moved his head as he tried to focus on Father MacDonald's disembodied face which seemed to be floating unsteadily in a mist. Gradually the mist cleared as Tim's vision became stronger and he recognised Father MacDonald. "I'm dying, Father," he whispered.

"Not just yet, my son. You're not dying," the priest smiled reassuringly, "You're recovering nicely and with some tender love and care from Maria you could make it to a hundred! Maria is here in the hospital, Tim. I'll go and fetch her."

Maria bent over him, kissing him and wetting his face with tears. Anne and Michael were allowed at his bedside for a few minutes and were thrilled when he recognised them. The ward sister came to draw screens around the bed and asked them all to wait in the corridor while a doctor re-examined Tim now that he had regained consciousness. After the examination, they were given a few more minutes to say goodbye and then advised to leave, Tim needed rest.

Michael was able to fit hospital visits into his work schedule at Manchester and within a few days after their first visit he took Maria and Anne to see Tim again. This time Tim was sitting up in bed, greeting them with smiles as soon as they entered the ward. Michael left Maria and Anne to talk to him while he spoke to one of the doctors.

"We're very pleased," said the doctor, "He's making good progress. But there is a snag, I'm afraid, the blow to the head and his coma have caused some memory loss."

Michael looked puzzled. "Memory loss? But he recognised us straight away."

"Oh, yes. The problem is he can't remember anything about the accident or what led up to it."

"The hit and run driver, I hope they catch him and prosecute," Michael said angrily.

"Neither Constable Simpkins nor my colleagues are convinced it is a hit and run case," said the doctor, "Tim sustained a single blow to the head, whereas hit and run accidents usually cause multiple injuries and that is what Simpkins has said in his report. The Manchester police asked for our opinion after consulting their own experts and came to the same conclusion."

"So where does that take us?" asked Michael.

"They've started their investigations already," said the doctor. "A detective interviewed Mr. Ryan yesterday – and I know he may have been slightly confused at the time but he did say he remembered visiting his mother and he even gave the police her address as his next of kin....But that's all he could remember."

Michael asked if the police had any theories about what actually happened.

"They said he could possibly have been injured elsewhere and then dumped at the spot where Constable Simpkins found him. They're investigating what Mr. Ryan's movements were from the time he left his mother's house up to the time Simpkins found him unconscious near Whitehouse Farm. They want to talk to anybody who might help with their enquiries. I expect they'll get around to you and your friends in the end."

"No doubt they will," said Michael. "Thanks for your time and patience. Just two more questions, doctor, if I may. When do you think Mr. Ryan will recover his memory and when will he be fit enough for the journey home?"

"Frankly, I don't know when he'll get his memory back, depends on circumstances. In Mr. Ryan's case something could have scared him so badly he's blanked out the incident because subconsciously he wants to forget it."

"You're saying it could take, weeks, months – is that it?"

"Perhaps years, perhaps never," said the doctor. "As for going home, it shouldn't be too long now, but you'll have to speak to his consultant about that."

A fortnight later, Michael brought Tim home from hospital. He dropped Maria and Tim off at their front door and before Anne could utter a word of protest he was speeding her to her own house. Anne didn't like that, she said there were lots of things they hadn't finished discussing - and anyway, she wanted to see the look on Tim's face when Maria told him about the baby. But Michael said the homecoming and the news about the baby were special for them and they should share those things together, alone.

Anne sat glum faced beside Michael, then realizing he was right and she had been wrong, she apologised for being such a nosey old woman and invited him in for a cup of tea. Michael smiled, he reached over and patted his aunt's hand fondly, "I thought you'd never ask," he said.

Tim and Maria stood facing one another in the living room, bending forward slightly, forehead touching forehead, rocking backwards and forwards. "They told me I've put on five pounds and I'm getting my strength back," said Tim dreamily in between kisses.

"Isn't that wonderful darling, and by this time next year you'll be strong enough to change our baby's nappies?" She leaned away from him a little to await his reaction which was slow in coming. In fact it was so slow,

Maria's heart skipped a beat, "My God, maybe I've made a mistake, maybe he doesn't want to be a father?"

When Tim realized the significance of what she was saying he took Maria in his arms and kissed her again and again until she thought he would never stop.

Anne waved goodbye to Michael and left alone for the first time that day she longed to share Maria and Tim's company again; there were so many questions she wanted to ask them. Eventually, this mix of curiosity and loneliness got the better of her. She put on her hat and coat and hurried round to Maria's intent on getting the latest news update!

Tim and Maria were in the garden when she arrived. Tim called as she came through the gate, "Come and see this shrub, Anne, if you look really close you'll see Mr. Tufty's starting to show his blossom ready for the winter."

"Yes, lovely," said Anne trying her best to sound enthusiastic. "Summer in winter, you told me before."

Maria knew Anne wasn't the keenest gardener in the world, "Tim, why don't we all go in and have a drink to celebrate your homecoming?" she suggested.

"Great idea," said Tim. "You two go ahead, just a few things I've got to do out here. Won't be long; join you in a couple of minutes."

"Don't do too much, Tim, the doctor says you still need lots of rest," warned Maria. Anne was already half way to the kitchen door.

"You've told him about the baby, how did he take it?" said Anne as soon as they were in the house.

Maria laughed, "How did he take it? Why, you'd think he was the only father in the world to hear him talk. And talk about talk, I had to stop him in the end - all he wanted to do was talk about what a fine boy the baby would grow up to be. Oh, he's quite convinced the baby will be a boy and when he's old enough we'll take him to splash in the sea, teach him to swim, build sandcastles with him, play football with him, see him grow up to be just as clever as Michael…"

Anne liked the reference to Michael. "Ah," she said, taking a sip of her sherry, "Isn't your Tim a lovely man?"

"Do you know, Anne, he's so excited about becoming a father I think he's forgotten about that interview with the police. And while he's so happy, I haven't the heart to remind him."

"Don't remind him then," said Anne.

"You're right Anne, let him stay happy for as long as it lasts."

"Has he remembered any more about the accident?"

"Funny you should mention that. Just before we went into the garden, I asked if he remembered White House Farm and he laughed - told me some yarn about Josie Appleyard and that policeman, Arnold Simpkins. Said they were making love in the kitchen while he was outside the open window drinking milk from a jug left on the sill – they didn't even notice! He left a three-penny bit on the sill to pay for the milk….sounds a bit far-fetched to me, you don't think that blow on the head's made him imagine things, do you?"

"We can easily check," said Anne. "Why don't you phone Whitehouse Farm and find out what really happened - about the milk, I mean!"

"You're right Anne. I've been wanting to phone Mrs. Appleyard to thank her for helping Tim after the accident, she'll be pleased I'm sure when I tell her that he's home and making a good recovery."

"Well, now's your chance," Anne was standing at the window looking out into the garden. "You'll have plenty of time, Maria; Tim's doing a spot more weeding."

Within five minutes Maria reported the result of her telephone conversation with Josie. "Tim's story was true," she said. "I only talked about the milk of course! You know, Anne, when I mentioned Whitehouse Farm to Tim it must have triggered something off in his memory. Perhaps that's how it will all come back to him in the end - a word, a question about a place or a person — and when it does it will open the door just that wee bit wider. Oh, Anne, I'm so glad you suggested I should speak to Mrs. Appleyard."

Tim came in from the garden. "Sorry I've been so long," he said. "Leave the garden for just a few days and the weeds take over."

Maria persuaded him to sit down and enjoy his drink. After a few sips he launched himself into the subject of fatherhood and a man's responsibility 'til his voice grew drowsy and he fell asleep, contentedly, in his armchair.

Chapter Twenty Eight

Towards the end of October a plain clothes detective came to interview Maria and Tim. He began by interviewing Maria but there was little she could tell him about Tim's journey to and from Doncaster, then he questioned Tim and made no more progress there. Tim wasn't able to add anything to what he'd already told the police when he had been interviewed at the hospital.

Maria accompanied the detective to the door and he confided that he thought Tim must have met someone, or called on someone after leaving his mother's house on Leger day. "He must know who that person is," he said, "If only he could give us a clue."

Maria frowned. "He said he couldn't remember."

"I know, the doctor said it might be quite some time before he remembers anything at all about the incident – if ever. It's a pity – we could be looking at a case of attempted murder here.   The West Riding police have been to talk to his mother. She said when her son left her house his sole intention was to return to you in Blackpool. Now we know the time he left Woodlands and also the time he was found on the roadside near Whitehouse Farm and he couldn't possibly have got that far on foot..... "

Maria interrupted, "Are you saying someone attacked him in Doncaster, threw him into a car, drove him as far as Whitehouse Farm and then dumped him there?   Is that it?"

"That's what we suspect."

"But why?   Why would anyone want to attack him.........?"

"We'll find out who and why in time, don't you worry, Mrs. Martinelli. If Mr. Ryan remembers anything, anything at all, you will contact us, won't you?"

Maria waited while the detective walked down the path and then she shut the front door. For a moment she leaned with her back against the door and closed her eyes; on one hand she was overwhelmed with relief that nothing had been said to identify Tim as a deserter, on the other hand she was now worried about the possibility of him having enemies in Doncaster. What sort of people were they who had driven Tim all the way into the hills and left him for dead?   But once Tim got his memory back he'd be able to tell the police and these people would be arrested. She drew some comfort from that.

She found Tim busy with pencil and paper, quite unperturbed by the police visit. "What do you think of this one, Maria?" he said, showing her a sketch of a crib, "I've got the tools and enough wood, I'll make a start on it today!"

In the afternoon, Maria had a phone call from Tim's sister, Martha; she was ringing from the local post office in Woodlands.

"What did Martha have to say?" asked Tim.

"She said that the police had called at the house wanting to know when you had left for Blackpool, and told them you had been injured on your journey back here and been treated in hospital in Manchester. The family know you are alright now, but they were all so worried about you...."

"You told her I was okay?"

"Yes, Tim, of course and when she rang off she was confident everything was fine."

"I must write to Mum," said Tim, "Tell her how good it was to see her again."

Maria thought perhaps now was a good time to test Tim, to see if something else would nudge his memory. She said, as casually as she could, "I asked Martha how she knew my telephone number; she said that you gave it to your mother, wrote it down on a newspaper cutting and put it in the wash-stand drawer in her bedroom - just in case she ever needed it."

"Well, if that's what Martha says, it must be right, Maria. I just wish I could remember." He went back to work on the crib. "No good worrying about my memory, love, and I've got more important things to do – this crib isn't going to make itself."

The days flew by, now they were into November and Tim was busy getting the nursery ready. He'd taken all the planning out of the hands of Maria and Anne. "It's the father's job" he insisted, so they left him to get on with it.

On one wall of the nursery he had painted a scene of sea and sand with children making sandcastles, on another wall a view of the local park; there was a blue sky and a sun shining overhead, grass, trees and flowers below and groups of children playing on swings and roundabouts.   What caught Michael's eye and stirred his imagination was the brightly coloured hot air balloon Tim had painted on the third wall, it was manned by three jolly circus clowns leaning out of the balloon's basket. A group of people waved to them from the top of Blackpool Tower. "I'm not much good at painting people," Tim said and started to explain who they were.   "You don't have to tell me where I am, I'm the one holding the baby!" exclaimed Anne. She was right, and then she identified the others, Michael, Francis, Tim and Maria.

"You'll be expecting a call from the Vatican next," said Michael – "Restoration work on the Sistine Chapel ceiling. This is fantastic, Tim."

Tim put an arm around Maria, "I'm not going off to paint anyone's ceiling, Michael, from now on my place is here with Maria and the baby and…." The phone rang and stopped him in mid sentence.

"I'll get it Tim; your hands are all paint!" Maria pointed to the mark his hand had made at her waist and flung him a cloth, "Don't you dare touch anybody 'til you've used this,"

She was back within seconds, out of breath from running up the stairs.

"You shouldn't dash about like that," Anne chided.

Maria spoke quickly to Tim. "It's for you love, your brother, Bernard, he made it plain it's you he wants to talk to, not me!"

"Bernard?"

"Yes, Bernard. Hurry, he says it's important."

"Bernard, wants to talk to me? I can't believe it!" Tim bounded down the stairs two at a time.

Michael glanced at his watch. "D'you know Tim's been on the phone for ten minutes. Ten minutes! I wonder what's keeping him?" Maria and Anne were asking themselves the very same question when Anne put her finger to her lips, "Shush, I think he's coming back."

Tim sat down on the only chair in the room, he looked dazed.

"What is it Tim, your mother, she's not ill is she?"

"No, no, it's not bad news," he stood up and held Maria close. "It's not bad news at all Maria, in fact it's the very best news, ever," his eyes were shining now, "Bernard was explaining to me the gist of a very important letter Mum had received from a department in the War House," Tim smiled, "Bernard never calls it the War Office, always says War House. He didn't read from the actual letter, Martha's put the letter in the post – he said I should get it first thing tomorrow. You see that letter changes everything....!"

"Please Tim," pleaded Anne, "Tell us what it says."

"Well, according to Bernard, the letter reads something like this – "The man Timothy Ryan, presently undergoing treatment in a Manchester hospital, is not Timothy Ryan the deserter."" Tim looked around at them all. "That's the important bit, isn't it? I don't know who that Timothy Ryan is but it's **not** me."

For a moment there was silence and then they were all talking at once, asking questions. Tim put up a hand, "Listen," he said, "At first I thought it was a mistake, that's what kept me so long on the phone, but Bernard insisted it was true and that I'd read it for myself when I got the letter."

Maria suggested maybe there had been some sort of amnesty. Michael wasn't having that, "Amnesty! Time to forget and forgive! I very much doubt it. You want to know what I think; I think it's all been a glorious botch up. But don't knock it Tim, take my advice, once you get that letter, say nothing. With that in your possession, you are a free manDo you hear me, Tim – free!"

The following morning the letter arrived. Michael was there with Maria and Tim when the postman delivered it. The wording was almost exactly as Bernard had told Tim over the phone. "Nothing wrong with Bernard's memory," said Michael after he'd read the letter. "Look after this, Tim. Put it somewhere safe."

Tim didn't need a second telling; he went upstairs and tucked the letter away in one of the dressing table drawers. Now at last they could get on with plans for the wedding!

Maria had phoned Father Macdonald with the news and made arrangements to see him after lunch when Anne turned up, breathless and apologetic. She explained that she'd seen a beautiful outfit in the window of the posh dress salon next to Maria's gift shop. "Couldn't resist it," she said, "It's so gorgeous I went in and bought it for the wedding, just needs one small alteration. They said it will be ready for me in a couple of days."

Anne noticed that Maria was now wearing her engagement ring proudly on her finger. "Have you decided what you're going to wear for your special day?"

"Not yet," said Maria, running her hands over her waistline. "Something tells me I'll have to be careful about the size."

In the afternoon Tim and Maria met Father MacDonald in the presbytery. He gave them dates for the bans to be read out and assured them the wedding could be arranged for the day of Maria's birthday.

"Couldn't be a more perfect birthday present," Maria said and they sent a telegram to Tim's mother inviting all the family to the wedding on the twenty third of December.

At last the wedding day dawned. It wasn't a bad day for the time of the year, no snow and not too cold and, thank goodness, it was dry! There was a lot of cloud about but every now and again the sun found a gap and brightened things up a bit and Anne said that was a good omen for the future.

Michael was best man and with the wedding ring securely tucked away in his waistcoat pocket he accompanied Tim to the church. They were at least half an hour early. "Got to make sure we don't keep the bride waiting," Michael said, "Make sure everything's perfect."

The Yorkshire chara arrived and drew up a discreet distance away from the church. As soon as Joby put the handbrake on, the passengers' began to disembark; out they came out in a steady stream that seemed to be never ending.

"Looks as if Joby's brought the whole of the West Riding with him," said Michael. And he and Tim went to greet them and guide them all into the church.

Tim was delighted to see his family again, his brothers Bernard and Jim, his sister Martha, her husband Tom and young Tommy and Margaret, excited to be by the sea at last. His older sisters, Polly and Anne were there with their children, and Long Andy, Short Andy and even Freddie Payne the Woodlands milkman had come to join in the celebrations. Josie and Arnold Simpkins were the last out of the chara, Joby had picked them up on his way over the Pennines. Josie showed Tim her wedding ring, she and Arnold had married a couple of weeks ago and Arnold's mum had gone to live with them at Whitehouse Farm. Contrary to expectations, his mother was very happy living with them and they had absolutely no qualms about leaving her to look after things whilst they were away - with Arnold's mother in charge, the farm couldn't be in better hands!

When all the guests had been ushered into the church, Michael and Tim waited in the porch for Maria. "I wondered why Bethan wasn't with the family, she got an invite," Tim said. "But Jim tells me she volunteered to stay behind to look after Mum so Martha and Tom and the children could come."

"Jim introduced himself to me," said Michael, "No sign of Frau Weisskopf, though - did he say why she wasn't with him?"

"As a matter of fact, he did - calls her Trudi - said she stayed away in case she caused embarrassment." Tim chuckled. "Perhaps she was right, can you imagine the situation if the whole trio had turned up – Bethan, Mum and Trudi?"

"Mass starts in ten minutes, Tim," said Michael. He looked out from the porch and saw the wedding car arriving with Francis and Maria. "Come on Mr. Ryan, let's go into the church, it's time you were getting married…"

When Tim knelt at the altar rails with Maria beside him, he felt that his life was renewed, he was starting life over again and with the person he loved most dearly. As the chords of the final hymn rose from the organ he sang with such fervour, most of the congregation lowered their voices to listen to him. Anne whispered to Michael, "He sounds like Peter Dawson, the singer on the pier!"

After Father MacDonald's final benediction and the witnessing ceremony, the bride and groom walked up the aisle and out into the sunshine. A large gathering of onlookers were waiting with bags of confetti poised ready to shower on the couple the moment they stepped through the church gates.

The wedding party posed in groups on the steps in front of the porch to be photographed. Anne looked resplendent in her elegant pink dress and fashionable broad-brimmed hat. Anne was content, she'd achieved what she wanted to achieve - today she was Maria's Matron of Honour. Maria wore a pale blue silk dress with knee-length skirt, a low waist line and a loose pleated bodice. She wore her hair up, her short veil held with Tim's tiara, and as she smiled up at Tim with her arm linked in his and surrounded by family and friends she seemed to radiate happiness to all those around her.

A young woman had joined the onlookers outside the church gate but stood slightly apart, not mingling with the crowd. She stared intently at every member of every group as they were being photographed. As she abruptly walked away, John Beswick noticed her. "See," he whispered excitedly in Michael's ear, "That woman, it's her. I'll swear it's her. I told you she wasn't dead!"

Michael looked from their vantage point on the church steps and her appearance left him in doubt although, yes, there was something familiar about her walk. There were no doubts in the mind of a little girl holding her mother's hand at the back of the crowd. "Betty, Betty," she called, "It's me, Fred........." but the child's call went unheeded and the woman disappeared round a corner.

The photography session was over, the photographer folded his black cloth, collapsed his tripod stand and made ready for his next job. This was the moment the crowd were waiting for, at last they could shower the bride and groom with confetti. A car dressed with white ribbons drew up at the kerb, Tim took Maria's hand, Francis took Anne's arm and together they got into the car and waved to the crowd. Maria was more than contented, she was married to the man she loved and soon she would have their baby. What more could a woman wish for?

Michael helped the chattering guests back onto Joby's old bus and set off with them to follow the car to the wedding reception at Cecelia and Joseph's restaurant. It promised to be the perfect ending to a perfect day.

Lightning Source UK Ltd.
Milton Keynes UK
UKOW051913191011

180587UK00001B/1/P